King of
Clark Street

DIANE DRYDEN

CAPSTONE
FICTION

WATERFORD, VIRGINIA

The Accidental King of Clark Street

Published in the U.S. by:
Capstone Publishing Group LLC
P.O. Box 8
Waterford, VA 20197

Visit Capstone Fiction at
www.capstonefiction.com

Cover design by David LaPlaca/debest design co.
Cover image © iStockphoto.com/Diane Diederich
Author photo © 2007 Larry Samson

ISBN: 978-1-60290-057-8

To
my sister,
Linda

ONE

His name was Leon McKee, and he was now pretty much homeless. The only reason that he had applied for the job as night watchman at the cleaners was to get off the September streets and into someplace safe and warm.

Leon had never planned on being homeless. Edith, his wife of over thirty years, had been gone for almost a year, and her death had left him feeling so destitute and alone that it didn't matter to him if he went on with life or not. Nothing could have prepared him for the brutality of her death. It was incredible to believe that as she crossed a Chicago side street carrying her small bag of groceries that she would be hit by a speeding car. Her tiny body had been thrown onto a neighbor's front porch only two blocks from home, breaking almost all her bones. It was over so quickly. The doctors said that she had died on impact and was mercifully spared even a moment's agony.

One of his worlds ended that day and another began.

He was barely twenty when the Japanese bombed Pearl Harbor, propelling him into an immediate future in the military. But after all the physical training and mental discipline, he ended up staying Stateside in the payroll department for all of his service years. Worst of all, he was stationed at Fort Bliss, Texas, the entire time, a place Edith decidedly did not like because of the oppressive heat and the multitude of bugs and sand. But the survival scenarios that he once learned years ago were coming back to him now, making life on the street a bit easier.

Everything changed when Edith died. Leon found that there wasn't much use going home after work because there was no one there to greet him, no supper on the stove. Leon wasn't a drinking man, so the bar on the corner never lulled him in to drown his sorrow in booze.

He often found himself sitting in his old recliner for hours on end, morbidly reviewing his life and trying to figure out where the years had gone and how they could have left him so alone and so empty. He and Edith were the original odd couple, in that they were seldom apart. She had occasionally spent time with friends from church and for a while he bowled on the team from work, but most of the time they spent their off hours together. They were each other's only friend.

Some of his darker thoughts included his decision to bury her locally. He spent long hours of regret, realized that he should have taken her body back to southern Illinois for burial. It was where she was born and where generations of her family had been buried. In his grief he had never thought of it, so he buried her in a cemetery close by and found himself there more times a day than even he knew was healthy. But he couldn't comprehend that his wife and only true friend was really gone. He couldn't accept the truth of it and began slowly spiraling down into a deep abyss of grief.

He constantly reviewed their lives together and thought of the first home they owned. It was a traditional Chicago bungalow they had bought as soon as he was discharged from the service. They made it their goal to pay for it as quickly as they could so the majority of his paycheck went toward paying it off. Through Edith's careful planning they were able to live off the little they had left each week. Being a small house, there wasn't a lot of upkeep.

Most of the neighborhood bungalows were made of brick or had a stucco finish, but they found one oddball that was sided in wood. They bought it because it was affordable. Eventually they upgraded the wood for what the salesman called "carefree steel siding." Their yard, like all the others, was no bigger than a postage stamp and required very little care. But now the grass grew long, and the house was neglected. The garbage cans were full of takeout containers and cereal boxes and milk cartons. Most of the downstairs windows were grimy with a combination of dust and frying grease (before he gave up trying to cook), but he didn't care.

His retirement from the plastics plant left him with days of leisure time, a healthy amount of money in the bank, but no one to spend it with. He was fit, fifty, and incredibly lonely. He also had the distinct impression that God left him when Edith did.

Leon found that walking helped. Chicago was a big, marvelous city that spread out in all directions, creating little finger neighborhoods as it continued to roll outward into the suburbs. He and Edith had lived in their own little finger neighborhood for over twenty-six years, and it had become home. His mid-1940s neighborhood was the result of the frenetic building boom after the war, and all the houses appeared pretty much the same. Each house had five cement steps on the right side, a door at the top of the stairs, and a small landing. Each house had a large window to the left where, inside, most everyone placed two chairs and a hideous lamp in between them. Leon often commented that there seemed to be some unwritten contest to see who could buy the largest and most hideous lamp. Many of the truly dreadful ones were covered from top to bottom with wildly tangled grapevines with romping cherubs and all done in solid "gold" with a tall white shade. The fact that the lamps truly overpowered the little living rooms didn't seem to matter.

Each house also had a garage in the back of their lot next to the alley. Their garbage cans were there too. It had always irked Leon that first he had to lug the groceries all the way to the house from the garage; then he had to truck the garbage all the way back out to the cans. It was funny how often he thought of that now. He thought about how daily life had been, and how much he had taken it all for granted.

For all practical purposes his world, as he knew it, had ceased to exist. He felt utterly and completely alone.

As Leon's walks became longer, he found that he spent even less time in the old neighborhood; after all, it had been years since he even knew his closest neighbor. Many of the recent ones had trouble speaking English, and Leon was tired of trying to communicate. It seemed like the last ten years or so the neighborhood was constantly changing as different nationalities of people moved in and moved on. So on he walked, often yielding to the sun's warm offer to doze on a park bench while he listened to the bustling sounds of life that surrounded him. Supper at the downtown Chicago Pacific Garden Mission became more and more frequent. When he found that he could stay the night if he attended a church service first, he drew cold comfort from the words of hope in Christ that he heard. His heart had hardened when he lost his wife and he was not about to allow God to make amends.

The ad read, "HELP WANTED, man for night watchman from 7:00 PM until 7:00 AM, Thursday through Sunday. Contact the Band Box Cleaners & Laundry, 5417 N Clark Street, Chicago. No phone applicants." Leon thought the ad amusing: "No phone applicants." How could you apply by phone when there hadn't been a telephone number given? Who would want to work for someone who put in a peculiar ad like that? But he found himself curious and decided that it wouldn't hurt to see the place.

A bus ride with one transfer took him past Wrigley Field, home of the Cubs, and soon after he was in a section of Clark Street that anyone could see was once a bustling place of commerce. Now, like so many other city neighborhoods, it had deteriorated to boarded storefronts, graffiti, and here and there a business that was working hard at surviving. Next the bus passed a sign that read "Andersonville, Home of the Swedes since 1855," and it seemed like a thriving community full of ethnic shops like Ma's Bakery, Schott's Deli, and Erickson's Market. Rows of neat brown brick row houses lined the side streets.

Like other cities, Chicago neighborhoods quickly changed from block to block; from safe and busy ones to the "You don't want to spend any time there" ones. When the bus rocked to a stop in the middle of another neighborhood struggling to stay alive, the driver let him know that this was where he was to get out.

The Band Box Cleaners & Laundry stood in the middle of an odd three-store grouping of throwbacks to the Victorian Age. All three shops looked exactly alike, like three cupcakes attached at the hip. Each had an elaborate roof peak covered in the front by the woodwork style that was called "fish scale" because of the way the wooden slats were rounded at the ends and then attached in a tight overlapping pattern, row upon row, like scales on a fish. All three buildings had false fronts, making their one-story building seem like two. Each had a door in the middle that was recessed between two display windows that overlooked the front and the area leading to the door. Each store didn't appear to be much wider than twenty feet. Both the cleaners in the middle and the beauty shop to its left had long lost trying to maintain

4

any semblance of window display for the public. The Sunny Days Flower Shop on the right of the cleaners did sport huge flower urns and massive displays of silks that belonged more in the 1920s than the sixties.

Contrasting these once-upon-a-time beautiful buildings was a modern-style, one-story, flat-roofed, yellow brick building. It had two long and high horizontal windows, known as ranch windows, and awkwardly hugged the side of the Victorian-style beauty shop. The name J.D. Donnelly, DDS, was written on the new sign facing the street. On the other side next to the florist was an abandoned two-story boxy frame building that, from the elaborately painted names on the windows, once housed a butcher shop, Nylecks Purveyor of Fine Meats, on the main floor. Upstairs the signs in the windows boasted a CPA on one side and a "Music Lessons Given" window on the other. The music sign was not a professional sign like the CPA, but had been written by hand and on cardboard that now was faded along with the building. The building stood completely empty, as did the lot next to it. The block ended with a drugstore that was open and doing business but had wire cages on the front windows.

As Leon lingered over his coffee in the One Stop Coffee Shop across the street, he continued to watch for any signs of business at any of the three old Victorian has-beens. Every once in a while a woman holding her head scarf tightly in place would dart furtively into Madam's Boutique for her weekly wash and set and probably a bit of gossip. Leon noticed that the women were old, like the neighborhood around them, seemingly stuck in a past that never changed or moved forward in the slightest.

Several people stopped by the flower-shop window even though the windy September day was twirling leaves around in front of the shop. The cleaners was a different matter, though, because there was a slow but steady stream of customers. Some were obviously taking in their stuff, and some were picking up cleaning or laundry. Leon hadn't even realized that there were places that still did laundry. As he sipped his coffee, he thought about the years he and Edith had used a laundry service. He had hated the tedium of itemizing every item to be washed, right down to the socks and handkerchiefs. Edith had always been the one to check off each item after the returned piles, wrapped in paper, were opened on the bed. As soon as he could, Leon put a washer and dryer on layaway so he would never be subject to that mindless task again.

Around noon, a young girl, maybe sixteen years old, dressed in a very tight sweater, a tight, very short skirt, and no coat, exited the building and headed for the coffee shop. She had the typical bouffant hair and lipstick so pale that she looked like death warmed over. She made up for the lipstick in her eye makeup though—lots of black. The woman behind the counter called her Sandy, and she picked up two containers of the soup-of-the-day—clam chowder, Manhattan…the red stuff, not the Boston white. This was one of the things that Leon liked about Chicago. There were few set standards for anything: clam chowder colors weren't written in stone and just about anything would catch on here. Anything, that is, except politics. Mayor Richard J. Daley was one person who made sure that politics didn't change unless he wanted them to. Another unwavering fact was that the north side residents would pretty much support the Cubs, while the south side remained loyal to the White Sox: Wrigley Field vs. Comiskey Park.

His curiosity about the shop and its odd ad finally got the best of him. He finished his blue-plate special of a hot meat loaf sandwich on white bread with a dollop of real mashed potatoes and delicious beef gravy, then wandered over to the cleaners and went in.

The tall, relatively thin woman, somewhere near his age, glanced up from behind the U-shaped counter when he came in.

"Picking up?" she asked.

"No, actually, I've come to inquire about the job."

Her name tag said Vivian, and she studied him over her half glasses. As she stared briefly, he wondered if he shouldn't have given his appearance a bit of polish. It had been so long since he needed to be presentable for anything that he no longer cared how he looked. The gospel mission had showers and washing machines so on that front he was okay, but there were definite signs of wear on his clothes and shoes and hair and fingernails, for that matter. The only thing new on him was the day's copy of the *Chicago Tribune* newspaper under his arm. He had always been a *Trib* reader, passing up the *Sun Times* years ago, even though the *Times* was smaller and read more like a book. He liked the look of the *Trib*. He liked the crisp red, white, and blue banner on the front page. He figured only the commuters who rode the train in from the suburbs to the city every day read the *Times*. It made sense because it was smaller and easier to fold in order to read, thereby not disturbing their neighbor's space. They might be stuck with the other paper, but for his dime, it was the *Chicago Tribune*.

She took a piece of scrap paper from the stack by the side of the cash register and asked his name. As she wrote the information, Leon realized that if she asked his phone number, he would have to make one up. He supposed that by now his phone had been cut off from service; it had been months since he had even been home. By the time she asked for the number, he had made up an excuse that he was getting a new one because his last one had belonged to a doctor and he was receiving calls all hours of the day and night. She appeared dubious but began telling him about the job. She gave him a quick tour, including an introduction to Sandy, who turned out to be the only other employee, and then back out to the front. "You can stop in tomorrow after 10:00 AM, or call and I'll let you know what I've decided." She handed him a piece of paper on which she had written the phone number of the shop.

Leon didn't think he even had a chance for the job. The lady didn't seem very interested in asking too many questions about him—like did he have any work experience as a guard? He had told her about his years at the factory and his time in management at the same plant and for the first time, he told someone about the death of his wife. This Vivian person was a hard one to read, so he was left with his own thoughts about the job.

He still wasn't even sure if he wanted the job, or any job for that matter. He owned his own house and his severance pay was in the bank drawing interest. But there was something exciting about being back in the rat race, having a purpose to his day. There was more energy to his walk as he thought of a possible job opportunity even if it was only a night watchman at a run-down cleaners.

The weather was warm for September so he skipped taking the bus back to the mission; he needed time to think about his real motives for this move. He started to walk and think. Was it the job? After all, how much of a crime threat could there be that they needed a night watchman? Did the graffiti on the abandoned building mean there were actually gangs in the neighborhood, or had they only marked their territory as they migrated through? And, just how much crime threat could there be to a small, derelict cleaners? For goodness' sake, what could be of any value to rob? But, on the other hand, this could be his opportunity to have a warm, dry place to sleep without fifty other men snoring in his face and even get paid for the effort. The thought of going back to his own house never even entered his mind.

By Saturday two weeks later, Leon had "worked" several nights at the cleaners and was actually looking forward to being there each night. The first nights he'd been there, his only weak attempt at setting up a crime deterrent system was to leave the light on in the back workroom and the radio playing in the front part of the shop. When this was done, he'd sack out on a pile of draperies that were lying against the back wall in the workroom. According to their cleaning tag, they had been there for over a year and he had a feeling that the draperies (or "drapes" as they were always referred to in the Chicago vernacular) would be there for years to come, the way Vivian had of never discarding anything. Thankfully, every morning he always managed to wake up by six and be finished in the bathroom before she arrived.

Her arrival always followed the same pattern. After seventeen years working there, he supposed that this was so ingrained that she probably didn't have to think of her next move. At 6:30 sharp every morning, Monday though Saturday, she would unlock the front door, reach to the right and flip on the lights, walk through the opening in the counter, taking off her coat as she walked through to the back. She hung her coat on the hook, placed her purse on the bottom shelf near her workstation, then she proceeded to make her ritual coffee. Even though Leon was getting into his own personal routine, he intentionally threw her completely off schedule one morning by having the coffee made and a bag of donuts from the coffee shop across the street on her workstation table. He could see her struggle with accepting this effrontery to her perfectly timed life, but with all the graciousness she could muster, she managed to mutter a low, "My, what a surprise, thank you."

To add insult to injury, Leon stuck around and took out the cup he had bought at the Goodwill store the following day and poured a cup for himself after filling hers. He watched her again struggle with the need to stick with her unforgiving routine and the pleasantness of being waited on and catered to.

"I was thinking that it would make more sense," he ventured boldly, "if we either moved this little worktable to the other side of the room, or maybe invest in another table so we could have our coffee sitting down together." He hurried on. "I would imagine that I could pick up a table pretty cheap at the Goodwill store. In fact, I saw one there yesterday that would be perfect; I think it was only four dollars. Certainly the company could afford one old table?"

As soon as the words left his mouth he was surprised that he had said them. Just because he got the job it didn't give him liberties to run the place. But he had seen her love for thrift from the scrap papers that she produced by cutting up used envelopes to the way she would re-use the coffee beans each day until the coffee pot's holder got so full she had to dump them. He wondered if he should mention that she really should recycle them at this point in a garden plot or a house plant somewhere, seeing she had taken such pains to save them as long as possible already. But he didn't. In fact, he knew almost nothing about where or how she lived. He knew that she took the bus because she always arrived walking from the west and she never drove a car that she would have parked behind the store in the alley and then come in the back way.

After a short pause Vivian said, "I suppose that it would be a good idea if we had another table over there by the hand sink. We would have more room now that there are three of us here on Saturday mornings. Especially if you're going to continue to bring donuts."

It had been a long time since Leon had to figure out a woman's motives. Edith had always been so straightforward, but now here was this woman who normally treated him strictly as an out-of-sight employee, and now she was saying that she thought he should bring donuts every Saturday. Or is that what she was saying? Maybe this job wasn't such a good idea.

TWO

By late November Leon was puttering around the cleaners late every night, not only the Thursday through Sunday that he was hired to work. He was still sleeping in the back on his well-used bed of unclaimed draperies, to which he added a pink bedspread and an orange afghan from the Goodwill store for warmth. Some mornings he just managed to be up and his bedding put in the storage room before Vivian arrived. This worried him so much that he bought a small alarm clock for insurance; it helped that Vivian paid him in cash each week. It would do no good to have her know that he was there primarily to sleep. But actually, when he thought about it, he wasn't only sleeping. He had tinkered with several of the washing machines and got them to working. He oiled the hinges on both the front and back doors and cleaned out the accumulation of odds and ends from the front windows. They seemed bare now, but they were clean. He had purchased (with her approval) not only the table for their break time but found four almost matching chairs, which, after he painted them a dark green, did indeed make them look alike.

He had also (with her approval) started to clean out thirty years of accumulated junk in the two storerooms that stood side by side in the back. He always followed her condition that she was to inspect everything before he threw it away. She even had to inspect the stuff that was obviously ready to go, like the cleaning solutions that were way out of date or containers of clothes soap that had obviously gotten wet and were now just one big block. But he didn't mind going though everything with a fine-tooth comb because it meant that he could stay on a bit during the day so they could be together.

Business remained steady and there was something about the

homey smell of laundry soap and fabric softener. He didn't care for the dry cleaning odor and wondered if anyone ever really did get used to its sour smell.

"I don't think it smells sour," she would say when he said anything about it. "Besides it's what pays our salaries and I would imagine that in time you'll get used to it. Have you ever been in the back of a print shop? Now that's a smell that no one should ever have to go to work and smell all day. I think it's possible that it causes cancer in some people," she said with womanly authority.

One morning (with her approval) he spent hours looking up phone numbers and making calls about disposing of the pieces of old washers and dryers that had been put behind the building. These were all those old relics that were no longer fixable, and he found that he could sell them as "white goods" to a dealer and get a little cash for them. Vivian had to admit that she had never heard of such a thing. He wasn't sure if it was a compliment or only a statement. Knowing Vivian, he figured it was only a statement. The company he found said the cleaners would even be included in a monthly pick-up route, without a fee, if they wanted it. He'd ask.

He lobbied tirelessly to use the resultant cash flow towards both an old secondhand refrigerator and possibly an apartment-size stove that had recently come into the Goodwill store and was being saved in the back just in case she said yes.

Vivian surprisingly relented and when both appliances were finally installed, she even commented that it was becoming quite a nice "break area." He thought of it more as home.

Several weeks later, when he was pretty sure that she was softening, Leon bought some wood that turned out to be endless trouble getting on the bus because of its size. It was from a lumber company several miles away so he could construct a rough counter next to the hand sink. Vivian mentioned that it was beginning to feel more like a living quarters than a break room, but she hadn't said no to any of the purchases.

She hadn't even said no when Howard, the guy who ran the ancient hardware store across the street next to the coffee shop, helped him out with the tools he'd needed for the construction of the counter.

Howard also contributed unlimited advice as he stood and watched Leon work, making comments he thought useful and drinking all the coffee in the pot. Naturally it was understood that Leon would make any other purchases that he needed for the project from the hardware store in exchange for the free advice.

Normally during the day (when Vivian no doubt thought he was home sleeping after "working" all night) Leon walked Clark Street and visited stores up and down the blocks. He talked endlessly to the guy who ran the shoe store and lamented with him about the lack of reliable help. The girls at Lee Optical weren't too sure about him at first as he tried on endless eyeglass frames and asked how he looked, but eventually he won them over like he usually did strangers and soon was content to merely wave to them each time he walked by.

He became a regular at the big Goodwill store, six blocks farther down on Clark Street, and had nothing but respect as to how it was run. He'd often take a dozen donuts down to the shop around nine and as he and the manager, Pete Dake, ate the pastries and drank Pete's horrible coffee, Pete would tell him again and again how the business was run.

Pete said that when items came in, they were all put in the back room and initially inspected. If the items were dishes or shoes or furniture, they were either tossed because they were unsalvageable or they were cleaned, priced, and put in carts to go out onto the shelves. If the items were clothes, that was completely different. Each item was first checked for appearance. If it passed that test, it was sized and put into piles. Clothes that were good but needed washing were washed right there in the back room and dried in one of the two big commercial dryers because they received a lot of clothes.

If the clothing items were beyond hope, as many of them were, they were sent upstairs where they were freed from their buttons and cut into strips. The buttons were collected and sold, the cotton cloth was sold to one company for rags and the synthetic fabric pieces went to a company that manufactured insulation for new car and truck doors.

Leon had noticed the constant change of people who worked there and Pete told him that he often "employed" temporary people during the day to help sort clothes and when he found that many of them could not even read the sizes on the labels, he started an elementary reading class that ran each Tuesday: sometimes with a full classroom, other days he was lucky if one showed up.

Each day these sporadic drop-in "employees" worked, they were allowed to take three items home at no charge for their "wage." Leon often helped Pete unload trucks on Wednesdays because it was the slow day at the cleaners. Pete would "settle up" with Leon by letting him pick out something for free and if it was something big, he even dropped it off at the cleaners after the store closed—no charge.

One afternoon in mid-December, when the Band Box Cleaners & Laundry had finally slowed down from their pre-Christmas rush, Leon was waiting for Pete to deliver his latest freebie, a lovely and not-too-ancient sofa that had cost Leon three days of volunteering. Sandy, who was on a last ditch work/study program from the local high school— meaning she worked more than went to school, but it was better than dropping out—found that the table and four chairs was a perfect place to pretend that she was doing her homework.

Leon wandered into the cleaners around three o'clock in the afternoon in order to be there when the sofa arrived. He shook a dusting of snow from his latest find at the Goodwill store, a genuine WWII Army down jacket, fur-lined hood and all, and sat down at the table with Sandy, teased her that he came in from the cold with only one purpose and that was to "check her homework." He had been kidding with that comment, but she responded with "I wish someone would take an interest and check it." He pressed her further because Vivian had mentioned that the reason Sandy stayed on after her work hours were over is that she had a mother who was seldom home and didn't seem to interested in her own daughter's future. She winked when she made the comment about the mom not being home, so Leon was left to his own imagination.

"So, what is it you're working on?" He sat down and took off his coat.

"Who knows?" She all but yawned the answer. "Who cares anyway? I don't see the point. When would I ever use this stuff in real life?" She managed to say all this while she endlessly twirled the only strand of hair around her finger that wasn't heavily teased and sprayed, while continuously taping her pencil on the table.

14

Ah, the old questions and the equally old excuses. How many of the classes that any of them had taken during their school years translated into what any one of them was doing now? But still, maybe it wasn't the learning of the subject that was important; maybe it was learning for learning's sake that was the key. It was the process of understanding that was important.

It was a tough sell, but Leon thought he had made a few inroads with his little speech, and she did agree to one tutoring session a week from both Vivian and him to help with her current homework assignments in physics and biology. She had one last chance to pass both courses or be kicked out of school completely. He'd have to spend a bit of time at the library himself to stay ahead. Thankfully it was the beginning of the Christmas holidays and he wouldn't have to do anything about it for a few more weeks.

Leon had to admit that the well-used, five-foot tall, secondhand Christmas tree that Pete gave him (no, begged him to take!) was a little shaky, but it did spruce up one of the shop's front windows. He bought little twinkling lights for the tree with the cleaner's petty cash fund over at the hardware store. Leon liked the new little lights they called Italian lights, and for his money he'd give up the big Christmas tree lights forever; not only were they heavy on the tree, but they got hot and that worried the always careful Leon.

He had taken an entire evening and devoted it to making chains out of old, multicolored cleaning tags that Vivian had decided for some reason to keep. They had been in the storeroom for years. They actually made a pretty addition to the lights; they reminded him of the paper chains he had made in elementary school.

After assembling the tree and putting on the lights and decorations, he placed it in the front window and then decided to wipe down the front window to make the tree easier to see. As soon as he started he realized that this would have been easier to do before he put up the tree and in the daylight instead of by the dim lights of the streetlights outside, but it was too late now. Naturally when he was finished wiping the one window, he realized that he had to clean the other window to match.

It was hard to tell who was more surprised that Saturday morning when both Vivian and Sandy arrived at the same time and saw the little tree was brightly lit, dispelling late-December's dark morning. They were both surprised to find the front door already unlocked, the coffee ready, donuts on the table, and their hired "security" man looking all the world like a cat who had swallowed the cream.

Vivian brought in her own surprise as she pulled out a still-warm breakfast casserole, plus plates and silverware from her trusty old black oilcloth bag. Leon thought that the people on the bus must have been surprised to smell such luscious food smells instead of the usual, sometimes-disgusting, public transportation odors.

Because business at the cleaners was practically nonexistent three days before Christmas, they all sat down without any pressure from the usual harried customers, and ate their surprise holiday breakfast, then finished up with donuts from a new chain called Amy Joy Donuts that Leon had found only yesterday.

Leon said the Milwaukee Avenue donut shop looked like a strange, futuristic building that was painted a kind of aqua color and resembled a space ship with it's funny legs sticking out like a spiders', but the donuts were made fresh every hour and the place was always busy.

Sandy surprised them all when she shyly handed them her end-of--semester Christmas grades that had improved dramatically, which Vivian immediately posted on the fridge making it feel even more like home.

"Oh, wait a minute," Vivian said as she removed the grades from the fridge. "You'll want to take these grades home and show your mom. I'll bet she'll be proud." She was always trying to mend the huge rift between Sandy and her mother.

Sandy responded with a teenage, "Nah, don't bother. My ma could care less about my grades, and besides, she hasn't been home much anyhow. She has new interests."

"What do you mean she hasn't been home? Do you know where she is?" asked an always concerned Leon. "Is she going to be home for

Christmas?"

"Not only don't I know where she is, or what she's doing, or who she's with, I don't care. It's like I've run out of caring and I could care less about Christmas. Besides, why should this year be any different? We have never had one of those Christmas carol holidays; no silver bells and holly. Most years we don't even have a tree; that is, unless one of her boyfriends brings one over."

Vivian distracted Leon and Sandy by getting up and clearing off the table noisily, thereby ending the painful conversation that would not have any satisfactory conclusion for any of them. Soon the two women were inventorying the end-of-the-month dry cleaning that hung in their clear plastic wrappers by the workstation while the little radio played their highly advertised "Twenty-four Hours of Christmas Carols Every Day until Christmas" and then they started on the storeroom inventory of supplies.

It was well-known that Vivian was a stickler for inventory. She believed that proper inventory was the backbone of any good business. Not only did she refer to the supplies as inventory, but also to the cleaning and laundry that hadn't been picked up. People that didn't pick up their cleaning after a month received a personal phone call. Two weeks later if the stuff was still there, they received a letter threatening that the Band Box Cleaners would not be responsible if they did not respond in person and that the cleaners retained the right to get rid of their stuff if they didn't come and get it. Two weeks after that, a final letter saying was sent out saying that their items were gone, off to Goodwill or some other place.

But the items were never really gone. Vivian didn't have the heart to carry out her implied threats, but the customers must have thought it true because once that final letter went out, almost no one came in inquiring about their items. Little did they know that their items of clothing or household articles had joined the many others in the storeroom, or as Leon called it, "Death Row."

When the inventory was finally finished, Sandy idly wiped the washing machines, both inside and out, as Vivian fiddled with the radio to find a station that was playing peppier Christmas music as she sat down to type out some final notice letters.

Ever since her husband died, Vivian spent Christmas the same way every year—alone. Her family lived nowhere close and the few family members left were busy with their own families and traditions. After sending out the appropriate greeting cards, she began her own routine that she made work each Christmas. First she would go to the early morning service at her church, singing every carol with unbidden tears in her eyes, walking both there and back if it wasn't icy or too much snow. She used to write scathing letters to businesses who didn't shovel their walks during the winter, but after a few years of fruitless attempts, she finally gave up and just detoured onto the street or just took the bus, or some years if she was really depressed, an expensive taxi to the church.

After the service, in which the wonderful old story of Jesus' birth was portrayed by the primary class, was over and the coffee hour had come to an end, she would return home and fix a nice dinner for herself. Then she would lie on the sofa and listen to a new Christmas cantata on her stereo, trying not to sink into the dark depression that was always ready to descend if she wasn't very careful. She worked hard filling all her day to avoid being lonely. While her husband was alive, they always had fellow businesspeople in for Christmas dinner and they always had a Christmas tree in the window, a live one in the early years and then an artificial one after he had his stroke. After he died, she didn't see the point of it, so she sold the artificial one at a curb sale and she was finished with that part of the holiday…finished with it until now.

It had also been years since there was a tree in the window of the cleaners and one that Leon had gone to the trouble to put up and decorate was a welcome change. She had to admit that Leon's presence there had been a welcome change too. She knew that he slept in the back on the floor—you'd have to be blind not to notice—and she knew that he probably took the job just to avoid the cold, but she didn't really care. There was something about him, something so genuine and something so sad.

Christmas finally came and went with each of them handling it as well as possible. Soon much of the winter was over. All three—Leon, Vivian, and Sandy—constantly reestablished their relationship, and deep friendships were beginning to form. Sandy was doing much better at school and even her attitude at the shop was changing, even though her home life seemed to be pretty much the same. Leon was the one who attended her parent-teacher conference, upon her invitation, and learned that she had tested out to be a lot smarter than she let on. Her teachers were impressed with her recent work, but not surprised that she could do the work. Leon teased and said that the homework was getting beyond his capabilities, and maybe he should pick up a night class or two or maybe even attend class with Sandy.

She was not amused.

THREE

By spring Leon had been accepted as a regular neighborhood guy and he was meeting with the unofficial "town three," as they called themselves, at Nell's coffee shop every morning. There was Howard from the hardware store, Dennis from Sunny Day Floral Shop and Leon from the cleaners, and they would solve the problems of not only Chicago, but also the world. They almost always sat at the table by the front window and stared across the street at the three old faded buildings, listening to the Wally Phillips' morning show on Nell's radio that was nestled on the shelf along with the wooden salad bowls. They would have preferred something less intrusive, but Nell, like so many Chicagoans, was an avid fan of Wally's and always did the "twenty-penny exercise" each morning no matter how busy she was. She would drop the twenty pennies carefully onto the floor and then pick them up one by one, bending at the knees, while Wally played music with a beat that made it all easier and almost fun. Thankfully for them, she did this in the kitchen.

Dennis had often lamented the sad demise of what he called the Three Painted Ladies and he was always championing the lost cause for refurbishing them. He informed them that the name *Painted Ladies* came from the Victorian Age when houses were colorful and overbuilt and overpainted and overendowed with *gingerbread* and that the term was either used as a derisive one or as a compliment, depending on how the speaker felt about real painted ladies. But evidently the absentee owner of the cleaners cared nothing about painting and refurbishing; evidently all he cared about was having the rent paid on time. No one had seen him in years and Vivian communicated to his office by phone, but always spoke to his secretary who said that she would pass on any messages. Vivian said that he probably abandoned them years ago for sunny Florida and she didn't blame him.

"They could be real show pieces if they were painted back to their original grandeur," Dennis said for the third time that morning. "I've seen some on both coasts that would knock your socks off!"

After Dennis left, Leon asked Howard, "So, how much paint would it take to do only the cleaners?"

They sat a while longer as Howard wrote lists of figures on his napkin and finally came up with the answer in gallons. It was quite a few gallons even for only the exposed building front because the wood was old and it would drink in more paint than normal. "It must be thirty years or so since those buildings saw paint," Howard said as he paid for his coffee, left a tip, and waved to Nell as he left.

Before Leon broached the subject of possibly buying paint for the building with Vivian, he made one last visit to the flower shop next door to talk to Dennis a bit more. There was never a worry about disturbing Dennis because he wasn't ever really busy and he seemed to have endless knowledge about Painted Ladies.

Each morning that they met, this possible painting project of Leon's gave the coffee guys a new focus and now their conversations included information on various paint sample squares from different paint manufactures brought by Howard, while information on Victorian color placement came from Dennis. They even exchanged their regular table by the front window for a table in the back, because as long as they could, they needed to keep this a secret; not only from Vivian, but also from the entire neighborhood. They especially needed to keep it from anyone there in the coffee shop. There were lots of people who would be more than happy to get involved and lend them their nonexistent expertise. Leon figured that once he had Vivian's approval he would paint the front door first to get the people on the block ready, and then, when the controversy died down about the blue door, he'd quietly start on the rest, including finding a guy to repaint the Band Box name on the glass in the front door and the side windows. Nell knew her customers well and was suspicious by their table change and she made sure their coffee cups were kept full at all times, while obviously trying to overhear what they were speaking so softly about.

When the final six colors for the building had been chosen, Leon waited for the right moment to approach Vivian. With Easter right around the corner, the Band Box Laundry & Cleaners was busier than ever cleaning curtains and drapes and summer clothes along with an influx of mud-spattered wash loads. Spring was spring wherever you lived, and mud abounded everywhere, universal.

Not only were they wildly busy, but other things had changed at the cleaners too: One night Leon had "come clean" to Vivian about sleeping in the back. She appeared appropriately surprised and they had a long talk over a take-out chicken supper from the coffee shop. Nell had extended her store hours to evenings because she had recently bought one of those new chicken boasters where the chicken and the potatoes were not only deep fried together, but also deep fried under pressure. Because the chicken was crispy on the outside and tender on the inside, the broaster was an instant success and people well outside the neighborhood were coming in for chicken to go and to eat in. Nell was thinking of putting on more help and extending her hours.

The evening turned pleasant as they toured the back of the work area and decided that instead of a pile of draperies, she wouldn't mind if he fixed up one of the now clean storage rooms for his personal use. She didn't ask about his past or why he chose to live at the cleaners.

"Wonders never cease," was the only way he could think of it after she had left to catch a late bus and he was cleaning up their takeout and putting the shop to bed.

It was right after the spring rush at the cleaners that Leon felt the time was right to ask about painting. Since business had been good, and was actually getting better, Leon started to wonder if it was Nell and her new chicken clientele across the street that made them more visible.

His confidence was pretty high because by now, all three guys knew the names of the paint colors by heart, because they had chosen hues, rejected and had chosen again many times until they felt they had finally gotten it exactly right. Howard had even worked out quite a discount if the cleaners would put a sign in the window saying they bought all their paint from him taking advantage of his expert color choices. Leon had given up waiting for a time that was perfect and decided to just jump right in as soon as there was a lull in any day.

Not only did Leon have the colors written down that they'd anguished over and the close-as-he-could-figure cost on the sheet of paper, but Dennis had also taken the paint chip samples and glued a cutout replica of the shop to show how it would look when it was finished. The other two agreed that Dennis had missed his calling and should have been an architectural painter, if there was such a thing, because the sample picture was terrific.

Leon gave it his biggest sales pitch ever, but he could see right away that it was a sales job that wasn't getting anywhere. She did bring up viable questions that truly had no answer. "What would be the use?" was the biggest one, and Leon had to admit that she was right. Business was decent for this neighborhood's standards and because the taxes would go up as a result of the refurbishing, she was sure that their rent would go up too. Not to mention the fact that it really wasn't up to her. Leon had forgotten that fact. Since the owner never showed his face, it was easy to forget that he even existed. But he did, and Vivian was right; he would have to be consulted.

After Leon finally convinced himself that the painting was never going to happen, it was less than two weeks later that he had the go-ahead to begin. Vivian agreed that he could start with only the door to see how it looked. She had the authority to decide from then on if he should continue. He asked no questions, but went right across the street and bought the paint, "only for the door" he told Howard, and winked.

As soon as the shop closed at noon on the Saturday of Memorial Day weekend, Leon painted the door. First he made sure that both Vivian and Sandy had gone home before he began to paint, often stepping back and squinting his eyes to get the full effect. Howard had been right. The old door drank in the paint and he used the entire quart on this one project. He made sure that he had removed all traces of paint from his hair and nails before he met Vivian at Lincoln Park on Monday for her church's Memorial Day picnic. No errant paint splotches were going to ruin his surprise.

The holiday bus schedule was different than the regular one, so he was a little late for the picnic, but the people were welcoming, the day warm and sunny, and the mouthwatering hamburgers hot off the grill. Vivian introduced him as her friend, not employee, and several women gave her that special signal women give to each other that says, "Nice catch!"

By Tuesday morning the painted door was the talk of the coffee shop and everyone had to admit that the blue door looked pretty good: strange on the old faded building, but good. Vivian's comment was that she continued to think that maybe they should live with only the door done for a while. *Honestly, you would think that after the fun they had at the picnic that she would be more supportive. After all,* thought Leon, *who was the reason she almost won the water balloon toss? Who was the reason she even joined the balloon toss? And wasn't it he that got soaked when it burst in his hands?* Sometimes he thought she was as stuck in the mud as the old women that supported the beauty shop.

Sandy's only comment was that the door looked "cool."

Then the strangest thing happened; business picked up even more, and it was not uncommon to hear a new customer say something like, "I drive this way every day on my way to and from work downtown and I never noticed you before!"

It was difficult not to gloat, so Leon busied himself with raking behind the shop and cleaning up every bit of junk so he wouldn't be tempted to take any credit. He even cleaned behind both the flower shop and the beauty shop (with their permission of course). After the entire back was clean and the Dumpster in the alley was full, he installed a new light behind the cleaners, taking down the old rusty metal one. Howard had called this new one an automatic security light and said that it would come on automatically when anyone walked in front of its beam. Leon mounted it above the back door and could hardly wait for nightfall so he could see if it worked. When he finally felt it was dark enough, he stepped out of the back door, sure enough, the light blinked on. Howard had said that he could set it so it would come on at different distances from the door. It wasn't until the door closed behind him as he reached for the ladder to adjust the sensor that he realized that the door was locked and he would have to skirt all the way around the beauty shop and the dentist and go in the front door, stopping at the coffee shop to get the key. Progress always seemed to come with a cost.

With more business, Leon was often pressed into service and he could usually be found in the front working the pickup counter or trotting across the street for their lunch order. He refused to help sort laundry, though. "Some things just can't be borne" was his answer to the laundry job. "A man has his limits!"

Sandy had opted for six weeks in the summer with shortened work hours so she could attend summer school to catch up with her class. Vivian was seriously considering hiring another part-time employee or two to fill in for Sandy. She didn't want Sandy to think that her job was threatened, but on the other hand, she really needed more people to work.

"Look at it this way," Leon said. "Maybe she'll decide to go back to school full-time, and then what would you do? I know she loves it here; in fact, there's no doubt that we're more of a family to her than that constantly migrating group at her house. I think it would be a really good sign if she did drop back in to school and graduated with her class next year."

After the shop closed and Leon was relaxing in his recently purchased, used, orange-and-brown plaid reclining chair while reading the day's paper, he couldn't help think about the turnaround in business. It couldn't be because he painted the door. But there didn't seem to be another answer. Next door at the florists, business hadn't picked up because of the door painting, and the other stores on the block didn't seem any busier, except for Nell's.

For some strange reason, he also started thinking more and more about his own house and what amounted to his former life. He kept thinking that maybe he should go back and check on things, if nothing else, for insurance sake. By now all the windows were probably broken and there might even be strangers living inside, destroying his life of almost thirty years. More of him didn't care than did care. He knew that some day soon he would have to do something, but not now, not yet. He did decide to stop at the Goodwill store tomorrow. It had been such a long time that he'd been there he wondered if Pete would even remember him.

Leon didn't know why he hadn't thought of it before. Over morning coffee he mentioned to Vivian that the boards underneath one of the front windows needed to be replaced and suggested that maybe he could get at these during the week. She said "fine" absentmindedly as she thumbed through applications for a new employee. He knew as soon as the old boards were replaced with new boards that they would stick out like a sore thumb and she would have no choice but to let him paint so it all looked the same. Then maybe he could slowly do the rest of the front.

It took almost a gallon of medium blue/gray to cover both sides of the shop beneath the windows. Howard came over and said they had done a good job on the colors because the new light color was a perfect match with the darker blue on the door. The light salmon color trim that Howard had picked and Leon had added around the windows and doorframe complimented the two blues better than any of the guys hoped.

"Now if I can only think of a way to work my way up the sides and continue on across the front."

"Sounds easy to me," said the self-proclaimed expert on women, "Start on one side, say you forgot, and maybe you should go as far up as the front windows on each side and see what she says."

Vivian didn't say anything. She was becoming a different person now that a new full-time employee named Margie was starting her training period. Leon had to admit that he was a bit disappointed, because he liked sparring with the boss and now she was more interested in running the business than she was in him.

After Margie was hired, things began to change with her presence, and Leon didn't like it. For the very first time, his little storage room "apartment" had its first ever padlock on the door. Not only did he not want Margie to know that he was living there, he didn't want her anywhere near his room for any possible reason.

In the evenings he often reclined in his chair, his paper unread, wondering what was going on. Everything was beginning to change again. He had just gotten comfortable with his new life, and now things were different again. How hard was it to live a life that was steady and predictable? His life with Edith had been steady and predictable, and he had gloried in it.

It was the middle of summer. Hot sun glinted off the roofs of the cars that parked in front of the cleaners as people picked up their clothes. The glare from 10:00 AM and on practically blinded anyone leaving the shop. Howard had finally found some scaffolding for Leon to use, and as soon as the shop closed for the day, he assembled the scaffolding and resumed his painting. He was grateful that it not only stayed light long into the evening, but that the hot air would help to dry the paint faster.

He had always hated painting. In fact, that's why he and Edith had their house sided. It felt odd to be so happy with the work he was doing. But things had changed. He had changed. Or had he? He had to admit that he still liked the past better—both the one he shared with Edith and the way things used to be here at the cleaners, before the infamous Margie.

Rave reviews were what Leon received when the coffee shop filled up on Monday morning. He shared the praise equally with Howard. Both mentioned many times that morning that Dennis had played a big part in it too, as they wondered why he was not there to receive his share of the praise. He was always in early on Mondays to order his blooms for the week. The Sunny Day Floral Shop was still closed later that day and most of the week. There was no note on the door, and no one seemed to have any information, not even Nell, the best-informed neighborhood know-it-all. The flower delivery trucks came; the drivers knocked, inquired at the cleaners and the beauty shop, and finally left.

All the people in the neighborhood who knew Dennis were surprised that none of them knew where he lived or, for that matter, very much about him. No one could remember the license number on his car or even the number on the delivery van. Surely the van would be easy to spot. How many other yellow vans had their sides splattered with pictures of flowers and his name on both doors written in the shape of flower stems? But was this serious enough to call the police? No one could remember if he had family and besides, it was very possible that he might be at some convention or maybe enjoying a week away from the petals on vacation somewhere. Granted, business was usually slow in the summer and fall, and he was always complaining about the fact that people grew their own flowers in the nice weather. If it weren't for summer weddings, he said, he'd be dead in the water. It was truly odd, though, for him to leave and not tell anyone, especially his delivery people. By the end of the week the flowers in the large glass cooler by the cash register started to wilt and some of them began to die.

The police questioned everyone on the block and set up a temporary and makeshift office at the coffee shop. They were there so much taking up valuable space that Nell threatened to name a donut after them. Not only did they not appreciate Nell's sarcasm, they only ordered coffee.

They were a full week into the investigation when they found his mutilated body on the south side of the city in a Dumpster next to an abandoned factory. His yellow flower van had been picked clean for parts. He had been killed in a way that the police said resembled a mob hit. Did any of them ever suspect that he was "money laundering"?

It was hard for anyone to believe that Dennis had been killed because he had been making the bulk of his income on the shady side of the street. But evidently, he was doing what the police called skimming—taking some of the mob money he was depositing as legitimate sales of flowers and making it his own. Dennis found out, like so many others, that you can run, but you can't hide. But it still was unbelievable for anyone to accept. Not mild-mannered Dennis!

After the lawyers located his next-of-kin in South Carolina and they came north and picked through the inventory, the rest of the shop stuff was sold on the curb in front of the store by a disinterested cousin. Dennis had a will that had been simple and uncontested, so in no time at all, his building joined the others that had been abandoned. Vivian bought one of the huge urns that had stood outside his shop. "In his memory," she said. Leon was touched and surprised. They moved it in front of the cleaners, taking all three of them to lift and drag the heavy cement planter.

It took the talk about Dennis a long time to die down. The entire strange episode was the main topic of conversation wherever anyone went. Even the *Tribune* covered the entire story, in two days' papers, pictures and all. The *Sun Times* gave it only one column, six inches in all.

FOUR

A pall had been cast over the neighborhood and local folks lowered their voices when they talked about the guy down the block and what happened to him. Margie, their flaming red-haired employee, made her usual wild speculations and shared with anyone who listened that she too had lived an adventurous life and it was lucky that she hadn't got caught. Thankfully, Margie was a heavy smoker, and because the dry cleaning solutions were highly flammable, she had to go outside to the back alley to smoke. So she made it a habit to smoke fast, stubbing out the remaining cigarette in a coffee can of sand carefully so she could relight the same cigarette and smoke it later. She liked to point out to the girls that Leon had provided the coffee can "just for her" and she always gushed when she said it, as though it had been a labor of love. Unfortunately for her captive listeners, as soon as her quick smoke breaks were over, she returned to endlessly "natter" on about her vast knowledge of the underworld.

It was going to be a long summer.

Leon was surprised when Vivian briefly mentioned, while she grabbed bites of her lunch at her worktable, that she wanted to talk to him after hours. He figured that she meant her work hours, not his. He usually left by noon or one and didn't return until 7:00 PM, when the place was closed and empty. He knew Margie was very interested in him because he was the only one there wearing pants and she made him uncomfortable with some of her comments. He had run into lots of women like her all the years he worked at the factory. She certainly didn't keep her interest in him a secret and didn't seem to notice that he seldom responded to her comments. He learned long ago to give this type of woman a wide berth and absolutely no encouragement.

But today was Margie's day off and Vivian dropped her bomb as she began the conversation by asking Leon if he might want to work with Howard on colors for the outsides of the empty flower shop. The owner of the buildings had contacted her and said he liked the results of the paint job on the cleaners and maybe the place next door would rent faster if it were painted. She also said that he would pay very well to have it done.

Up until now, Leon hadn't known that the guy that owned the cleaners also owned the flower shop. Vivian said that he also owned the beauty shop too, making him the Painted Ladies' keeper. Immediately Leon thought that eventually he might end up painting all three of the buildings. It was good news and bad. He'd made friends with paint, but he wasn't sure if he wanted to be that good of friends. Vivian did add that she could make another call and see if they could hire a professional painter to do the "fish scales" and all the elaborate gingerbread at the top so Leon wouldn't have to.

Funny, Leon thought. *How could a guy who lives in Florida full-time know what the buildings are looking like? Did someone send him a picture? Didn't Vivian say that as long as the rent got paid, he didn't care about the cosmetics?* He was about to voice his question to Vivian, but she continued to talk, making it impossible to interrupt.

"I had no idea that she was such a flake," Vivian said as she examined her store-bought salad for foreign objects—like the new arugula lettuce she didn't like but was showing up in every salad in town. "And I didn't know she was a smoker. Do you know how much time she spends outside? I need an employee here all the time...not one only in-between smoke breaks!"

Ah, Margie, he thought. "So, why don't you talk to her about this?" Leon asked. He casually reached over and speared her discarded greens. He found he liked the peppery taste.

"Mainly because I never thought to ask her these questions before I hired her. This is somewhat my fault. It's been a long time since I had to hire anyone."

"How about back when the store was busy—when the whole neighborhood was different? Back when dinosaurs roamed the earth?"

"Very funny! But things *were* different then, including me. Mainly because I was just an employee, not in management. There were a total of six of us working here. Most of us were part-time, but that was all I wanted at the time." She picked out more of the offending greens and continued, "When I realized that my husband and I weren't going to have children, I wanted something to do with my day. It wasn't a real popular idea around our house, though. My husband had a very good income working for an oil company, and I certainly didn't need to work. But he was gone a lot..." She stared down at her salad. "Not only was it lonely, but you can only do so much charity work and attend so many church meetings for the social activities. Besides which, every time I got involved with some committee, my husband would breeze home and make other plans for us the night I was supposed to do something. Finally I didn't volunteer anymore.

"I felt like I was letting so many people down each time, even though they all said they understood. One afternoon, when I was early for the downtown bus, I walked up a few blocks for something to do, and thought that I'd catch the same bus a bit farther up on Clark. As I was glancing into the shopwindows, I noticed the cleaners had a cardboard sign that said HELP WANTED. I walked in and got the job immediately and started two days later."

"What did your husband say?" Leon asked, wiping his fingers on his pants.

"He didn't say anything for almost three weeks because he was in the Far East on business. When he got home, first we had a bit of a fight; then he reluctantly saw my point of view. I think it embarrassed him that I wanted to work...because then people would think he wasn't a good provider. Image was everything to him. He even shortened his last name from Dumbrowski to Dumbro when he started moving up in the world. I thought it was silly, but he said that people didn't hire people with obviously ethnic names. I said that all names were ethnic but lost the battle. I rebelled, though. He used Dumbro, but I still used Dumbrowski. It was probably the boldest thing I ever did. And when it came to my new job, I held my ground there too because it was something that I really wanted. He reluctantly gave in. He had to give in because he was leaving again and probably realized that I was determined to do this.

32

"I worked here for seven years. Then my husband had a series of strokes and died within two months. Needless to say, I was in shock. I was not at a loss for money because he had invested in his company and left a sizeable nest egg for me, but for the first time, I felt truly alone in life. My boss here at the Band Box gave me all the time off I needed and he worked around my schedule when John was sick. After it was all over I could have gone somewhere else and worked full-time, but this was all I wanted. I made some very good friends here in the shop and up and down the block. They were more like family to me than just coworkers. Some days it's hard to believe that my husband's gone and I've been here for almost seventeen years. Not to mention that most of the friends I've made here in the neighborhood have died or moved on."

Leon fiddled with his coffee cup while he waited for her to return from her sentimental journey.

"But, I guess that's all pretty much water under the bridge. The real subject is, what am I going to do with Margie?"

Leon loved his little "efficiency apartment" that had been his home now for over six months. It was all he could ask for. This former storeroom was only eight feet wide and ten feet long. The two outside walls were made of concrete block and the other two of wallboard. The door going out to the workroom was on the eight-foot wall.

As soon as Vivian suggested he move into the room he immediately abandoned his bed of old draperies and purchased a twin bed frame and mattress from the Goodwill store. Vivian had surprised him with a bedskirt (a part of the bedding he could have skipped) and matching bedspread, both of which had been moldering in Death Row for over two years, according to their tags. With a fresh washing, they turned out very nice. Thank goodness they were not flowery. He had slept under flowers all his married life, and now he was quite pleased with a solid brown spread and a brown plaid dust ruffle.

Leon added a bookcase made out of decorative cement blocks that separated the standard two-inch-thick wooden boards. Leon had always loved books, and he was an avid reader. His little library now boasted one hundred and eight volumes, mostly from the Goodwill store, all used, read, enjoyed, and put there on the shelf to be read again. Any book that he didn't like either went back to the Goodwill or was given to the local library.

Vivian had surprised him at Easter with a lamp for the upturned orange crate he called a bedside table. He didn't have the heart to tell her that there were no outlets in the room and the only light was the bare sixty-watt bulb hanging in the middle of the ceiling. But he wouldn't have moved the lamp for anything.

He loved the one high window on the wall that faced the alley. The streetlight gave a soft glow to the room. A large, lone elm between the light and his window provided nightly entertainment as its branches swayed back and forth, reflecting on his wall and ceiling through the window squares.

Sandy had made three solid brown throw pillows in her home economics class for his bed. He found her kindness very touching, but pretty much stored them in the corner, never understanding what women saw in throw pillows. Before Margie came and he was able to leave his door open during the day, he made sure that he placed the throw pillows on the bed so Sandy could see that he liked and used them. It didn't sound like compliments came Sandy's way too often from her family, so he liked filling in the gap. He always found it odd that Sandy had no problem with him living at the cleaners in a storage room. She never questioned or commented on it. Some days he got the impression that, if Vivian offered, Sandy too would move right into the other storeroom.

Once Margie started working, Leon took his eight-foot bookcase boards over to the hardware store and had Howard cut them in half. He then bought more decorative block and made four short shelves where there had been only two long ones and turned the bookcase so it was perpendicular to the wall instead of up against it. This way, the view of his bed was almost blocked off if the door was accidentally left open. He took no chances, though, and made sure he was always up and out before she arrived...and his new addition of a padlock was firmly closed. It amazed everyone that Margie never asked what was in there. It seemed to be her mission in life to know everything about everybody.

FIVE

It was a hot Monday morning in mid-August. The miles of city cement that held the heat overnight now fiendishly radiated it back as the sun awoke for another scorcher. As Leon crossed the street, dodging the morning commute of cars and trucks after having an early morning cup of coffee with Nell before she opened the shop to the public, he had to admit that he had more problems with his nerves now than he did at sixteen. He got nervous every time he thought of actually asking Vivian out on a date. All that caffeine at Nell's probably hadn't helped either.

It had been almost a complete year since they'd met. He tried to think of it not so much as a date, but as two friends going downtown for the Venetian Water Festival that was held every year in Grant Park right on Lake Michigan. They could eat lunch at the concession stands, walk a lot, maybe get a cab and go to the Planetarium, the Aquarium, or even the Field Museum, then back downtown for the boat parades. There wasn't a lot to plan...maybe they should just kind of let the day unfold.

He was happy to see that they were still alone. The infernal Margie hadn't come in for the day yet. As Vivian was taking the money out of the floor safe behind the counter, he stepped up behind her and started to ask if she would like to go into the city on Saturday. Because she hadn't heard him behind her, she raised her head without thinking and whacked it on the open drawer of the cash register. She sat back down on the floor rocking back and forth and rubbing her head.

"Let me see it," Leon said as he tried to pry away her hand.

"No, no, no, it hurts too much."

"But I've got to see if it's bleeding."

"Okay, but wait a minute; it really hurts."

When she finally stopped rocking and rubbing, she removed her hand and he gently parted her hair. "No blood. But you're going to have quite a lump."

"Great, just what I needed. I have to work on the letters to the customers today about their late pickups and I need to work up an ad for the neighborhood paper about our fall drapery cleaning prices. Maybe I should call Margie and see if she can come in today and help."

"Nope, I think that's a terrible idea. I'll fill in if you need someone. Sandy's working later, right? We could do fine by ourselves if we had to."

"So, I shouldn't call Margie?" She had gone back to rubbing her head.

"Absolutely not. The only reason I would recommend you call that woman is to fire her. It would be a happy day if she never walked in here again."

"Leon, I thought you liked her," she said with a teasing tone in her voice.

"Like her! Are you nuts? She is the bane of my existence. I'm tired of arranging every one of my days so I won't have to be anywhere around her. I even have to watch what I say and how I say it whenever she's working because she always gives it another meaning. What would she say if she knew that I was going to ask you to go to the Water Festival this weekend? She'd find some harebrained meaning behind it."

"What did you say?"

Leon blanched but continued. "My intentions were not to scare you half to death. I only wanted to ask you if you wanted to go with me to the Venetian Water Festival down at the lake. It's all weekend, but I think that Saturday afternoon and night will be the best time to go. I've always liked to see the boats all covered with colored lights shooting water into the air."

He had stopped talking, but Vivian hadn't answered. The silence grew as he waited. By now they were both sitting on the floor as she said, ever so slowly, "I don't know what to say. I was hoping that it wouldn't come to this. It's not that I don't like you, or care about you, but…"

"I understand," he said as he stood up, closing the cash drawer. He reached down to help her up.

"No, I don't think you do. John and I had a marriage of convenience," she began with a shaky voice. "He earned lots of money and was gone all the time. I stayed home looking like the perfect companion. But our marriage was empty." She sat down gingerly on the stool behind the counter. "It was just a shell…just a joke really. Even after he had his stroke, I couldn't find love anywhere inside myself even though I looked as long and as deeply as I could. I don't know if I ever loved him, or if love finally died through the years."

She gazed directly at Leon. "I realized as he lay there unable to do anything for himself that I was there out of duty and nothing else. I cared for him like I would have cared for a patient in a hospital: good care, but no personal attachment. I felt so guilty at the funeral when people came up to me and told me how sorry they felt for my loss and how hard it was going to be for me without him. But as time went on, I realized that I wasn't grieving because I missed him. I was hurting for all the things we never had. For all the love that I was denied."

She had turned her back on him now. Reaching for her purse, she opened it to grab a tissue to wipe the beginning of tears from her eyes, then turned to head for the door.

But Leon was right behind her, taking her into his arms and drawing her close. "I am so sorry. I can't imagine any man not loving a wife like you." He breathed the words into her hair. "He must have been a complete idiot to not see how wonderful you are, to see how giving and thoughtful and caring you are." He raised her face carefully so he could gaze into her eyes. "I could care for you."

He didn't kiss her, even though he desperately wanted to. It wasn't time; her heart was a long way from being healed and whole, and he could wait as long as it took.

He hugged her again, then gently pushed her to arm's length, and smiled. "So, what do you think about this weekend?"

The smile that stole across her face was like the sun coming out after the rain. "I think it would be wonderful."

"Good. Now go home, take some aspirin, sleep a little, and let Sandy and I handle business today. I'll call you around noon to see how you're doing, and most importantly of all, don't call Margie!"

This time it was she who reached up and kissed him lightly on the lips. "Leon McKee, you are the last of the truly good men."

It was with a great deal of trepidation the following day that Leon got on the number twenty-two bus and asked for a transfer to the bus that went to his old neighborhood.

This was a task he would have put off indefinitely, but he knew that his house insurance would be up very soon because he always mailed the check the third week in August, right after Edith's birthday. He always joked and said that it was her birthday present and that, if the house burned down, they would spend her birthday anywhere in the world she wanted. She always pointed out that by the time the insurance paid off the claim, they would be too old to go anywhere except for the old people's home.

Thinking back on the narrow routine that held him so tightly, he realized how painfully predictable he had been...even to the paying of their bills exactly the same time almost to the day each year, making the same joke each time. How could he have been that way? Didn't it drive Edith nuts? Was it only compliance on her part or maybe frustration with a man who was so predictable, so dull? He had never thought about it before and he was not prepared to think about it now, but it was time to face the music and see how much damage an empty house could sustain before being condemned by the city.

Walking slowly from the corner to approach his house from the front and not from the alley, he noticed that the neighborhood hadn't changed much. As usual, there was no one in their miniscule front yards, even though it was a beautiful summer day. People in this neighborhood weren't the kind to sit on their front steps, or stoops, and just hang out. They didn't spend too much time in their backyards either. They were pretty much house dwellers, like he and Edith had been. Maybe people in the suburbs put in pools and a barbecue pit, but here in the city, a backyard was primarily a spot to mow and to use occasionally for a graduation or a Fourth of July family gathering.

He didn't want to look, but as his house came into view he was dumbfounded and thoroughly confused. It was in perfect condition. The lawn had been newly mowed, and there were pots of red geraniums on either side of the door. There wasn't a year's worth of papers and litter in the yard, and the mailbox wasn't overflowing with flyers. The windows were even washed. He wasn't prepared for this; it was almost more ominous than seeing it falling apart.

Walking slowly up the steps he removed the front door keys from his pants pocket and wondered briefly if they would fit in the lock. The house certainly did look like it had new owners. When he unlocked the door, the stench from the old house hit him full-force. He realized that he was holding his breath—both from the smell and also in expecting to meet someone living there as if they owned it. A glance through the rooms assured him that he had been the last person in the house. He sat down in his old reclining chair to try to puzzle out the mystery.

The doorbell startled him. Going cautiously to the door, he opened it a little and peered out on a diminuitive Asian man. He held no briefcase or salesman's sample kit, so Leon said, "Can I help you?"

"Are you the owner of this house? My wife saw you go in, so she thought I should come over and check." He added quickly, "I'm your neighbor."

"Oh, sorry, I didn't know that. You see, I haven't been home for nearly a year, and I don't know anyone anymore."

"We wondered where the owner was, so we asked around and the people across the street, the Wakowskis, said that your wife died suddenly several years ago and about a year ago you never came back. They thought that maybe you went to live with one of your kids for a while."

"We didn't have any children." he said slowly as he ran his fingers through his hair. "I was staying with friends, though. But I'm confused. What happened to the house? Or should I say, what didn't happen to the house? The outside is beautiful, flowers and all!"

"Even though I had never met you, when I heard about your wife and your going away, I started doing a few things around your yard. Like taking in your papers and saving your mail. I started shoveling your snow from the walk to the door for the mailman, and I kept up the maintenance even when winter was over. It was just as easy to mow your front when I did mine. I didn't do your backyard though, so I'm not a saint."

"I can't believe it. Why would you do such a thing?"

"I guess I would have wanted someone to do that for me if I was on the other side of the coin."

"Please," Leon said as he opened the door wider, "please, come in for a minute if you have time."

"Thank you, no. I only have a little time before I have to be home to make a few business calls. I'm in the import/export business, and I have a little shop down on State Street. My son and his wife run the shop now, but I still like to help out with the buying. My son is a smart businessman, not as smart as his father yet, but soon." He smiled when he said that, creasing his eyes until they almost disappeared in his face.

What a pleasant man, and what an amazing thing to do! Leon thought. *To care for a stranger's house...for almost a year as though it were his own.*

"I don't know how to thank you, Mr.... I'm sorry. I don't even know your name."

"It's Watanabi."

Leon wasn't sure if that was his first name or his last name, but he reached through the partially open door and took his neighbor's hand to shake it. He found himself bowing automatically. "I don't know what to say. I thought that the house would be a mess, with broken windows and a lawn that was nothing but weeds. I never expected this, never."

"I am very pleased to do it for you. I knew that you would come home one day after you had your great shock." Watanabi turned to leave, then added, "Shock is funny thing. I saw a lot of it in the big war. Many of my people had shock. Many of my own family. But now you are home, and I will bring over your mail later."

Later, thought Leon as he gently closed the door. *Later.* He wanted to be back at the cleaners helping get the front pickup area ready for the coat of soft green paint that he and Howard finally agreed on so it would look as nice as the outside. *Later.* What was he supposed to do about *later?*

He wandered the house opening drawers and closing them, opening closets too and not really seeing anything in them. He removed a pizza box from the kitchen table that still had one piece of pizza on it that had actually turned a dull gray. He didn't even remember leaving it. He then cleaned out the refrigerator of food so ancient that it was welded to the bowls, so he threw the bowl and all in a garbage bag. Garbage? Was he even still getting a pickup? They billed every month, and if you didn't pay, they didn't pick up. But that was silly. What would they have picked up? This being away for a year was complicated.

He thought of going over to the neighbors to retrieve his mail, then realized he didn't know in which house his neighbor lived and had no idea how to find out. He picked up his phone to see if it was still working so he could call Vivian and let her know that he might not be back until the next day. No such luck. The phone was dead.

He went back upstairs and took a blanket off the bed and brought it down to the sofa. If he was going to sleep there, he would not sleep in the bed; there were still too many memories that he did not want to face. Someday he would, but not now.

There was canned ravioli in the cupboard, so he opened a can and ate the contents for lunch directly from the can because there was no gas for the stove. He had forgotten how good the ravioli tasted, so he opened another can and ate that one too. A little lunch gave him the energy to go through his important papers and to add some things to his gray metal security box so he could take it with him when he left and go through his former life when he got back "home."

Watanabi came again around 3:00 PM. Would Leon care to come to his house for tea? If so, then he could help Leon take his mail home.

The house next door was in pristine condition. To Leon's joy there was no hideous lamp in the window. It was odd, though, to step inside the common beige 1940s Chicago brick house and suddenly be transformed into another world.

The living room was sparsely furnished, but beautiful in its simplicity. Walls gleamed with silk fabric, and scrolls with oriental script graced the walls instead of pictures. The furniture was dark and shiny—absolutely beautiful. There was the slightest scent of incense in the air. Watanabi was urging him to "sit, sit" on the sofa as his wife came with tea. She too was a tiny woman and even though she was in American dress, she gave the impression that she was in a kimono by the way she walked and carried herself. She set the tea tray down and stood with her eyes down.

"Now Takako," Watanabi said gently, "we have been in this country too long to not break out of our old traditions. Look up and meet our neighbor, Mr. Leon McKee. He's the man whose name is on all this mail." He gestured toward two huge plastic garbage bags against the wall.

"That's all mine?"

"That is all the regular mail. Your other mail, the junk stuff, is in boxes in our garage. We did throw the flyers away though."

Leon sat back against the sofa and sighed. "I'll never get through it all. It will take me forever."

"Maybe so, but a cup of tea will be a good start. Takako, will you pour some tea for our neighbor? I hope you like jasmine tea; it will soothe you."

Back in his own house, he knew he needed a plan. Most of it seemed to involve his car. He checked to see if it was still in the garage, and it was. If it started, he could pull it around the front and load the mail that he and his neighbor had carried over. He had planned to spend the night in this house that used to feel so familiar, but the thought of leaving was more compelling than the thought of staying. All the memories were suffocating him, and there was no escaping them while he was there.

Watanabi had given him a business card, and Leon had written down the phone number of the cleaners. He had offered several times to pay for a year's worth of yard work, but his neighbor flatly refused even the smallest sum.

"To be a neighbor is not for sale. I do this for kindness. Your country has been very kind to my family and me. We came a few years after the war, and even though there was much objection by many people, both here and back in Japan, we knew we would do whatever we had to do in order to stay here. So this is our thank you to whole country."

SIX

Leon came in the back door. Vivian looked up, startled. The only one who even used the back door was Margie going in and out for her endless smoke breaks and the supply delivery guys, but none of the guys were due for another month and Margie was off that day. Leon almost always used the front door. Why the back door this time?

"I wonder if you would mind me parking a car behind the building for a few days." He appeared exhausted.

"Not at all. I didn't know you had a car."

It was as though he had something else on his mind because it took him a few beats before he worked through her questions to finally answer. "Well, I sort of did, do, and sort of didn't. But I have one now for who knows how long."

"Okay," she said slowly, thoroughly confused. He certainly didn't share a lot of his life. Where would a formerly homeless guy get a car? Surely he hadn't stolen it! Even though she was dying to know the whys about this new vehicle, she didn't ask. She simply went back to counting the money from the day's business so she could close and leave for the day.

"So, what did you decide about the crusade next week?" she asked over her shoulder.

Silence. Noting his confused expression, she continued, punctuating every word. "You know, the Chi-ca-go-wide Bil-ly Gra-ham Cru-sade, the end of next week?"

Still no reply, so she continued, "The one you said that you would go to with me? Remember, I'm singing in the choir? Alto? Third row back? McCormick Place? Do you remember any of this?"

It was the final straw that broke his back. It was the last little bit of information that pushed him over the emotional edge. He started to cry. He was so emotionally drained that he didn't move or even go into his room to hide his tears. He just stood there like a three-year-old and let the tears roll down his face.

She was next to him in an instant, putting her arms around him and rubbing his back. She didn't say a word, but when the storm was over she led him to the sofa and sat down next to him. She held his hand for a while and then got up to get him a glass of water.

He sat there blowing his nose and wiping his eyes but still not saying a thing.

"Do you want me to stay, or go?" she asked gently. "I'll do whatever you want."

When he didn't answer, she realized that he couldn't answer. He had gone somewhere unknown to her and was dealing with things she couldn't fathom. There were times very much like this with her husband, toward the end, as he dealt with things in his own life that he later asked her forgiveness about…things she never knew and did not let herself dwell on once he died. With John, it was over, all of it, and she was not about to hang on to any of it. Let the hurts and the old memories and the new knowledge of things gone by die with him.

But with Leon, it was different.

She took the afghan from the recliner chair and covered him as she helped him lie down on the sofa. She bent and kissed his cheek. "I'll see you in the morning." She started to walk away but came back and whispered, "Give it all to God, Leon. He's the only one that knows it all anyway and can heal it all, whatever it is. Besides," she added with a smile, "he'll be up all night anyway."

Even though Vivian arrived early the next day, Margie arrived even earlier and was there when Vivian came through the door into the back room.

"I thought I'd get an early start," Margie said, as she was spooning coffee into the basket of the percolator and looking around for Leon as she pushed her bright red hair seductively behind one ear. "I brought in a coffee cake from that great bakery down from my apartment—the one I was telling you about on Milwaukee Avenue, Gladstones. That's the one that if you go on Saturday morning, the line to get in the shop is clear around the corner! I thought maybe we could have an early break, just the three of us."

"I'm not sure where Leon plans to be today," Vivian said with a touch of ice in her voice, relieved that he was not still asleep on the sofa. "I think he said he had to be downtown for something," she lied.

"Oh well, I guess that's the way it goes. Besides, I'm leaving early today myself to go downtown."

"Did I know that?"

"Well, I was going to ask you if you'd mind me leaving a little early. I'm meeting some of my friends downtown and then we're going to the Venetian Water Festival. Ever gone?"

Horrors! Vivian was thrown into a panic. Now what to do if Leon did feel up to still going? Would they want to take the chance of running into Margie and probably her equally clueless friends?

"Um" was the only word Vivian got out before Leon walked through the front door with a big smile. He walked up to Vivian, gave her a peck on the cheek, and practically sung, "Good morning!" He nodded politely at Margie and headed to the coffeepot while asking Vivian pointedly, "Are we still on for tonight?"

Vivian's heart was bursting as she crossed the room and put her arm through his. "Of course!"

"Well then, coffee all around! Look—someone's brought in a coffee cake. Let's have it now. I'm starving!"

Margie spent her half-day in the front of the shop not talking to anyone. She was even seen going across the street to the One Stop Coffee Shop to use the bathroom.

The entire weekend was wonderful. It felt like it flew by. Vivian was absolutely euphoric when she opened the shop on Monday. They had taken Leon's car downtown and even found a parking place on the street, so they didn't have to pay for parking. The festival was wonderful, the evening was warm and sultry, the food was the best she'd ever eaten and the city's building lights, especially all the ones on the famous Michigan Avenue buildings, were at their finest, not to be outdone by the beautiful Buckingham Fountain lights and water show. Best of all, they never saw Margie or any of her friends. She didn't bring up anything about the way Leon acted on Friday night or on his complete change of personality on Saturday. She just enjoyed their time together, no questions asked.

But that Monday morning there was a note on her work desk from Leon saying that he wouldn't be in until late in the afternoon. He was busy reconnecting.

Her day deflated instantly. *Reconnecting*—that couldn't be good.

SEVEN

Reconnecting, what a wonderful thing, thought Leon. *I've needed to reconnect with a lot of things for a long time, especially myself.* He was beginning to understand that he had been hiding behind his routines and his ruts for so long he lost the joy of living and the excitement of the unknown. But things were going to change. As he lay on the sofa, he had done exactly what Vivian suggested. He gave it all to God. He poured out his heart for a long time, bringing up all of his past, his present, and his future. God in return supplied the Bible verses that Leon had learned as a child as soothing comfort for his broken spirit. When the surrender was finally finished, he slept like he hadn't slept for years.

In the morning the world was new, and so was he.

He started at the hardware store and talked to Howard, ordering more paint for the other buildings and ended up helping move some stock around in the back because the store had been so busy that neither Howard nor his one employee had had time to get ready for the truck that was arriving shortly. Leon then stopped in at the coffee shop and gave Nell a hard time about the White Sox. He trotted down quite a few more blocks and grabbed a bus to the Amy Joy Donut Shop for a coffee and a bit of gab with the guys at the counter, thinking all the time that he should have driven his car and made the trip shorter. It was hard for him to remember that he owned a car. But then, if he had been driving his car, would he be able to find a parking place in order to stop at a flower shop to order some flowers for Vivian? Walking into the fragrant display room filled with flowers and ribbon, he instantly thought about Dennis and the terrible way he died. He wished again that there were something he could have done to help Dennis over his financial humps so he wouldn't have gotten involved with those people. And if he had been then where he was now with God, maybe he could have shared his faith too. *Why,* he wondered, *do we always try to find a quick way out of our problems?*

A tiny woman, whose name tag said Dottie, interrupted his thinking as she asked if he was looking for anything in particular in flowers. He quickly ordered some beautiful big "football" mums that would be delivered to Vivian later that day. He thought they smelled awful, like dirty feet, but she loved them. He got three of the gold ones and even bought a vase for them. Not only was he smiling, but almost started whistling as he resumed his walk. It reminded him of his father. His father used to whistle all the time; he jingled the change in his pocket when he walked. Nobody even carried change in their pockets now, but his father always had. He remembered his father had been a happy man...until the 1929 stock market crash. Then everyone's world seemed to change.

Leon stopped dead in his tracks. "Thank you, Lord. I'm beginning to understand now." He realized he'd become exactly like his father was after the crash. He had been going though life with a dog-determination in order to "make it." Everything he had done mirrored the way his father had done it. Starting with being emotionally closed to those dearest to him, going on to his constant fear of not having enough money, or of spending too much money. Now, suddenly, all these years later, he understood. Best of all, in an instant he understood that he didn't have to be like his father, and it didn't really matter that he had money in the bank and a house completely paid for. What mattered most was that if it were all to disappear overnight, he had what was most important: his newfound relationship with God and, he hoped, Vivian.

Now he was smiling so widely people automatically smiled back. He turned the corner and wandered down to the Goodwill store. He hadn't seen Pete for months and he felt like a good long visit.

As usual, there was a truck being unloaded in the back, so he stopped to help. Pete introduced him to a skinny young man who looked all of twenty years old and was helping out and added, "You really need to sit down and talk to this guy. You wouldn't believe his story!"

"Oh yeah?" Leon said. "Well, I've got the entire day to hear it, so it better be good."

Later that day he shared the story with Vivian over another takeout supper of chicken from the café. Nell was expanding her service and was now offering her grandma's recipe for coleslaw by the pint along with the chicken and broasted potatoes. It was evidently a big hit because the place was always full of folks coming, going, and stopping in for takeout.

Even though Vivian had a worried look, she hadn't said anything negative. His flowers were in the middle of the table.

Leon started in telling her about his day. "This guy's story was hard to believe, but then this entire day has been hard to believe. He's a skinny kid by the name of Johnny. I didn't catch the last name. Up until several weeks ago, he was sleeping in the park with his guitar."

Vivian gave herself more chicken but didn't say anything.

Not being sure if she was even interested, he began to watch her as he talked. "Anyway, he kind of joined the drop-out society and decided that he didn't need to work and that he could make enough money busking with his guitar."

"Busking?" she interrupted and asked. "What in the world is busking?"

"I asked the same thing," he said, relieved that she was taking an interest. "It's the term musicians use when they play music on the street or on the El platforms for donations."

"Ah."

"So, anyway, he found out that life on the street wasn't all he expected it to be and after bragging to his parents that he didn't need to be like they were and be a part of the 'establishment' rat race, he ended up pretty much a transient. That's when he decided to show the world that he was doing fine, and he invented the slug-bag."

"Slug-bag?" she said, like a parrot that repeated phrases.

"Yeah, he bought a five-by-seven-foot tarp and sewed it together with some heavy string through the grommet holes to form a sort of sleeping bag. I guess it looked like a great big gray garden slug when it was finished and he was in it. He was living over in Lincoln Park underneath one of the big pine trees. He said if it weren't for the tree roots, it would have been perfect. The low tree branches kept the rain off and he was virtually hidden from view. He showed other people the bag, hoping to make a few bucks producing these for them, but he forgot that his "buying public" didn't have any money. That's why they were living under the expressway overpasses and in the parks and abandoned cars. Many did scrap enough cash together and made their own bags and also coined the phrase "slugging it out" when they used them.

"Anyway, he got tired of living underneath a tree and fighting off the real bugs and it definitely wasn't good for his guitar to be out in the elements, even though he did have it in a plastic garbage bag. When he heard that rooms were available over on West Madison—skid row—for a dollar a night, he decided that anything would be better than sleeping on tree roots. He was wrong. It was less than a week, and he'd had enough of the one-dollar rooms. They were dirty, noisy, dangerous, and he was always worried that someone was going to steal his guitar. He said he felt safer sleeping in a park than there. Anyway, a guy he met outside of the flophouse asked him if he wanted to buy a refrigerator box. He said that he had no use for a refrigerator box, but thanks for asking. The guy said that in the long run it would be a sound investment for his twenty dollars because it would be somewhere he could have some privacy and get away from these loonies to sleep."

" 'Twenty dollars? Are you crazy? I haven't got twenty dollars!' " That's what he told the guy. He had the money, but he didn't want the other guy to know for lots of reasons. He got him down to eight dollars and arranged to give him the money when the guy gave him the box, all the time asking himself what he was going to do with a box."

Vivian's eyes started to wander around the room, so Leon really got into his story. "So later that night he gets delivery of this box and now he's stuck. According to Johnny, the guy who sold him the box said something like, 'Look, if I was yous, I'd find me an apartment building that's a little run-down. I'd park the box next to the building and maybe people would think that it was around some pipes or the air conditioner or somethin'.'

"Johnny said he thought it was a screwball idea, but one that just might work. He said that he balanced the thing on his head and carried it for blocks and blocks until he found a place that might work. He put the box down under the fire escape stairs next to the building. He also said that whoever took the refrigerator out of the box did it by cutting around the entire bottom and then probably lifted the box off. They then rolled the fridge off the bottom cardboard and threw the bottom into the box too. What he needed, he figured, was duct tape to attach the bottom again and then decide where he wanted his door.

"He said he slept in the box the way it was that night, and the next morning he slid out cautiously and headed for a hardware store for some duct tape. On his way back he stopped to watch some guys at a construction site and noticed that they had pallets of stuff—all wrapped in plastic. He got the guy's attention and asked if he could have the plastic. The guy told him to come back at lunchtime when no one was working, so he wouldn't need a hard hat, and take all he wanted. Bingo! Now he had a box, yards and yards of plastic, and a new roll of duct tape."

"This is getting harder and harder to believe," she said.

"But it's what he told us, and I really think it did happen. Anyway, he got all the way back to his new digs before he said that he realized that he would need a knife of some sort to cut any sort of a door. He stowed the plastic and the tape inside the box and headed straight back to the hardware store for a pocketknife. He said that the guy who helped him wasn't the same guy as before and he thought for a while that he wouldn't sell him a knife because he looked like a 'hood' with his slicked-back hair, white T-shirt and jeans. He figured that the only thing that made him appear credible was the guitar he had slung around his back. Evidently the guy believed him because he sold him the knife."

When Leon paused for breath, Vivian asked, "More chicken?"

"Ah, no thank you; now where was I?" He stopped as she glanced at her watch. "I'm not boring you, am I?" he said with a bit of sarcasm.

"Actually I find it fascinating, but if you'll notice, it's almost eight-thirty, and I still have to go home."

Leon glanced at his own watch. "Eight-thirty. I can't believe it! Where did the day go? I have so much to tell you, and I haven't even told you what really happened to me! It's so much more important than this story."

"And I haven't told you thank you for the flowers. I could hardly believe it when the flower shop guy delivered them. He insisted on giving them directly to me and wouldn't leave them with either Sandy or Margie. I was quite surprised. Thank you."

"Well, get used to it Sweetheart," he said in his best James Cagney impersonation, "cause you're gonna get more!"

The lightness that she had felt in the morning when Leon breezed in and gave her a kiss returned to her now. When he said that he was going to reconnect, he meant with his friends, not the ones that caused his grief last night. She sat back down and said, "I suppose I could stay a little longer."

"Okay, but only a little bit. I don't like you riding the late buses."

She smiled a bit sadly.

"Anyway, to make a long story short,"

"Too late!" she cried.

He didn't get it. "Anyway," he started again, "after he fixed up his box—'put on the plastic weather siding' is how he termed it—he headed back downtown to look for some sort of secondhand store, maybe an army/navy place. Now that he had a 'home,' he needed a pillow and maybe even a bedsheet. When he found the store, it turned out to be the Goodwill and Pete was out back, as usual, unloading a truck. The kid volunteered to help. Lucky for him there was a big load of camp bunkbed-sized mattresses in the truck. Evidently they had come from a Boy Scout camp somewhere up in Wisconsin that got all new mattresses from money from somebody's estate fund. Pete said to separate them into two piles as they took them off the truck. One pile was the saleable ones and the other for the ones that evidently held some very scared or homesick kids.

"Pete said they would give the smelly ones to a local animal shelter for the dogs to use, since they wouldn't mind the odor. Anyway, this kid, Johnny, asked how much the good mattresses would be sold for. Pete said he had no idea because they never had this many of one thing before and he wasn't sure if he wanted to sell them cheap and get rid of them, or price them up a bit and hope for the best.

"Anyway, the kid ends up with one of the best ones for helping out and he leaves a happy guy. And with that, my dear, I'm going to stop so you don't miss another bus!"

He helped her up from the sofa, pulling her into his arms as she stood. He caressed her hair as he said, "I can't wait to tell you everything that happened today. I don't know why I started with the story about Johnny and Pete, because I have something much more important to tell you. Not tonight, but soon."

She moved her head as if leaving, but his hand curved her face to meet his. "I care for you so much, Vivian Dumbrowski. You have changed my life, and I have never been so happy." He was amazed how easy it was to actually say the words. And now he was going to take full advantage of this newfound freedom from his old self.

She felt like it had been forever since she had been kissed so thoroughly as Leon kissed her. She was breathless when he finally, tenderly pulled away.

"Leon," she began.

He didn't let her finish. He maneuvered her towards her work desk for her to pick up her purse. "I'll see you in the morning."

"Good night," she said softly, closing the door behind her and then crying all the way to the corner.

EIGHT

The following day Sandy arrived at 7:00 AM and began loading the washers. Vivian was a little late, something she was starting to do more and more often. Margie blew in around ten, announcing to one and all that she was getting married and moving to Miami, Florida. She stated very loudly that an old flame who had always been madly in love with her had asked her to marry him. He owned a golf shop near Miami and he vowed that he would stick around in Chicago as long as it took until she said yes. As she talked, she was cleaning out stuff from her shelf. Before leaving, she said, "Here's my address in Florida, and you can send my check there. Oh, by the way, I quit!"

The bell attached to the front door had hardly stopped clanging before a stunned Vivian yelled out "Yahoo!" to which Sandy added a loud, "Amen!" Neither one could believe what just happened, nor could they wait to tell Leon. Or, said Vivian, maybe they shouldn't tell Leon yet, but keep him on the hook awhile longer. Sandy, with her seventeen-year-old wisdom, said that it was too cruel, so they decided to tell him as soon as he came in. Besides, the way they were grinning, he probably would figure it out for himself.

Lunch for the three of them at the cleaners was like old times with sack lunches and a box of Amy Joy donuts for dessert. They were all sitting down and talking nonstop together, taking turns to go when someone came to pick up or drop off cleaning or wash.

"It's been a long time," said Leon, pushing back his chair and balancing his coffee cup on his stomach.

"Too long," said Sandy. "I can't tell you how I've missed this."

"All right, young lady," said Vivian sternly. "You've got a lot of catching us up to do, so you might as well start right now. How was summer school?"

Giving absolutely no heed to the jobs at hand, the three friends sat for almost an hour talking comfortably together. Sandy announced proudly that she had passed all her classes. She admitted that she was still having trouble with physics though, but she had caught up enough to be going back to school full-time in another couple of weeks. It even looked like she would be able to join her class and graduate alongside of them.

Sandy had grown up a lot that year. Gone was the extreme makeup. She looked so much softer and cleaner somehow. Her hair was still teased and sprayed into a style that Leon called "early African Ubangee," but they were happy about all the other changes. There was excitement in her voice now when she talked about school and her summer school friends. Both Vivian and Leon were also relieved to hear that she was finally finding a better group of kids to hang with. No one asked how things were going at home; it was uncanny that they both decided to avoid that subject until the timing was better. After all, this was a day of celebration. No more Margie!

That was the good news. The bad news was that they would have to go through the process all over with more applications for another employee. Business had picked up considerably, and maybe both a full-time and a part-time person were needed.

Sandy noted that the coffee shop across the way had its window trim freshly painted, and said she'd heard that Nell herself had sewn the new half curtains for the windows. She had picked a one-inch green-and-white-checked fabric, and it matched the new green paint around the window perfectly.

"Was that her husband who did the painting?" Leon asked Vivian.

"That's what Howard said. Someone told him that he had been injured on the job somewhere and spent a lot of time at home feeling sorry for himself. When Nell had some plumbing problems at the café, he came in to take a look so she wouldn't have to call a plumber. He hadn't been in for a half a year or so and he couldn't believe the changes that you made on this building. He saw that you had started to paint the old flower shop to match and I guess that's all the challenge he needed. Howard said that he came right in and bought the paint and even with his 'injuries' he got the job done in one afternoon!"

"I noticed that the hardware store is doing a little sprucing up itself," added Sandy. "His wife must be doing the front display window because it looks much better. I like the display of rakes and the baskets of leaves that she has in it now. She's even got packages of spring flower bulbs! Remember how it always was more of a catch-all for odds and ends?"

"You're right! I guess when you work here every day, you don't notice the changes. But ever since Leon painted the front door, everybody's been slowly sprucing up or painting something." As Vivian talked about Leon she put her hand on top of his and patted it.

Sprucing up is not the only thing that's changed around here, thought Sandy with a smile on her face.

NINE

Leon knew now that there was no more waiting. Fall was unpredictable in the weather department and the outdoor painting had to get finished. Leon was tired of waiting for Vivian to contact the building owner so he could contact some painters so they could get the rest of the Painted Ladies finished. The owner was probably having trouble finding painters that didn't cost an arm and a leg, so Leon began to ask around. He started making what seemed like endless phone calls. People who said they'd be out to do estimates never showed up, or some showed up, took a look at all the gingerbread trim and backed out of the job. Finally they found a company that would do it. Actually, Howard found someone. The guys he'd found originally said they couldn't start until late September, but their other job had fallen through, so they were ready to go *now.*

Overnight the scaffolding was put up, crews assembled, and between Leon and the painting crew, all three buildings were completely finished within two days— gingerbread, fish scales, and all.

Leon and Howard sat in the front window of Nell's café, parted her new curtains when she wasn't looking and stared at the finished product. All their endless color choosing, all the waiting, it was hard to believe it was finally finished. How many times had they changed colors? They couldn't remember. As long as these nine colors were only on paper, there had been no risk. But now their choices were there for all of Chicago to see. Leon was sure that everyone was thinking about Dennis at some point, but no one brought up his name. He had been the lynchpin for this whole enterprise. His full color "artist's rendition" of the three buildings still hung in Leon's room tacked to the wall.

The beauty shop's main color for the bulk of the front wall was lilac with the fish scales painted in a soft purplelike color called Heliotrope. The front door was done in a medium purple they called Tempest and the gingerbread was Suntan, a soft yellow. They had added just a touch of soft salmon to the top gingerbread trim.

The cleaners in the center had the bulk of the building in a gray/blue called Grecian Urn for the main color, Gold Buff for the fish scales, and Volcano, a darker blue for the door, and the gingerbread trim with a light touch of the soft salmon here and there in the other trim.

The old flower shop, which was still vacant, would have pleased Dennis, who thought green the best color in the world, with Willow Brook, a soft sage green for the main color, Suntan for some of the trim and the fish scales and Pale Copper, a dark tan for the door and the gingerbread. Because there was a little bit of the soft salmon left, they used the final bit on the trim over the door to completely coordinate the three buildings.

It seemed like almost everyone on the block knew all the color names by heart and every single shop owner and employee stopped by to comment on the choice of paint, the weather, the Cubs and Sox, anything to make conversation. It was probably Nell's biggest day for sales. That's what gave Leon what he thought could be his greatest idea yet.

He hurried across the street and found Vivian in the back ironing shirts and talking to Debbie, the young woman who owned the beauty shop next door. He had never formally met Debbie, and to his knowledge, this was the first time that she had ever ventured anywhere besides her shop and her car. He didn't want to interrupt their conversation, so instead of talking to Vivian, he found a pencil and paper, sat down at the table, and wrote his thoughts. "This could be good," he muttered to himself.

Sixty hand-written invitations were ready to go in less than two days and Leon, Vivian, and Sandy all agreed that they needed to be hand-delivered instead of mailed. They had debated long and hard as to who would get one and they even called Howard over to help with the decisions.

"I say we just do our block," Vivian said, giving earnest voice for her idea. "If we go too far we lose the 'family' feel."

"I respectfully disagree," added Leon. "There is something that is happening here that we cannot confine to only our block. Besides, what is the Chinese restaurant that's two blocks down and one of your favorite places for take-out lunch going to say when he finds out he's not invited? And how about all those crazy Swedes? Would you risk missing a dinner of Swedish meatballs swimming in white gravy and a soft piece of limpa bread smothered in butter to go with it?"

He had a point and she conceded. She looked to Howard for help.

"Don't look at me. My wife and I think it's the best idea that anyone has had for a long time. We'd be happy if it was only the cleaners and the hardware store!"

In the end it was Sandy who made the decision. She had come into the back room after helping more customers than she had seen for a long time. "Wow, when did business pick up like this? When I left for the summer it wasn't like this, not even on our busiest days. The entire neighborhood's changed. It's like urban renewal or something."

"Okay, that's it. We invite everyone we know and then some. The more the merrier." Vivian stood to help in the front.

"All they can say is no," said Howard, throwing water on their fire.

The invitations read:

The Three Painted Ladies, 5400 block, Clark Street,
cordially invite you to the first ever block party/potluck
to celebrate not only Labor Day,
but also the new spirit
in the neighborhood of brotherly love
and the completion of the refurbishing up and down the block.

To be held on Sunday, Sept. 4, 1964
at 7:00 PM
in the empty lot north of Wilson's Drugstore.
If you bring the food, we'll supply the music.
Does anyone have tables and chairs we can use?
Please contact the Band Box Cleaners at 555-6264
or stop in anytime.
P.S. Nell from the One Stop Coffee Shop says that there will be free
coffee with each piece of pie every day until the party.

Not many people appreciated the part about brotherly love, but it was Sandy's idea, and they didn't want to discourage her now that she was doing so well.

Vivian said that invitations usually didn't include requests for things, especially tables and chairs, but this was a first on all counts, so what was the difference? It was going to be fun, even if they ended up being the only ones there!

Leon thought it was unusual to have a sales ad in an invitation, but Nell was really getting into the business.

By hand-delivering the invitations, Leon got a better chance to meet even more people up and down the street for three blocks each way. At each stop he asked if anyone had a line on some music they could hire, cheap. He got all sorts of offers and lots of requests. So far it was pretty evenly divided between requests for Swedish music (he should have realized that), and some of the younger crowd wanted rock and roll. Sandy voted for Peter, Paul, and Mary; old people voted for a polka band; and several even suggested they get that new group they had all seen on the *Ed Sullivan Show*—the Beatles.

"Like that's ever gonna happen," Leon commented to the drugstore guy, Don Wilson.

"How about a mariachi band?" Don asked as he filled prescriptions in the back. "My wife's brother's group might be available."

"Mariachi…that's Mexican, isn't it? How much?"

"Believe me, they work cheap."

"So, is that because they're no good?"

"Naw, they're very good, but they don't get much call to play around here."

"I would suppose not. How can I get hold of them?"

"I'll have Maria call them as soon as she comes in, and they can contact you. I know they'd appreciate the work."

"So, if you don't mind me asking, why does your wife's brother play in a mariachi band?"

"Because that's what he did in Mexico. He's working in landscaping now, and playing gigs as a second job."

"So he's Mexican?"

"Yeah, why?"

"No reason, I guess I didn't know that."

"That would make my wife Mexican too," Don said as he stopped what he was doing and stared directly at Leon.

"You mean that person at the front counter is your wife?"

"No, actually that's our daughter, Rosa."

"So, where's your wife?"

"She's home now, upstairs. You know we live upstairs, don't you?"

"Actually," Leon said thoughtfully, "I didn't know any of this."

"We bought the building a little over eight years ago with money my father had left for me in his will. I was an only child and my old man wanted me to be a doctor. I did pretty well in medical school but couldn't handle the suffering part of the patients. I guess I was too soft. Maybe you could say that I would rather be a behind-the-scenes soldier, so I opted for a few more years of schooling and became a pharmacist. My father never forgave me…well, maybe he had because I was still in the will for the entire estate. But to my face? Never. When I married Maria, it put the icing on the cake. He never even talked to me after that."

"Wow, who knew? Kind of like *West Side Story*."

"Kind of." Don grinned. "But you notice—I haven't died like the guy in the movie did."

"Thank goodness." Leon paused and thought about his words

before he added, "Are you ever worried that more people, besides your father, object to this marriage?"

"Well, if you've noticed the wall facing our empty lot, you'll see graffiti that was put there for us. I won't tell you what it says, but I can tell you that there were plenty of nights that we lay awake for a long time, hoping that these young punks wouldn't take the notion and rob us or, worse yet, burn down our building. If they did burn down the building, not only would we have lost everything we owned, but also we probably would have died in the fire. And robbery is just one of the reasons we put the metal bars on the windows and keep them on all the time. It doesn't look real good, but we're not taking any risks."

"But it's old graffiti, right? There aren't still people out there that would do something to you?"

Don put the plastic bottle full of pills into a box marked *Ready* and continued, "I think we're pretty safe now. I guess we can finally paint over the writing and symbols now."

"Is there a reason you didn't do it right away?"

"Gangs are like male cats. They mark their territory, even if they're only passing through, so if another gang comes in, they see the territory is spoken for and they usually keep on going. It's when the new guys decide to stick around that it gets nasty."

"Wow, I've got to get out more. I didn't have a clue."

"It's a fact of life man...life in the big city!"

Leon was all the way out the door before he remembered the music. "Hey, can I get that phone number from you for the band?"

TEN

The permits were all filed with the city, the mariachi band booked, (they did work cheap) the tables set up, and the Christmas lights that Howard donated for the occasion were strung between the buildings and along the side of the abandoned building that flanked the empty lot.

Leon had made it his special job to paint over the graffiti on the abandoned building. He had hardly started when two of the guys who were sitting at the coffee shop saw what he was going to do and came over to help.

"Fiesta? Whoever said that it was a fiesta?" Leon was complaining to Vivian and Sandy as they sat down for a quick lunch. "Just because there's a Mexican band doesn't mean it's a fiesta!"

"Whatever we call it, it's going to be wonderful, and when this is all over, I'm going to make you sit down and tell me the rest of the story about that Johnny guy."

"You've got a deal."

"Johnny who?" asked Sandy. "And whatever happened with Peter, Paul, and Mary?"

To say the party was a success was an understatement. Their long potluck table ran the gambit from enchiladas to moo moo gai pan and was heavy on the Swedish meatballs and cinnamon rolls brought by the Villa Sweden restaurant gang.

The police showed up, but only out of curiosity. Even though people started out in their familiar groups, it wasn't long before everyone was mixing and moving their chairs around away from the tables so they could sit and talk sports, politics, or business.

Late in the evening, Vivian finally cornered Leon and led him away from the noise of the band and the well-wishers. Everyone there wanted to say thanks for the great idea and to tell Leon that when he got in the painting mood again to contact them and they would let him paint their buildings. The only quiet place she could find was back in the cleaners at their own familiar well-worn table.

"Okay, what did you mean the other day that you had something important to tell me?" she asked as she sat down heavily, pushing out a chair for him with her foot.

Leon thought for a moment, then remembered the conversation. It took him only minutes to candidly share the amazing things that had happened to him that day—from going back to his house and facing his past, the realization about his father's life and finally understanding that he had no obligation to live up to someone else's ideas. He told her about his marriage to Edith—how it was all right, but predictable and unexciting. He told her that he often wondered if Edith was disappointed in him in some vague way. She never said anything outright, but it was a persistent feeling he lived with.

He also told her about taking her advice and giving it all to God. "I know that Jesus is my Savior. I accepted him into my heart when I was seven at a summer camp. I guess I kind of lost touch with him the past twenty years, though. Whenever anything came up, I handled it without his help. I guess in reality I gypped myself out of having a really close relationship with him because I never invited him to be an active part of my life. That, in retrospect, was a very stupid and selfish decision on my part. Things could have been so different, or better yet, *I* could have been so different. I regret the way I've spent many of my years."

Vivian was dabbing at a few tears when he finished. She stood and walked to the sink. She turned and started to say something.

But at that moment Howard came in through the front door. "Hey, I think the one-hundred-cup coffeepot must have blown a fuse at the café. Nell wants to know if we can plug it in here."

Vivian gave a final swipe at her eyes and bustled forward. "Of course. Let's use the plug in the front. It's loaded for bear, and we never use it for anything. Gracious, I don't know what they were thinking when they did that." She knew she was babbling, but couldn't stop herself. Their talk was over, and she didn't get to tell Leon the most important thing *she* had to say.

Tuesday morning everyone was smiling through the haze of a four-hour night.

"Next time we do this, it's got to be on a different night, not Labor Day Monday itself!" said Debbie as she lumbered in and sat at the table next to Sandy. "I'm glad I don't have anyone in my chair until ten. I'm so tired. It's a good thing that all I've got booked today are just wash and sets. Cuts could be dangerous. It was fun, though, wasn't it?"

"I agree," said Vivian as she poured a cup of coffee for Debbie and the fourth one of the morning for herself.

"Hey, who was the guy with the camera?" Sandy sipped her coffee gratefully.

"Which one? I don't know why people take cameras to things like that. It's dark—how good can the pictures be?"

"Beats me," said Sandy, stifling a yawn.

"Sandy started school full-time today. It's her senior year, you know," Vivian mentioned to Debbie.

"I remember high school," said Debbie with a sigh. "I can't say I liked it, but my parents said they'd pay for beauty school if I stuck it out and graduated with my class, so I did. I guess, looking back, I never have regretted it. Isn't it funny how we look back at our life regretting things and not regretting things that we never thought we would?" She picked up her coffee again, drained it, and put the cup on the counter.

"Well, I've got a whole day of business today, so I better get cuttin'. Ha, get it? Cuttin'?"

Vivian gave her a weak smile as she sailed out and Sandy let out a groan. Before she reached the front door, Debbie turned and asked, "By the way, who was that cute guy named Johnny? Somebody said that he worked at the Goodwill store. I guess I'll have to start shopping there more often!" With that final comment, she was out the door and passing the front window at a trot.

"Must be nice to be so young and have so much energy," Vivian said sourly. Gracious! What was the matter with her? She was on edge and everything was beginning to bother her. "Must be the coffee," she said as she poured herself another cup. "And where is Leon? The guy has the advantage of sleeping right here; you would have thought that he would have been up and around for coffee, and isn't he going to bring donuts anymore?"

A customer came in so she sighed, got up, and officially started what she knew was going to be a long day.

Sandy wisely held her peace.

A writer for the *Tribune* called the cleaners around three. With the mood Vivian was still in, she admitted later that she wasn't very courteous to the caller and only perfunctory in taking his name and number.

Leon had spent the bulk of the day cleaning the empty lot and hearing lots of compliments as he stopped here and there in the neighborhood. He had never felt so happy. Telling Vivian everything, absolutely everything last night was the best thing he had ever done. Somehow he felt cleaned, renewed.

When he finally landed back at the cleaners at closing, he noticed immediately that Vivian looked beyond tired. "I think you need to get an ad in the paper for more help. You look completely done in."

Vivian glared at him, grabbed her purse and sweater, and stormed out without even saying good-bye.

"What did I say?" he asked the air.

ELEVEN

The phone was ringing when Vivian arrived the next day at her usual early morning time. It was the *Tribune* again and she was just about to hang up when Leon opened his door and came out. "One moment please," she said into the phone and called Leon. "It's for you."

"Must be more compliments," he said as he took the phone and covered the mouthpiece with his hand. "It's probably Mayor Daley's office wanting me to run for public office...possibly an alderman or something, maybe king."

She wasn't amused.

After a short conversation, in which his part was mainly "yeah and uh-huh," he hung up the phone with a puzzled look. Vivian was beginning to load the washers; the hum of the machines that had always been so soothing was now grating on his nerves.

He didn't know if he should go across the street to the hardware store and discuss this news with Howard, or stay here and try to talk to Vivian. He glanced over at her as she slammed washing machine lids down and threw clothes into the dryer and decided that it might be safer if he left for a while.

He and Howard slipped over to the café to their usual table and Howard said, "Okay, shoot."

"Remember the guy taking all those pictures at the party?"

"There were lots of cameras at the party. Which one?"

"I don't know which one, but evidently he was with the *Chicago Tribune* and he asked around at the party and now he wants to sit down with me and talk about the neighborhood."

"You're kidding. What's his name?"

"The guy who does the stuff for the magazine section that comes out with the Sunday paper. What's-his-name."

"Oh yeah, that helps."

"You know who I mean, don't you? He did that piece about cemeteries?"

"Yeah, I think I do. So what are you going to do about it?"

"I guess I'll sit down and talk. What could he possibly want to know?"

"Well, if you ask me, maybe he thinks that you have something to do with the block changing like it has. After all, look at it. In the last six months we've gotten a record store, an optometrist, and a barbershop. Hey, I hear that Vivian already hired the barber's wife to work at the cleaners, Anyway, even Van down at his TV repair shop is buying the place next door and expanding his business. He's gonna move his family in upstairs when he makes that all one building too. It should be pretty nice up there."

"I don't think that's got anything to do with me. Neighborhoods are always changing in a city.... It's got nothing to do with me."

"So when you gonna see him?"

"He wants to set something up for next week. I told him I'd call. I only hope it has nothing to do with Dennis."

"I think that I'll put the padlock back on my door," he told Vivian later that afternoon. "I really don't want the people of Chicago to know I live here."

"So, just what do you want the people of Chicago to know Mr. Big Shot?"

Gracious, she was testy.

"I have no idea. I have no idea why he even wants to see me. All he said is that he was at the block party and wanted to talk to me. Maybe he has a newspaper route for me to handle."

Vivian softened considerably. "Listen, I don't mean to be so crabby. I don't know what's gotten into me. I'm sorry if I've been cranky.

Forgive me?" she asked as she slipped her hand into his. "I've got a lot on my mind and I've got to find a way to get it off my mind before it drives me crazy."

He thought she was referring to the business and hiring new employees, but he was very wrong.

Vera started to work at the beginning of the following week. She was indeed the wife of the barber, a guy named Joe. They seemed to be somewhere in their late fifties. She was a "ball of fire," according to Vivian, and with Sandy working part-time again during the day, and every other Saturday, it looked like life was going to calm down a bit. The guy from the newspaper called back and said that there were some late-breaking stories that were filling his time and asked if they could arrange something for a week or two later. That was fine with Leon. Whether it was an alderman's job or an investigation about Dennis, he could wait.

Rain seemed to be the order of the day for the entire last two weeks of September. The cleaners, once again, became a haven of peace. Even though it was dark and dreary outside as the endless traffic hit the same potholes and splashed water onto the cars parked alongside the sidewalk, inside the cleaners it felt as cozy and comforting as being back in the womb. The washers hummed, the dryers made it warm and pleasant, and even the whir of the automatic track, which held the dry cleaning as it revolved from the work area to the front, added to the calm.

People spoke more softly for some reason. Today Vera brought over a casserole to bake for their lunch, and Joe was going to join them at noon. Chicken and rice swimming in mushroom soup slowly baking in the oven; the soft, sweet smell of fabric softener; steam hissing from the iron; and donuts from Amy Joy on the table. It couldn't be nicer.

It made it hard for Leon to leave, but there was a job that he had put off way too long. He had phoned Watanabi at home that morning and arranged to meet him at his store on State Street at 11:00. It was time.

He was whistling again when he came in the shop at closing. Vivian and Vera were wiping down the machines and cleaning up the kitchen. Rush-hour traffic had finally let up and lights in the neighborhood began to come on in the houses and go off in the shops up and down the block.

When Vera left, Vivian stayed around awhile toying with the idea of a long talk, but it had been another busy day, and to tell the truth, she was too tired to talk. It seemed like she was tired all the time, so she just said, "Night," as she left.

Leon was still thinking about his meeting with Watanabi and hardly noticed that she had gone. When he first came back, he had felt good about what he had done, but now he was beginning to have second thoughts. Now he hardly knew exactly how he felt about what he'd done. Maybe it was time to start walking again. He thought better when he walked.

Johnny was at the Goodwill with Pete when Leon stopped by. "I didn't realize you guys were open this late," Leon said as he grabbed a chair behind the big counter and joined the two men.

"Normally we're not. We got to talking, and with the rain making the entire day dark, it was hard to tell when it was closing time. We didn't have any customers to remind us, since we're always slow at the end of the month anyway. I just looked at my watch before you came in and saw how late it was. But if you've got time, you've got to hear this story."

Leon turned to Johnny. "There's more to tell about your box adventure?" he joked.

"Yeah, it gets stranger and stranger."

"Really? Okay, shoot."

"Well, you know how I was sleeping in the box?"

"Your eight-dollar steal?"

"Yeah, that's the one. Well, the mattress I got here was a perfect fit. The place I found to put my box seemed to be pretty safe and I was actually getting a decent night's sleep, so I decided to look for a job. Even though I had a place to sleep, it didn't come with, you know, accommodations so I still needed to find a bathroom somewhere that I could use without having to buy something. There was a gas station down about two blocks. I thought that maybe I could strike a deal with the night manager. Maybe if I did some work around the place, I could use the bathroom to clean up and shave each day. He's a real lazy bum, so he said that if I cleaned both the men's and women's room every night and checked them every morning that not only could I use the bathroom for my personal use, but that he'd let me use a locker in the back for my clothes."

"Great."

"You're not kidding. The job was easy. After a week, I realized what a find I had made. I slept remarkably well and no one bothered me. I was also clean and, because of the locker, I had a place to keep another set of clothes. With all of this going for me, I figured it was time to see about some sort of real job. After I was finished cleaning the bathrooms one night I sat and read the want ads before I threw the papers away and saw that St. Joseph's Hospital needed orderlies."

"Isn't that the hospital down by Lake Shore Drive?"

"Yeah, that's the one. No bus transfers needed, just a straight shot down. I wasn't sure what an orderly was, but I thought it wouldn't hurt to ask. Well, not only did I get the job, but get this—I get to wear hospital scrubs, change in a locker room, and have access to hot showers. It couldn't have worked out better. Now I had a steady income, a locker room with a shower at my disposal, a place to sleep that was still pretty safe, and a second job at the gas station that now pays in cash for as long as I want it."

"That's unbelievable," said Leon. "You're really quite an entrepreneur."

"Thanks for the compliment, but I also found myself homeless again right away."

"Somebody discover you and make you move on?"

"I don't think anyone at the apartment even cared that I was there. Evidently they had one of those absentee owners, and rumor was that the place was for sale. Lots of the apartments were empty, and there was no super living in the basement. When something broke, they had to wait a long time to get it fixed, if they ever did. I suppose that's why so many people started to move out. But my problem was more rain than the lack of a super."

"I hear you about absentee landlords; we've got one in our business too," Leon commented.

Pete added, "I imagine that cardboard doesn't hold up too well in the rain,"

"You've got that right. Even with all the plastic I had on it, and being right up alongside the building and out of the main downpours, it still was starting to sag."

"So?"

"So, he moved in here," said Pete matter-of-factly as he rose to finally lock the front door.

Leon peered around at the showroom floor for a possible spot where Johnny would be camping out. Pete saw him looking around, smiled, and said, "No, not on the floor. We have a group of rooms upstairs that we 'rent' out for free to those who really need help. We only make it on a month-to-month basis to make sure that we're helping instead of enabling."

"*Enabling?* That's a big word for this part of town. What does that mean?"

"Keeping people from not facing up to their circumstances. It's when other people feel so sorry, they take on the responsibility that the other guy should be taking. We use the rooms upstairs for people that we feel are really trying to make a change for the better and they just need a little help from a friend to get started again."

"Wow, who knew? I think that's great."

"It's not only that news. When Johnny isn't working at the hospital, he's still a big help around here."

"So," Leon asked, "does that mean you are or are not still working at the gas station too?"

"It means I'm not. They canned the night manager and I was making enough at the hospital, so we kind of parted company."

Pete added, "And if you've noticed, the trucks that are usually in front of our loading dock for hours now aren't anymore. Johnny's got all the employees helping out when it comes to unloading. He's even devised a system of sorting it right away. He said that he had taken a business class about sorting mail."

"Mail? You've lost me. You're handling mail now?"

"Nah," interjected Johnny. "The principle of sorting mail correctly says that an efficient way of handling the daily mail is to handle it once. In other words, don't look at it, put it down, then go through it again and again later. In a business class at school we learned to handle it once; as we went through it, each piece had to go somewhere. Some went directly into the garbage, some went into a pile to be handled immediately, and other stuff goes into a pile that will be dealt with by somebody else."

"That's the principle that he uses here for the trucks. Instead of unloading everything in a pile, it gets sorted as it comes off the truck. Stuff for the Dumpster goes directly to the Dumpster like always. Everything else finds a home on the sales floor right away. It's put at the end of the aisles, cleaned and tagged on the floor, and then shelved immediately. The whole thing works remarkably well. In fact, now our employees have their own departments instead of working the entire store. It's amazing. Now they have more pride in their own sections. It's funny to hear them unload the truck, the way they brag about *their* departments, and how excited they are when stuff comes in for their section."

"I can't tell you how great this all is," said Leon. "There's a world of people out there, people we know"—he eyed Pete—"and people we've never met who do all sorts of things, good or bad, that we have no idea about. Like the guy named Dennis who used to own the flower shop next door to the cleaners. You wouldn't believe it, but he...."

After a few "for instances" about Dennis, and some about the Wilson family who ran the drugstore on the corner, and Nell at the coffee shop, he could have continued more stories far into the night, but Johnny had to be at work by 6:45 the next morning. Even though it was late when Leon let himself in the darkened cleaners, it wasn't as late as it could have been if all the stories could have been told in their entirety. Truth be told, he had a wonderful time.

TWELVE

As usual, the Cubs were having a losing season, seventy-three wins and eighty-six losses. Why should 1964 be any different? You would think that avid fans would be used to it by now, but "once a Cubs fan, always a Cubs fan." They had long ago in the season, along with faithful WGN announcer, Jack Brickhouse, begun their yearly mantra of "wait until next year."

Leon had tickets for the three games the Cubs were to play against the San Francisco Giants, October 2-4 at Wrigley. Howard could only make the first two games, and Vivian said she'd like to go to the last one with him.

It was only twenty blocks down to Wrigley Field and Leon suggested they walk. Vivian suggested they didn't, and maybe to save time trying to find a place to park Leon's car, maybe they should take the bus. They took the bus. The Cubs took the series and even though there was no hope for the year, the end of the last game pumped fans and the mood was high in the city.

To celebrate the exciting win, they caught a cab and took it up to Al's for Italian beef sandwiches. As Leon leaned against the high counter that faced the street where customers stood to eat, beef juice running down to his elbows, he watched the always-busy Ontario Street traffic. It was the right time to let Vivian in on his recent activities.

"Remember I told you that I had a house southwest of the city?" he said as he reached for even more napkins.

"Yes," she said as she replaced a steamed green pepper onto her sandwich and took another bite.

"Well, I sold it last week to the guy next door—that Japanese man who had been taking care of it."

"You sold it? You *sold* your house, just like that?"

Leon got the impression that she wanted to add, "Without consulting me?" but he couldn't be sure.

"Yeah, I felt that the time had come to make a clean break of my other life and the guy's been a gem about mowing and all. Anyway, I had to do something. He wouldn't take any money for all the work he'd done and with winter coming, I couldn't see him shoveling my walks again. And there's no way that I was going to go back each snowfall and do it, so I sold it, lock, stock, and barrel."

"When you say 'lock, stock, and barrel,' you mean everything inside too?"

"Everything. The day I was there I took all the important papers. There was nothing else there that I wanted or even needed. Besides, where would I put any of it?" He laughed at his own statement, but it was obvious that Vivian wasn't joining in.

"So, when does all this take place?"

"Oh, it's all done. I gave him a chunk of money off the cost of the house if he would take care of all the stuff inside. We came to an agreement that seemed to suit us both."

"I see." Her tone was icy.

Leon continued to watch the traffic as Vivian deliberately placed the rest of her sandwich into the waxed paper, picked up all her napkins and added them to the uneaten sandwich, and walked to the garbage can in the corner and tossed it all out along with her unfinished soft drink.

"Hadn't we better be going?" she asked coldly. "There's work tomorrow." She walked stiffly out through the door, out onto the street, and down to the corner to wait for a bus. It was clear that there would be no taxi ride back that night.

Sandy was a bundle of news and information the following day as the three ladies sat eating lunch together.

Things were going well at school and she liked her classes, especially her D.E.—Diversified Education—class. It was the course that enabled her to work half the day and go to school in the mornings. There was also class time that went along with D.E., and in it they studied marketing, displays, appropriate dress for employment, and learning how to act in an interview.

"It's really interesting. I guess I didn't realize that any of this existed," she told her friends. "I guess I never thought much beyond high school and my immediate future. I'm beginning to like retail a lot more and I'm thinking of going on to college, although I heard that Marshall Fields might have something opening up in the display department. I think it would be so much fun to do that! Wouldn't it be too cool to work at Fields!"

"Maybe you could even help with the Christmas windows," added Vera. "Joe and I fight the crowds downtown every year to see them. I hear they work on them all year. They must have an entire floor devoted to only the window display stuff. Some of the old ones they use Christmas after Christmas, so they must have to store them somewhere!"

"I would love to find out!" Sandy's eyes sparkled.

Conversation stopped as Leon entered and Vivian deliberately got up and went to the sink to throw away the rest of her coffee. "Well, I'd better get back to work," she said as she headed to the front, avoiding him completely.

"What's with her?" Sandy whispered to him after she was gone.

"Beats me," Leon said, watching her leave. "She's been this way ever since yesterday's Cubs game. I would have thought she'd be happy. They won the entire series after all." He headed to his room shaking his head.

"I think its love," said Vera.

"I think it's crazy," said Sandy, as she left the table to wash her hands and go back to the dryers.

The guy from the *Tribune* finally called back. Sandy took the call and called Leon to the phone. When he hung up, he said that he was off to downtown. "Don't wait supper," he joked. "I might come back as the new mayor. No, strike that, make it king!"

The short El ride down to the *Tribune* building was one of the longest ones Leon had made in a long time. He decided not to drive, not only because of the parking, but because his mind was going twenty different directions. He knew that he'd run into somebody because he wasn't concentrating. It had always fascinated him how so many people were at each corner waiting to cross when the light changed. It was like a sea of bodies at each intersection and he didn't want to hit any one of them. But he also didn't want to wait for them to cross, making him miss his light either.

The *Tribune* Tower was imposing, to say the least as it stood facing the Chicago River on North Michigan Avenue. It had a huge lobby with marble floors and columns. There was a gift shop to the left that he didn't even know existed. Maybe when he left he would stop in to a buy a souvenir of his beloved *Tribune*...maybe a cap or a cup, or pretty much anything with the Cubs logo.

A huge reception desk stood toward the middle in the back of the high-ceilinged lobby. Leon's shoes clacked as he crossed the distance and asked in hushed tones for the reporter that called him.

"Got an appointment?" the receptionist asked as she flipped open her book and placed a hand on the phone.

"Uh, yes, at two o'clock, name's McKee," he said, sounding like he didn't have a brain in his head.

A quick phone call and a curt, "Take those elevators to the eleventh floor and the girl at the desk will direct you from there," and she stared past him at someone else and said, "Yes?"

You can certainly tell why this city is not called the City of Brotherly Love like Philadelphia, thought Leon as he rode up the fast ascending elevator. *Would it kill her to....* The doors opened before he could complete his thought and he got out. He walked over to the desk, repeated who he was and whom he was there to see. This gal stared at him and said, "This is the eighth floor."

Okay, maybe he should just go all the way back down, out the door and back onto the street. He didn't want to talk about Dennis anyway, and he didn't want to get involved in any intrigue, especially with the mob. *Oh, that's right,* he said to himself as he once again boarded the crowded elevator, *there is no mob in Chicago. Yeah, sure,* he said as the doors closed and the car started upwards before he had a chance to push the mezzanine button.

When the doors opened, he checked to make sure it was the right floor. *Yes, eleven.* He stepped out into the busy hallway with phones ringing and people walking. He paused for only a second, then deliberately turned completely around and entered the express elevator near by, pushed the mezzanine button, sailed to the main floor, and left the building, completely forgetting to stop at the gift shop in his hurry to leave.

THIRTEEN

No one brought up his visit to the paper because the fall cleaning push had begun. By the time he returned to the shop, it was a very busy place.

Mayor Daley was running his annual fall Paint-up, Fix-up, Clean-up Campaign (the same one he ran in the spring), where the garbage men would pick up just about anything (without the traditional addition price) and all the city stores seemed to pick up the theme by running specials on everything for fall cleaning from rakes to weather-stripping and paint to new carpeting and furniture. It was time to clean and refurbish the nest before winter set in.

All of Chicago must have been in a cleaning mood too because there was all sorts of stuff in every alley waiting for pickup. Leon noticed this with interest as he rode the bus back home.

He wondered if maybe he shouldn't call Pete and see if he wanted to do a little garbage picking that evening. They'd done it quite a bit already during the summer and got some really nice pieces for Pete to put in the store. It always made them both wonder why some of the stuff had been dumped in the first place. One night they had picked up a brown, plush, old-fashioned rocking chair that not only was in excellent condition but still had the hand-made doilies pinned at the back and on both arms.

Somebody's grandma died perhaps? Leon thought there must be a story behind every discard—like the complete set of luggage they found on top of a perfectly good set of lawn furniture, dining table included. Were the owners coming or going? Another funny thing they noticed right away in the spring when they began their night work was that the better the neighborhood farther north, the worse the stuff they threw out. They had originally thought that it was how they stayed rich, keeping everything they owned and never buying new. Later on they heard someone else say that when the snooty people redecorated, they took their old stuff to their summer cabins up north. Wow, rich and stingy.

Leon and Pete did very well last May when it seemed like the entire city's rent was up and everybody moved. Living in a house outside of the downtown area, Leon was unaware of this fact. People in his neighborhood moved in and out at will, not only in May. Now that he lived right where the action was, he found Pete's assessment to be true; everybody moved in May, and seemed to take very little with them.

Thank goodness that Sandy came to work at noon each day now that school was in full swing. Between the three women, there was both job efficiency and a peace that reigned once again.

Everyone agreed that Joe, Vera's husband, turned out to be a real nice guy. He was maybe a few years older than Leon and they found that they had more and more in common as they got to know each other. Both of them had worked for years in jobs they were happy to have at first; then, as time wore on, they were too set in their ways to get out. Joe recently moved from working at the downtown's prestigious and historic Drake Hotel's high-end barbershop in the fancy mezzanine, to a little shop of his own that he set up across the street. He needed to stay working, but standing for hours at time, day after day was starting to take its toll on his body. He was hoping to establish a smaller clientele in his new shop. Vera had wanted to call the shop A Cut Above, but Joe won out, and Joe's Barbershop was painted on the front window. "I don't plan to be one of those unisex shops that do both men's and women's hair. Just for guys. Joe's Barbershop, period."

Joe suffered terribly from varicose veins and leg cramps like most barbers did from standing on cement for so many years. He had taken to wearing long support stockings, which helped somewhat, but he was secretly grateful that his business was slow, allowing him to sit down a lot more.

"That's why those rubber pads were invented," he told the group one day at lunch. "They go completely around the chair on the floor.

But I don't think it matters what you stand on. If you stand long enough on cement, you'll get leg problems."

"I heard that in Wisconsin they buy those padlike things for the cows to stand on in the barn," added Sandy, who was becoming more and more interested in trivia.

No one knew quite what to say to that one.

Sandy overheard the conversation Leon had on the phone with Pete about garbage picking after dark and asked if she could go along. She didn't have school the next day and her mother certainly wasn't going to care if she went or not, so "could she please, please, please?"

When Pete stopped to pick up Joe at nine, he didn't know that Sandy was coming along, and he had Johnny in the truck too. He had asked Johnny to come along and give them a hand and had forgotten to tell Leon. When they added Sandy to the front seat, along with the three of them, the seating was tight, but the mood for adventure was high.

It was almost 3:00 AM before the truck finally pulled into the back of the cleaners to drop Leon off. Leon told Vivian the next day that they could have worked all night because they kept filling up the truck, and they had to keep making trips back to the Goodwill to unload, but since Johnny had to be up by 6:45 for work they dropped both him and Sandy off, each at their own place around midnight, regardless of Sandy's protests.

"So, did they hit it off?"

"Who?"

"Sandy and Johnny. She's always asking about him and now she finally met him. Did they hit it off?"

"I have no idea and I really don't care. They're both way too young anyway, and both have questionable futures."

"And what do you mean by 'questionable futures'?"

"Well, she's flighty and he's ungrounded!" He was too tired to talk so he simply said the first thing that had come into his mind.

"You think that Sandy is flighty? After all she's been through—"

He stopped her by saying, "Look, I was kidding. I don't know if they hit it off or not, or if she's flighty or not. I'm beat, and I'm gonna go lay back down for a while."

Even after he left she continued the conversation by herself. By the time she finished reviewing all of Sandy's virtues, which she found to be many, Vivian realized how truly fond of Sandy she'd gotten in the past year...no, almost two years! Where had the time gone? Leon had been here for over a year himself, and where was that going? She was still musing when the bell over the door jangled, and she went to wait on another customer.

By the time Leon appeared an hour or so later, just in time for lunch, she whispered to him in passing so Vera wouldn't hear that she wanted to talk to him later.

Uh-oh, what have I done now? he wondered.

When Sandy arrived for lunch, she was absolutely bubbly. She talked incessantly about the fun they had garbage picking and about all the great stuff they got. She never mentioned Johnny once, but everyone could see that he fascinated her.

Leon didn't see a thing, and later that day when Vivian finally cornered him as he wandered through the cleaners with yet another can of paint in his hands, she grabbed his arm and told him to "sit Buster" as she dragged him to the table. She poured coffee for them both and asked, "Do you plan to let Sandy go with you guys again? Is this going to be a regular thing with the four of you? If it is, I would caution you not to take that poor girl. She's too easily influenced, and I think she's way too young to take up with that boy. Heaven knows that her own mother is a terrible example to begin with, but I wouldn't be able to live with myself if something happened to her because of that boy."

When she paused for breath and a swig of coffee, Leon asked, "Are you through? Can I get a word in edgeways now?"

"Oh, sorry. It's just that I feel more like a—"

Leon interrupted before she could begin again. "First of all, you aren't her mother, we are not her parents, and believe it or not, she's got a good head on her shoulders. She could be a far different kind of person with a family, or should I say, lack of family, like she has, but she's fine. Who else do you know that has come such a long way already? Sure, we've encouraged her and tried to guide her, but it had to be her decision to change. When I first came here, she was a completely different person. Remember Vince, that cheeseball with all those tattoos and the leather boots with the chains on them that used to drive by on his motorcycle and rev the engine? Every time she went out with him, I thought for sure she'd end up dead or pregnant or badly beaten. But now, she's back in school, working and making college plans. She's not the same person."

"I know, but honestly, I do feel like I'm her mother, and it's hard to let go. She's come so far to fail now."

"Don't you think that she has opportunities at school every day to get in trouble? Just because she obviously likes Johnny doesn't necessarily make it a bad thing."

"Ah ha! They did hit it off! Leon McKee, you are an exasperating man. You said that you didn't notice!"

"I said I didn't notice so I could get some sleep. But yes, they had a lot of fun together and I think it was all very nice. They seem to fit each other perfectly."

"Great—now I'm going to have to have a talk with her."

"I don't think that's necessary. Let's trust her on this one. In fact, let's help out by inviting both Pete and Johnny for supper some night."

"And just where are you planning on holding this supper? Here?"

"Where else?"

Supper it was on Saturday night and from the way they all talked and laughed everyone had a good time. Vivian's homemade lasagna went fast, the warm garlic bread didn't have a chance at being a leftover, and the cake for dessert (that Sandy made at school that day and brought) was a huge hit, even though it had a great deal of frosting on one side in order to even it out and make it level.

The conversation flowed as if those four people had been friends forever. Toward the end of the evening, Johnny told them about a guy he met at the hospital.

"He's not a patient. He works there, like I do, as an orderly. His name is Steve and, get this, he used to be a high-rolling trader in the commodities market downtown. Now he and his friend live in the office in an abandoned factory. Well, I should say that they only sleep there; they don't live there. He said that someone *could* actually live there because there's a shower and everything right in the office. He said that they wait until it gets dark and then climb up on boxes and pallets they've stacked against the outside wall and crawl in the back window."

For the first time since Leon could remember, Sandy didn't say, "cool."

"So, is that all you know about him and don't you think that's kind of odd?" asked Vivian, always the curious type.

"Yeah, that's pretty much all I know. He said that he and his friend Tony, another guy he originally met on the street, started talking one day while they were hanging around the beach or something and decided that maybe they would pal around together and see if they couldn't figure out how to get out of their situations without either one of them going to their parents for help. Each of them had also worn out their welcomes on the sofas of friends. The more they talked, the more they found out that they were uncommonly the same. Neither one was happy shifting around each night looking for somewhere safe to bunk, so they determined to spend what little money they had riding the bus trying to find someplace to sleep in a less crowded and safer neighborhood. They both agreed that it was smarter to become a team instead of trying to exist on their own."

"Why would it make it safer and smarter to be a team?" Sandy questioned.

"Because when you live on the street, you can't even take the smallest things for granted."

"Like?" she asked without thinking.

"I don't mean to be indelicate, but like going to the bathroom. To do this in the middle of the night you have to get up, roll up your bedding, whatever it is, and gather up all your belongings and find

86

someplace to, you know, go." Before she could ask why, he continued, "If you left anything behind while you were gone for only minutes, there would be a good chance that there would be nothing left by the time you got back. Stuff gets stolen all the time. I worried about my guitar constantly. I'm sure it would have been gone in a minute if I got sloppy."

"That's pretty sad—poor people stealing from poor people in the same condition," Sandy said as she reached for the knife to scrape off a bit of frosting on one side of the cake and cut another slice, offering it to Johnny.

"Yes, it is sad, but that's the way it is. I've heard stories about women and children in shelters for the night that didn't think and took their shoes off and put them under their cots only to wake up the next morning and find them gone. Naturally, no one knows anything as to their whereabouts and they have to leave barefooted."

"That's just cruel."

"Yes it is, but not uncommon. That's why it's safer and wiser to stay in pairs. Anyway, back to the guys. Evidently after they got off the bus in an area that they thought was okay, they decided to check out this McDonald's they thought they had seen from the bus and spend their final coins on lunch. Tony was sure it was one way and Steve was sure it was the other. When Tony took off in what Steve knew was the wrong direction, Steve told him that he would wait where he was so when Tony found out that he had been wrong, and Steve was right after all, they would then go the right way.

Steve said he was sitting in a doorway of an abandoned building enjoying being out of the wind and having the sun all to himself when these two guys in suits stop their car and get out almost directly in front of him. Because he had his eyes closed he said that they must have thought that he was another drunk sleeping it off on the street, so they talked to each other as though he wasn't there. According to their conversation, there was to be a corporate raid the next morning in the small factory across the street because of some misdeeds by the company where the state of Illinois was concerned, so they were going to go in early in the morning, seize all the records, and arrest the owners of the factory when they arrived. Steve couldn't tell if they were Feds or what. All this time he was also afraid that Tony would come back with the burgers and ruin everything, but it worked out that that right after they left, Tony returned, going on about this Italian restaurant he'd found that was looking for help in the kitchen. He explained the reason that he was late was because he talked to the guy there about a job while they were packaging the minestrone soup and hot garlic bread and he grabbed an application before he left, never admitting that he did not find the McDonald's.

"Steve and I have the same lunch time and we sometimes eat lunch together in the cafeteria, but there are so many other people around, we don't get much of a chance to talk about something for very long before someone else starts listening. He really doesn't want a lot of people to know where he lives."

"Or why," added Leon softly.

"He and his friend and I are going bowling on Thursday night if there aren't leagues, so if I find anything else out, I'll let you know."

"Cool."

Leon knew Sandy couldn't resist forever.

FOURTEEN

"I can't help but think about that young man Johnny was telling about who's living in the factory," Vivian said as she and Leon finished cleaning up the shop and making sure it was all spic and span for Monday. "By the way, I really do like that boy Johnny. He's got a lot going for him. I just hope he can get on his feet."

"Living in the *office* in the factory, you mean. And didn't I say that you'd like him?"

"I meant office. Don't be so picky. Anyway, you never said that I would like him. I don't even think anything like that ever came up."

"It's interesting, isn't it?"

"What's interesting?" she challenged.

"We sound like an old married couple with our halfhearted bickering."

Vivian stared at him only moments, then started to speak, deciding that she had to confess her secret now before she could change her mind again.

But before she could utter a word, Leon, who had turned to wash out his cup at the sink, asked, "So what about the young man living in the *office* of the factory?"

She visibly struggled with wanting to continue what she knew she should do and she had actually started to begin, but stopped to answer his question first. After all, she reasoned quickly with herself, there was plenty of time to bring up what she wanted to say about something else. And it would, no doubt, lead to a long conversation once she started, and it was already going on 10:00 PM. Better to wait.

"It's not so much living in the office of a factory that fascinates me, but how strange it must be to wake up every morning under a desk," she said. "Or to have a ringing phone that you cannot answer or a hot shower that you can't use. Why would they have a shower in a factory office? Anyway, you would think that would be something that you couldn't adjust to. And the thought that the authorities could come at any time for more files, or papers, or bookwork, and discover you would make me so on edge that I don't think I could sleep."

"I would imagine that the very fact they're young helps. They don't seem to worry about a lot. They're invincible, you know."

"I'm not so sure about that." She sat down on the sofa and he sat down on the other end.

"When I was only six years old or so, I didn't feel invincible when I had a sleeping experience that I'll never forget, and it only lasted one night!" Vivian said softly.

"Everyone seems to have a sleeping experience anymore. Pray tell, what could that have possibly been?"

"Okay, Mr. Sarcasm, I'll tell you whether you want to hear it or not. It was one fall in our summer cabin in Door County, Wisconsin," she began, ignoring his last comment.

"Is Door County that piece of land down at the bottom of the state of Wisconsin on the east side that juts out like a finger?"

"That's the one…but it's more like a thumb than a finger."

"Sorry."

"No problem. Anyway, my father was a high school English teacher, so he had the summers off. We lived in Milwaukee and he had inherited some money before I was born and he used it to buy a piece of property by one of the little towns in Door County way at the top. We were right on Lake Michigan and the cabin was wonderful. It was the standard type of cabin that was being built then. It had one long hall from the front porch to the back porch. On the right side in the front of the cabin was my parents' bedroom, then a living room behind it. On the left side of the hall in the front was my room, considerably smaller, across from theirs, with the bathroom behind it and the kitchen last in my row.

"Because the living room and the kitchen were both at the end of the hall, they were more or less one big room in the back. The cabin ended with a full back porch facing the lake. Other people who had cabins like ours used their porches for putting their tables and chairs on so they could eat their meals out there and watch the beautiful water, but not us! My father was a first-class pack rat. He had our porch so crammed with fishing stuff, which he never used because he had no patience with fishing, and boards and odds and ends and bits and bags of cement and pieces of one thing or another that he was sure that he would need someday in the maintenance or the upkeep of the cabin, that it was always too jammed for a table."

"Now I see where you've inherited your ability to save everything you come in contact with!"

"And just what do you mean by that?"

"For starters, let me point out your Death Row and then your scrap papers and then..."

"Okay, so I inherited the ability to know what to throw away and what to keep."

"I wouldn't call it that, but please, continue."

"Like I was saying before I was so rudely interrupted," she teased, "I will never forget the summers we spent there. Two cabins down there was a girl named June Mary, about my age, who always came with her grandparents for the summer. We never failed to have a wonderful time. We filled our days with stuff little girls liked to do then—like collecting rocks and acorns and moss. We'd play house for hours, using all sorts of leaves for dishes and sand for coffee beans. We'd paddle around the shore in her little boat; we'd swim all day and goof off. If it rained, we played paper dolls because we both had the same dolls and we each had different clothes for them. Sometimes we would spend all afternoon designing new clothes and then cutting them out of paper and coloring them in order to add to their wardrobes."

"Sounds wonderful," he interjected while she paused for breath.

She moved a chair and put her feet up on it. "One year when I was six...I already said, that didn't I? Anyway, one year when I was six there was some reason that we had to go up to the cabin in October. I think there was some sort of town meeting or something that affected our little area of cabins and my father convinced my mother that it would be fun for all of us—a quick road trip. I think the only reason he wanted us to go with is that he didn't want to go alone.

"We left early Saturday morning so we could get there in plenty of time for my father to attend the one o'clock meeting in town. We would then be back home in Milwaukee at suppertime. I had never been to the lake any other time except for summer, and it seemed so strange having no one else around. We had lunch in Green Bay, which if you remember is at the base of the thumb; then we drove up the peninsula. My father dropped us off at the cabin and went back into town for the meeting.

"The cabin was oddly quiet and very lonely so Mother and I took a long walk picking up treasures along the way to add to the mounds of collections that were already under my cabin bed in various boxes. In the late afternoon we decided not to wait any longer for Father to come, so Mother opened the coffee cake that she had bought at the bakery in Green Bay. We had a tea party—just the two of us—with the coffee cake and a thermos of hot chocolate that Mother had brought along from home.

"When six o'clock rolled around, we were both a little anxious about Father. There never was a phone in the cabin, and Father had the car. Each time we thought about walking into town, we decided to wait a little bit longer because it had started to drizzle and temperature had dropped, so we talked ourselves out of the two-mile walk several times. We were able to use our outdoor privy because the water had been drained from the cabin so it wouldn't freeze during the winter. After we had played all the board games several times it began to rain harder and turn colder. We both began to worry in earnest.

"Finally, at 6:30 my father arrived with hot beef sandwiches with mashed potatoes for supper, coffee in another thermos, and ice cream for dessert—all from the only restaurant in town that was about to close for the night. Isn't it funny what you remember? I never thought about it before, but I remember the meal completely."

Leon opened his mouth to comment, but she continued.

"He explained as we ate that the meeting ran hot almost from the start, but all of the cabin owners were represented, and they were able to pass whatever crucial matter was at hand. 'You'll thank me someday, Vivian,' he told me sternly while pointing a fork full of potatoes in my direction. I had no idea what he was talking about because after all that fresh air and that wonderful supper, I was getting sleepy. When I came back in after one more trip to the privy, Mother gathered all the afghans from the living room and announced that we would be spending the night at the cabin because it was too late to leave now. I thought it would be fun.

"Our cabin, like all the others, had outside shutters that were closed for the winter to keep out animals and people. Father had opened only the shutters that were on the windows in the kitchen for some daylight, so the rest of the cabin grew dark quickly. We found our way down to the end of the hall by candlelight and I was allowed to sleep in my clothes because my pajamas were lightweight summer ones made for hot vacation nights...not chilly and rainy fall evenings. I remember my mother piling blankets on and me curling into a ball on my bed, thinking that if I could fall asleep, I would get warm.

"I thought I heard musical chimes during the night in my sleep, and then for some reason, I finally felt nice and warm so I spread out and slept. When I finally awoke the next morning, I was surprised to find myself in the living room on the sofa and to see my parents sitting at the kitchen table drinking the last of the coffee and the hot chocolate combined. When my mother saw that I was awake, she said with a big smile that I should wrap myself in my blanket and come and look out the window. I had no idea what to expect. Maybe some animal or something? But when I peered out the kitchen window, the scene was almost surreal. There must have been over eight inches of snow covering everything in sight! It was like being blindfolded and then dropped into a completely different world! I couldn't stop staring because the sunshine made everything sparkle like diamonds and the rocks weren't rocks any more—they were strange little round mushrooms. And the fir tree boughs were hanging down like umbrellas that were closed. The lake was dark gray and nothing felt familiar; nothing was home.

"I remember my father saying that the rain turned to snow around midnight. He also said that snow at that time of year never lasted; it would be cleared off by noon.

"I asked how I ended up in the living room on one of the sofas, and Mom said that we all ended up in the living room on the sofas. It turned so cold in the middle of the night that they hung the heavy velvet drapery in the hall to block off the bathroom and the bedrooms isolating the kitchen and living room by themselves. Father then got the wall heater going and they pulled out the one sofa bed for themselves and put me on the other one. Mother had used every blanket and afghan she could find, and we all finally slept nice and warm. Now I understood what the music was that I thought I had heard: it was Father tinkering with the wall furnace and probably dropping the tools a few times.

"True to my father's prediction, the snow started to melt within the hour and we were on the way soon after, stopping in town for a big breakfast before leaving Door County."

"Not that I wasn't listening," he said as he yawned, "but what does this have to do with sleeping under a desk in a factory office?"

"I guess it's because it's so strange to wake up in odd places. I slept in that cabin for years before that night and years after that night, but that night still stands out in my memory as the strangest, most disconcerting night in my life. It was very unsettling to wake up somewhere that you didn't expect and to trade the familiar summer landscape for eight inches of snow!"

"Speaking of snow, and oddly enough, I had a similar experience, but mine involved an igloo."

"You did say, igloo?" It was her turn to yawn.

"Yep, I'll tell you quickly. Each year as a kid I would eagerly anticipate the mission conference at church. Our church supported a lot of missionaries. Each year six or eight of them would come to church for a long weekend, bringing with them all sorts of wonderful stuff like twelve-foot snake skins and ceremonial masks. Well, one year we had missionaries from Alaska. They were talking about the Eskimos, whom they called Inuit, and how they lived and what they ate and how they made their igloos. By the way, you don't want to know some of the stuff they ate, so I won't tell you."

"You're too kind."

He continued. "The best part of these missionaries to Alaska was that they were going to be home for an entire year and they promised as soon as we got enough snow that they would come back and help our youth group to make an igloo."

"Did they?"

"Yeah, they did! It took us an entire day to build it, but by the time we finished, it was a little lopsided but spectacular. It had to have been maybe eight feet across and the inside wasn't how the family igloos were. This was kind of a guesthouse model."

"Guesthouse? That sounds odd to me. I had no idea Eskimos had guests."

"I wondered that too and possibly the guy was making this part up; I don't know. I was young then and more interested in making an igloo than learning anything about it. I do remember that he said that most igloos were two stories."

"Okay, now I'm sure that you weren't listening when he said that."

"No, that part I do remember. He said that the original igloo would be built and the family would sleep and eat there. As the winter progressed and the snow kept piling up by the yards, they would make the tunnel longer and higher until they could build another igloo farther up and attach it to the first one by the stairway. They carved the stairs between the top igloo, which they used for like the living room and the bottom igloo was then the bedroom. I remember one of his kids saying that he used to have to drag his sleeping bag up the stairs every morning in order to shake out the sweat."

"Okay, now you're going to tell me gross things about sweat."

"Not if you don't want to hear it."

"Go ahead. It sounds disgusting, but tell it anyway."

"Their sleeping bags were all made out of animal skins, with the fur on the inside to keep them nice and warm in their 40-degree house. In the morning, everyone would take his or her bag up and outside, turn them inside out, and shake off the sweat. It froze instantly when it hit the frigid air and the kids said that it was actually beautiful as it dropped to the ground like tiny falling stars."

"I cannot believe you're saying this."

"I couldn't either, but remember, I was just a kid and I thought it was the neatest thing ever! Anyway, when we built this igloo with the missionary, there was a ledge that went around the entire inside that was about three feet high—that was where we were going to sleep. In front of this ledge was another ledge that was about a foot-and-a-half high, and that was kind of like a combination step to get up to the sleeping level. It was also a circular bench because in the very middle of the igloo, there was a bunch of snow that was packed solid and the top was smoothed so it looked like a round table."

"You actually slept there?"

"I was one who *got* to sleep there. In the entire youth group, four kids were picked each night to sleep over and we had to bring a sleeping bag and our parents' permission. I'll have you know that I was the first one to volunteer."

"Why doesn't that surprise me?" She rolled her eyes.

"Hey, remember that I was only eleven. Anyway, I know what you mean when you said that it was strange to wake up somewhere completely different from where you started, like waking up in a different world. We had one red candle stuck in the middle of the table that produced a little heat and it shed a soft light all night. We slept foot to foot and the next two slept head to head around the circle to avoid anyone kicking someone in the head during the night. I thought it was a blast, but I'll tell you that in the morning, it was truly strange to wake up looking at a wall of snow."

"Was it dark in there?"

"Only at night. We had the candle, so it wasn't completely dark. During the day it was quite light though."

"Strange isn't it," she said as she snuggled farther into the sofa, "all these experiences join together to make us what we are today. You wouldn't think there was enough time for everything we've experienced in our lives so far."

"Well, if you check the time, you will see that it's now after 11:30 and if you don't want to wait to take the 1:00 AM bus, it looks like you'll have to experience something else new—that of sleeping on this sofa and waking up here."

"Oh my gracious, I didn't realize that it was this late!" She got up quickly and paced the room.

"I could always run you home in my car. I have one, you know."

"Car, yes, your car. Well, I, er." She seemed oddly at a loss for words. She sat on the sofa again. "I suppose that I have no choice but to stay here. I suppose it would be all right. It seems comfortable enough," she said as she dug her hands into the cushions as though she'd never seen them before in her entire life. "Yes, I think that it would be fine."

Leon watched this performance as he stood by the sink. As she fluffed the cushions and took off the throw pillows, he slipped into Death Row and found two blankets that no one had ever claimed and said, "I've slept on this sofa once. It isn't bad."

"Right, yes, I suppose it will be fine. Thank you for the blankets. Will you be up early enough to wake me up so I won't be late for church? I'm supposed to be there early tomorrow because it's my group's turn to get the coffee ready for the coffee hour and we are combining our Sunday school classes so we can come up with some ideas as to what book in the Bible we want to study next."

"Not a problem, tell me when you want to get up and I'll set the alarm. Better yet, I'll get my clock and bring it out here for you and you can wake me up, although it's rare for me to sleep past six any morning."

They said good night and Leon waited for her to finish in the tiny bathroom before he tiptoed in to get himself ready for bed. As he was drifting off to sleep he thought how strange it was that the very thing she had just been talking about—waking up someplace strange—was about to happen to her again.

FIFTEEN

eon never heard the alarm clock ring and, according to his watch, it was seven o'clock. Amazed that he had slept so long, he took his time getting up, realizing that he had missed his chance to tell Vivian good-bye and to find out about her night. As he opened his door and entered the workroom, he was surprised to see her on the sofa still fast asleep. He practically ran over to the table to pick up the clock to see if it had been set wrong. No, it was set for six. Maybe she forgot to pull out the button that made it ring. He turned it over and sure enough, it was pushed in. He pulled it out and it rang. There, the clock worked. Naturally it roused her out of a dead sleep and she sat up wildly, trying to find the clock to turn it off.

As he pushed the button, she stopped thrashing and, almost yelling, asked, "What did you do that for?"

"What? Ring the bell? You said you wanted to get up at six and here it is seven. I would have thought that you would be grateful for the wake-up call."

She sat up, throwing her covers to one side. "I pushed the button in on purpose! I had a terrible night's sleep and around two I finally decided that they could do without me at church and I pushed the button in!"

"Well, you could have left me a note or something." He was now a combination of petulant and defiant.

"If you look at the table, *under the clock,* you will see that I did leave a note."

"Oh. Sorry."

She softened immediately. "I'm sorry too. I must be older than I thought. I had a terrible night's sleep and I don't know if it was because of the story I told you last night, or if I'm worse now than when I was six and can't adjust to anything new. All I know is that I could have walked home and gotten more sleep." She rubbed her eyes and Leon headed to the coffeepot.

"So, now that you're awake, what say I make some coffee and then I take you out for Sunday breakfast?"

She looked at her wrinkled clothes and then at him. "You're such a guy," was all she answered as she walked past him into the bathroom, closing the door very firmly.

He yelled after her, "So is that a no or a yes?"

She opened the door and glared at him. "Have you seen my clothes? They're all wrinkled! And I look a mess. I didn't sleep. Look at my hair!"

He pushed open the door and pulled her into his arms. "I think you look wonderful." He hugged her to himself and as he held her, he could tell that she was about to cry. "Don't you even think about crying! Listen, I don't think that a lack of clothes has anything to do with your tears. I think you're getting to the place that I was when everything finally fell apart for me."

His face was only inches away from hers and he spoke softly in her ear. "I don't know what's been eating you for a long time now, but you need to let things go. And that includes all the memories of that night at the cabin, all your inability to break your relentless routines. You need to let things go."

He pulled back a bit but still held her within the circle of his arms. "I don't know what it is that's at the bottom of your unhappiness, but you need to drop it off somewhere and never pick it up again. I did, and I've never felt so good. It was hard, hard, hard, but I did it. I just walked away. Remember what you told me? Give it to God Vivian, everything."

She slumped against him and started to cry softly. "But there's so much baggage that accumulates over the years. You learn to carry it so well that you don't realize that you're taking on more and more as the time goes by."

He kissed her hair. "That's the trouble. We pick up the stuff piece by piece, but when it comes to letting it go, it has to go all at once, not piece by piece. Just find a way to get it all out and over with."

She stood close to him for the longest time while he stroked her hair. He gently picked up her head to look into her eyes and saw that she was falling asleep. He led her over to the sofa, made her lay back down, and whispered, "Get a few more winks. I'll go get some donuts to go with our coffee."

When he came back almost an hour later, she was sound asleep. He grabbed a donut, filled a cup with coffee, and sat in his reclining chair next to the sofa. He read his beloved *Tribune,* the heavy five-pound Sunday edition, and fell in love with Vivian for the second time...or maybe it was truly for the very first time in his life

When she finally woke up several hours later, Leon was asleep in his chair with the comics spread out over his chest. Gazing at him fondly, she knew she cared deeply for this man, but it was so complicated. There were so many things that he didn't know about her. Well, actually it was just one thing, but it was a big one.

Because she had missed church that morning, Leon suggested they go to a late lunch somewhere downtown, wander around the city, then maybe go to the Sunday Night Sing down at the historic Moody Church in the evening. They could take his car, now that he had finally gotten his license and city permits up to date. Parking would be a problem, but it would be fun. It was such a beautiful day; maybe they'd sit on the huge rocks along the lakefront by the little Meigs Field Airport and soak up the sun.

He wouldn't make the same mistake today and take her to the planetarium. Last time they did that he went to sleep shortly after the lights dimmed and the constellations began slowly moving across the domed sky and the monotone voice began the narrative. Evidently when he started to gently snore, she got up and moved to the end of the almost empty row, pretending not to know him. She said that she had a good time anyway and was fighting sleep herself by the time the presentation was over. Maybe today it would be a good idea to just enjoy the weather and each other. Chinatown wasn't too far from the lake; maybe they should go there for a late lunch. Or maybe they should eat lunch downtown and then to Chinatown for supper, then Moody's. He seemed to suddenly be a man with a mission; he just wasn't real clear as to what it was.

She reminded him that she looked like something the cat dragged in, at which point he pulled her up from the sofa, assumed a grand attitude, and said in his best French accent, "If madam would kindly step to our Showroom of Fashion...better known as Death Row...she might be able to find some stunning creation made exclusively for her!"

She did. It wasn't what she would have picked to wear, but Leon liked it, so she said "okay." This day was not going to be easy for her, but suddenly she was game for anything.

Monday morning Vera asked Vivian if she had a hangover.

"That would be tough seeing as I don't drink!" Vivian responded with laughter. "No, we had the strangest weekend."

"You and Leon?"

"Yeah."

"So, are you going to tell me about it?"

"I've got to tell somebody."

"Thanks for the compliment."

"That's not what I meant. I knew that if I told anyone, it would be you. I really value your opinions and you seem to have a pretty good marriage."

"Well, marriage is marriage," Vera said as she hustled around putting her lunch in the fridge, then placing full baskets of clothes on various washers with their orders on top of each pile.

"That's an odd thing to say. What do you mean, 'marriage is marriage'?"

Vera took a deep breath, then talked as she sorted a basket of clothes. "Well, someone told me at my bridal shower almost forty-one years ago that marriage was 50-50. If you give 50 percent and he gives

50 percent you make one hundred, and you're both happy. That never really worked for us. I found that sometimes I gave 80 or 100 percent and sometimes it went the other way."

"I gave 100 percent all the time in my marriage and got about 5 percent back," Vivian shared with a bitter smile.

"It's unfortunate, but you hear that all the time. Makes you wonder about people, doesn't it? I guess I learned early that marriage is a lot of concession and compromise. Maybe trade-offs is a better term; you get something, you give something." She stopped for a minute and checked her list once again and moved to a different clothesbasket. "Like Joe doesn't care what color I want him to paint the walls, so he has no input and I make 100 percent of the decision. When it comes to our cars, I could care less what we drive, so it's his baby completely. Sometimes there are things that we both feel strongly about, so that's the time for compromise."

"But you seem to have so much respect for each other," Vivian said over her shoulder as she went to wait on a customer. When she finally returned with an armload of clothes for the dry cleaning machines, she started the conversation again. "So, how do you do it?"

"Do what?"

"Get respect from your husband?"

"Simple. I learned that you have to use him to make you easier to respect."

"Huh? Use him to make you easier to respect? I don't get it."

"Here, let me try to explain." Vera rested her arm on a washing machine and began. "I found out after we got married that it was easy for us to fall into the typical roles. He went to work; I stayed home and kept house. I mean, it was 1924 when we got married and that's just how it was. We had four children in a short time and I really did like being home. I think the kids got to Joe, and he started hanging out with the boys from work more often than I wanted him to. I was tired after a day at home with only children there, and I needed him to relieve me a bit. I never asked him outright if he would do it because I was hoping that he'd see how tired and plain worn out I was and automatically kick in. He didn't. His mother was absolutely no help because she raised seven kids virtually on her own because they were farmers living in

Iowa. I can't tell you how many times I heard about how she was able to get up at five in the morning, set the bread to raising, help milk the cows, feed the chickens and the calves, make the breakfast for her husband, children, and the hired hands, get the kids off to school and then put a full day of work in before lunch...which, by the way, they called dinner."

"So, what did you do? Go to your mom?"

"My mom died when I was twelve."

"I am sorry to hear that."

"Me too. I loved my dad dearly, but I would have given almost anything in order to have had a good mother. But anyway, I read an article in a magazine that changed everything for me."

"Some helpful piece in a woman's magazine like 'How to Put the Sizzle Back into Your Dull Life'?"

"Not quite. It was a letter written by a mistress to the wife."

"Are you serious? Oh rats, a customer. Hold that thought. I'll be right back."

When Vivian returned, Vera was back by the dryers. Vivian picked up another load of wet clothes, read the order sheet, and put the clothes in the appropriate dryer and walked back to where Vera was working. "So, go on...about the mistress." She whispered the last word.

"Oh the letter? It was kind of a long letter, but the only thing I remember was the place where she says, 'your husband wants you to be happy; but he doesn't want to be the one that makes you happy.' Believe me, I thought about that one long and hard. Next day I called a woman that I'd heard about—an older woman who had raised several of her own kids that were now grown and gone. I thought I could trust her with the kids and asked her how much for her babysitting services and what her schedule was. I got the information and that night after the kids were in bed I told Joe about this woman and that it would make me very happy to have him hire her so I could have a bit of time to myself and what did he think? He thought it was swell so I hired her (she turned out to be a godsend) and when she would take the kids down to the park for several hours each afternoon, I stayed home and slept. Sometimes I had a long, hot bath before my nap, but I slept every day she came. Now that I was in a much better humor, Joe started staying home more and even helping out with the kids—playing with them all on the floor. After I put them all to bed, there was time for just us…you know, us." She reddened a bit.

"You're very wise Vera."

"I don't think it was wisdom. More desperation."

"Desperation? I don't understand."

Vera picked up a basket, placed it on the washer, then rested her arms on top of the clothes. "After my mother died, her older sister, my aunt, moved in with us to help raise us. Eventually she and my father married. She was quite unlike the way I remember my mother to be because she nagged constantly and whined and complained until I wanted to leave home. You know, the evil stepmother thing. I knew that I never wanted to be like she was, so I was determined not to be. My father didn't seem to mind her behavior as much as I did. He was one of those guys who could put up with just about anything.

"But I knew there must be a better way than that to live in a marriage. Some days I wish I could read that article again—the letter from the mistress, but I guess I learned the one thing that I really needed to learn. It would be fun to read it all through. I think that marriage at any age can always use a little more zip!"

Vivian laughed as she headed up front to help another customer. "You amaze me, Vera. No one would ever tell to look at your sweet face who you really are inside!"

"And maybe it's better that way. But now it's your turn. What were you going to tell me about your weekend?"

104

SIXTEEN

Sandy came in at noon looking for Leon. She was not scheduled to work, but when she saw how busy the shop was she pitched right in.

"You're a lifesaver! Thank you," Vivian said as she stood folding clothes and marking off each item on the list. "I don't think we've ever been so busy on a Monday before."

"Maybe everyone's actually read your last ad about fall spruce-up and they're coming in because of it."

"But the ad mentioned bringing in drapes and slipcovers, not clothes!"

"Always the complainer," Leon chuckled good-naturedly as he entered the back room. "If it's slow, you complain; if it's busy, you complain. I don't know what to do about you."

He talked the entire length of the work area, entered his room, and closed his door before anyone could say anything else.

"I'll tell you," Vera said. "That man has changed since I first met him, and that wasn't too long ago."

"I'll say he's changed," added Sandy, "and I've known him for over a year. I think it must be love." She batted her eyelashes at Vivian.

"Okay, that's enough from both of you. He's a strange man, that's all."

"No stranger than others I've heard about," said Vera, eyeing Sandy.

"Speaking from experience?" added Vivian as she looked at Vera.

The three women broke into laughter as the washing machines churned and the dryers hummed and the bell over the door rang once again, making everyone groan.

"It's like this," Sandy told Leon later that afternoon. "I've met the head guy over at Marshall Fields and he said that they are hiring extra grunt help for the Christmas windows starting in one week. It would mean that I would work there instead of here and I don't know how I feel about it. I love it here, but I can't pass up this opportunity to actually work at Fields!"

"Have you mentioned this to Vivian? And what in the world do you mean by grunt work?"

"Oh, you know, hauling and running, nothing that would require any sort of schooling or experience. And I haven't said a word to Vivian...not yet at least."

"Don't you think that you should talk to her first? After all, she is the boss here."

"I know, I just thought that you might help me tell her. She likes you a lot and maybe it would be easier if it was coming from you."

"And what makes you think she likes me a lot?"

"You're kidding, right?"

"Yeah, maybe I am. Anyway, if you really want to work at Fields, I think we should tell her as soon as possible. By the way, is it only for the Christmas windows, or will it be longer than that? The windows are usually ready right after Thanksgiving Day, aren't they?"

"Yeah, they wanted me to start right away, but I told them that I had to give at least a one-week notice to my current employer. They didn't have a problem with that, but I know they would like me right away. I talked to my D.E. teacher about it, and he thinks that it's a great opportunity, since I'd like to do something like that for a career. My guidance counselor said that she would check out some scholarships for art and see about some local schools for me."

"Wow, you have been busy! Let's go talk to her now."

They left his room and returned to the work area, where both women were busy with even more piles of clothes. Sandy almost chickened out when she saw the workload, but Leon had started talking, so there was no turning back.

Vera was ecstatic and Vivian was happy.

"I can't say that we're not going to miss you. You are not only the hardest worker we have, but you also bring a lot of sunshine in this old place. But you need to make decisions now that will affect the rest of your life, so I'm glad you're going to get this golden opportunity!" Vivian gave Sandy a one-arm hug as she continued to fold clothes. "I say that you should consider staying on at Fields if they ask you to. We'll wait until you know more after the windows are done before we hire someone else. And you know, my girl, that there will always be a job for you here as long as you want one."

Sandy hugged everyone and left before she started to cry. It was tough to be eighteen, she decided. She was so full of happiness and sorrow at the same time.

Joe came over for lunch and since it was Leon's turn to cook, he walked several blocks down and came back with four orders of Swedish potato sausage, mashed potatoes, lingonberries, and limpa bread.

"Nothing like home cooking," said Joe as he dug in, "even if it's somebody else's home!"

At lunch Vivian once again told the story of her trip to the cabin as a child and waking up to snow. Leon added his about the igloo and Joe added his about the time he and his friend Freddy went winter camping.

"Well, it wasn't really camping. Freddy's father worked for this place that designed and made tents and camping stuff. He was always bringing home new equipment to try out. I remember the time he brought home a new tent they had designed for winter camping. I thought that was just about the craziest thing I had ever heard—winter camping! Who in their right mind would want to camp in the snow? Then his dad told us that they were doing experiments so they could present a new kind of tent to the government for the troops.

"Both Freddy's and my ears perked up. Being boys, we thought it would be the bee's knees to know the guy who invented the tents that the soldiers would use. But it didn't end there. When his dad saw our enthusiasm, he said that if we wanted to, we could be the first ones to try it out. He said that we could read the instructions, put it up in the backyard over the weekend, and make an official report of how easy it was to put up and how it responded to the snow.

"Well, if you thought we were full of ourselves, you'd be right. I went over on Friday night and the tent was lying on the living room floor. We goofed around until suppertime, at which time his dad asked if we had read the directions yet. We said no, but we would before we put it up."

"Needless to say, by the time we got ready, it was about nine and between the two of us, we couldn't figure out the instructions. Finally we just gave up. I slept on his sofa and he went upstairs to bed. When we all got up in the morning, his dad asked us how it went. He could see how it went because the tent was still in the living room with poles and stakes everywhere. But he was that kind of a dad; he wanted us to figure it all out by ourselves."

"We were determined to get it up and camp at least one night, so I was back later on that afternoon. We even passed up cake that his mom had made so we could read the instructions and get the tent up."

"How were you going to pound stakes in frozen ground?" Leon queried as he buttered more bread.

"We wondered about that too, but the stakes were sharp and we didn't have too much trouble. Anyway, we got it up, had supper, with that cake for dessert, and headed out. We took the new 'heat bucket' with us that had fuel in the bottom and kind of ran like a kerosene lamp. Naturally we were tired from reading the instructions on the tent, and it never even crossed our minds that it would be a good idea to read the instructions for the heat bucket. Ah, youth! Needless to say, we couldn't get the thing lit and we knew that we couldn't ask his dad, so we half froze until around 3:00 AM. Then we finally gave up and went in again."

"Gracious," Vera said. "You never told me that story."

Joe patted her knee playfully and said, "There may be a lot about me you don't know. I have depths yet to plum."

She removed his hand and squinted at her watch. "Well, plum yourself right back over to your shop, Mr. Smoothie. My mother says you're too fast and I shouldn't be seeing you anymore!"

"We'll just have to see about that." He pulled her into his arms and kissed her while he dipped her.

"Two can play at that game," said Leon as he grabbed Vivian and kissed and dipped her.

Both women pretended to be upset and told them to "get out of here and leave us alone. Unlike you, *we've* got work to do." But they said it while they were laughing.

SEVENTEEN

It was November, and the entire city started to bloom with colored Christmas lights. Leon had always thought there was no city that was as beautiful as Chicago during the Christmas holidays—or anytime for that matter, but especially at Christmas. All the stores were decorated both inside and out. Their windows, some done modestly and some done with all the lavish trimmings and lights, stood out on the dull gray streets. He had especially loved the sumptuous displays that Marshall Fields always did with masses of white and gold swags across the aisles on the main floor that draped from one huge Corinthian column to the other. And he had always loved the long row of golden trumpets that were mounted outside and jutted out from the State Street side of the store.

Howard joined them for lunch one day and was telling them about Candy Cane Lane. He said that it was a section of the city where every house had at least two fat, lighted pink-and-white candy canes attached to each side of the railings that led up to the porch. All the decorations, it seemed, were pink-and-white-striped plastic candy canes. Even the Christmas trees in the windows of the houses were white with pink ornaments. It did indeed look like Candy Land, he said. He also said that traffic always tied up for blocks and blocks as all of Chicago drove by slowly to gawk.

"Anybody ever have one of those flocked Christmas trees?" asked Joe. "We had one last year that had been flocked in a sort of a blue. It was beautiful, but the flocking fell off if you tried to hang anything on it."

"I think I prefer a green tree. I don't even care if it's real or fake, but I still like the green ones," added Vera.

"Does anyone like those new silver ones?"

"You mean the silver ones that have a light shining on it with a disk attached to the front of the light that had four sections on it, each one a different color? And as it revolves, the tree turned the color of the light, green, red, blue...what was the last color?"

"Who knows? I think they are disgusting," added Vivian. "They look like something that belongs in the far distant future. Some space alien's idea of Christmas."

"I think Candy Cane Lane sounds like fun," said Leon looking around at the others. "I think we should all go some night before they take it down. Maybe after Christmas, though, and avoid the crowds."

Everyone at lunch that day stared at Leon at the same time because, by now, they just knew that he rose to bait easily and would probably suggest they did the same thing after he saw Candy Cane Lane. After all, wasn't it only last week that they all celebrated with the drugstore family as they actually rolled back the metal bars on their windows during the day? Don Wilson said that now that the neighborhood had changed and the gangs were gone, they felt it safe to not only remove the bars; they also felt safe to live above the shop. Surely this and the news of Candy Cane Lane would spur Leon on to another neighborhood activity.

Leon returned their gazes with a little smile and kept on eating. It had been Howard's turn to cook lunch. Because his wife, Lois, had to stay and mind the store, she said that if he wanted to take lunch, he could find someone else to cook it for them. Ah Lois, a bundle of laughs.

Howard had done what Leon had done and bought their lunch to go. Nell was happy for the business and she made a big pot of her homemade red Manhattan clam chowder for the occasion. She also furnished hard rolls and butter, so it was a good lunch...especially since Amy Joy had two new donut flavors: a chocolate Bismarck with chocolate filling and a regular Bismarck with lemon filling and a lemon glaze. Leon had made a stop that morning to buy some.

Leon began meeting with the guys, Howard and Joe and Pete Dake from the Goodwill, again in the morning at Nell's. One morning Vivian thought she saw Sandy with them as she went into the front to wait on a customer. One of the guys who was looking over at the cleaners, saw Vivian staring out the window at them, so he closed the curtains.

She thought it a bit strange.

To say Christmas was in the air was a gross understatement. Traffic had picked up exponentially, and there never was a place to park anywhere both up and down the block. All the stores—the old ones and the new ones—were busy. The shop next door was finally rented, and of all things, it was rented with the intentions of making it into a flower shop!

"I wonder how Dennis would feel about that," Leon said morosely as he drank his morning coffee.

"I think he would be pleased," Vivian said as she explained Dennis to Vera. "I think it will be a little bittersweet, but nice. I'm sure the owner of the building was getting more than a little worried about this beautiful building sitting empty for so long."

"Don't start with the owner," Leon stormed. "I've never seen anyone in my life that could care less about stuff he owns. How rich could he be so that he doesn't care about his investments here?"

"Hard to say," said Vivian as she washed her cup. "What would you think of having a Christmas party here in the store?"

"When?"

"I don't know. Whenever it works, I guess."

"Who all are you thinking of inviting?"

"Well, it couldn't be many people. I don't think that this place would hold more that twenty."

"Twenty! Where are you going to put twenty people?"

"I don't know. I think we'd all fit. When I was single I always had more people than my apartment could hold. That way everybody thought it was a great party because so many people were there."

"Women."

"I also had them at night. That way all I had to do was keep the lights down low to save on the pre-party cleaning and just dust the phone and clean the bathroom."

"Once again, women."

"I thought it was very clever. I always had lots of candles; people thought they were for atmosphere, but they weren't."

"Okay, *clever* women."

"No, clever *woman*," Vivian said as she sidled up to him and kissed him lightly.

"I don't know if I'd do that missy," he said with his John Wayne voice. "It could get ya in a heap of trouble. Ah-ha."

"Oh yeah, I'd like to see you try."

He was about to try when the bell rang over the door, frustrating both of them. But the bell on the door made the bell in his head go off at the same time, and he finally realized what he was going to buy for Vivian as her Christmas gift. He hurried and put on his coat. By the time she came back into the workroom, he had gone out the back door.

He slipped and slid his way in the newly fallen snow behind the beauty shop and the dentist. He peeked around the corner to the front of the cleaners just in case Vivian might for some reason be outside, or maybe on her way over to the coffee shop. When he saw that the coast was clear, he waited for a lull in the traffic, then slipped across the street to the barber's to see if Vera just happened to be there today doing their books or some cleaning. She was! Life was good! God was good!

A brief conversation and the two of them were off, back across the street, around the dentist office, behind the cleaners, and into Leon's car. He could hardly stand his excitement and by the look on Vera's face when he told her, she was pretty happy about the idea too!

It took forever for his heater to kick in, so they left before it did. Leon talked a blue streak and Vera finally asked where they were going.

Leon started to laugh, "I have no idea!"

"Don't you think that we should stop somewhere and talk about this?"

Leon thought this was a great idea and thought about pulling into Amy Joy. On second thought, maybe it wasn't such a good idea. He didn't want anyone there to think that he was taking out someone else's wife, even though he was. He turned around and drove on until they got into the Loop and pulled into a parking garage.

"I know a little coffee shop on State Street. Let's start there and you can help me sort this thing out."

"Fine by me," said this experienced wife of forty-some years.

Christmas secrets were the glue that held together many new and old friends on Clark Street and added to the holiday excitement that year.

Arrangements were made for the four couples—Leon and Vivian, Vera and Joe, Howard and Lois, and Sandy and Johnny—to go downtown together in order to take in all the Christmas decorations and the lights and windows. *The Messiah* was being presented at the historic Moody Bible Institute in the Tory Gray Auditorium and they were planning to go. They decided to make a day of it: lunch at the Flame, home of the $1.99 flame-broiled steak, the three o'clock concert at the college, then over to State Street and Michigan Avenue for the windows.

Even though it was more than a little illegal, everyone crammed into Leon's old boat of a car—a midnight black seven-year-old, 1958 Cadillac, with its huge tailfins and all. To say they all had a good time was an understatement. They had a hilarious time...even cranky old Lois. Both Sandy and Johnny agreed later that everyone seemed more like eighteen-year-olds than the ancient ages they really were.

EIGHTEEN

They had to get rid of Vivian.

Their meetings at the coffee shop were over, and it was time to act. There were only three more weeks until Christmas, and everything had been planned and everyone in place to do their part.

Pete, from the Goodwill, made several clandestine late-night stops at the cleaners and knocked three times on the back door, getting into the spirit of the conspiracy. Leon's room was so full that he started hiding things in Death Row under undelivered draperies and blankets.

When everything was finally there, the plan was for Leon to pick up Vivian and take her somewhere for the day the following Sunday. Business had gone into its usual pre-Christmas slump, so he knew that there was no reason for her to want to stop in at the cleaners for any reason.

When he told her that he would pick her up for church she panicked visibly. "That's sweet of you, but why don't I simply meet you here at the cleaners?"

Leon knew that he had to keep her away from the shop because work was going to start around seven in the morning.

"It's no trouble to pick you up. You know, after being here over a year now, I still don't know where you live."

She sat at the table and looked at him. "I suppose I should tell you now...." was all she was able to say before the phone rang and a customer came through the door at the same time. "Would you get the phone? I'll go to the front."

By the time she got back she had thought of a good excuse. "I have to be at church early," she told him. "I'm on the coffee committee again and I don't think it would be fair to have you get there over an hour early and just sit around. We usually put on the coffee, get out the rolls, and have a time to visit. I think you would be bored silly."

It seemed like he'd bought it. "Great, how about if I met you there and we can spend the day together? I was thinking of maybe driving out to the suburbs. They've got that new mall out in Mount Prospect. They call it Randhurst and it's supposed to be the first one in the entire state that's all under one roof, maybe in the whole U.S. I heard it's got a restaurant in the middle under a domed roof. We could eat there."

"Randhurst? What an odd name."

"That's the place. It's on Rand Road and Elmhurst, so they combined the road names and called it Randhurst. There's also one on Golf and Milwaukee that they call Golfmill."

"Kind of the one on Harlem and Irving."

"But they call the one on Harem and Irving, the Harlem and Irving Plaza."

"Oh, right."

"Some people call it the HIP, but I don't think it will catch on. Anyway, how about it—a little drive and lunch in the suburbs?"

"Only if it isn't bad weather. Now that they've got the snow cleared away, all we need is an overnight freeze to make the roads bad again."

"It will be great, trust me."

"Oh, so now you control the weather? Say, whatever happened to you being king of Chicago? You never said what happened that day you went downtown to the *Tribune* Tower."

"I'll tell you all about it tomorrow," he said. "Oh, by the way, the phone message was for you. Someone from church said they couldn't make it on Sunday to help fix the coffee and wondered if you would come to their rescue and help out instead."

Oops, she thought. *Caught in a lie.*

As soon as Nell's coffee shop opened early Sunday morning, they were all there; Sandy, Leon, Johnny, Pete, Vera, and Joe.

"I don't know why we couldn't have met at the cleaners for coffee," groused Leon who had to get on a coat and boots just to cross the street.

"Because," Sandy said patiently, "I want to give you a visual of what we're going to do so we're all on the same page. Being over here we can see the entire front of the cleaners, both windows."

Honestly, now that Sandy had been kept on at Fields, she was really getting into the verbiage of the business. "A 'visual'?" Leon said. "What next?"

After the plans were reviewed and coffee drunk and Nell's donuts eaten (nowhere as good as Amy Joy's but he didn't tell Nell that), they all trooped across the snowy street to the cleaners to remove all their secret stash of decorating stuff. Vera had brought a casserole and popped it into the oven on low. By noon everyone was so hungry that they could stand it no longer and broke for lunch amid the paper and decorations, the wood and the tools, the wardrobe choices, and the stuffed dog.

Leon missed most of the day because, after shoveling the front walk, he left shortly after nine so he could be in time for Sunday school at 9:30. He had to admit that he liked Vivian's church. It was a good thing. He would need to talk to the pastor soon.

By the end of Sunday, Vivian and Leon had traveled directly to the suburbs and did indeed like the new mall. They found gifts for almost everyone on their lists, even though they weren't even looking. All the way back into the city they debated important issues, such as: did they like the Wiebolts Department Store in the mall better than the one downtown? And, was it a wise decision to eat in the restaurant under the dome, or should they have eaten at the Corned Beef Center on the main floor?

Because of the snowy streets, it was almost seven o'clock before Vivian and Leon arrived back at the cleaners. Leon dropped Vivian off at the corner to catch her bus because she said that it was too far for him to drive to take her home. He said that he would be glad to wait with her until it came, but she said that it would arrive any minute and by the time he parked the car behind the cleaners and returned, she would be gone.

Leon worried most that she would wander down to the store for something and ruin the surprise so as soon as he parked the car, he ran down the alley to the corner, but her bus had already come and she was gone.

Unknown to Leon, the secret Christmas workers—weary but very happy—had worked continually and finished before three.

Monday morning was dark and dreary and perfect for the surprise. Sandy had called in sick to school and she and Leon were there and ready when Vivian came walking up the street. As she approached the shop, hundreds of Christmas lights in the window popped on and she stopped dead in her tracks, mouth open, and stock-still.

She stood still for the longest time. When she did move, it was to back up into the street to get an even better look at the two windows.

As she entered the shop she was shaking her head and smiling. "And who's responsible for the windows?" she asked Leon who was sitting at the table in the workroom calmly drinking coffee.

Sandy popped up from behind a washer and said, "Surprise!"

"Surprise is putting it mildly. I would say more like shock! I thought Leon might put his little tree back up, but I never expected this," she said as she hugged Sandy. "I think you're behind this, aren't you?"

"Well, I guess I am with a little help from a few of my nearest and dearest," she said as she crossed the room and put her hand on Leon's shoulder.

As Vivian gave him her special smile, he added, "Vera and Joe and Pete and Johnny might have helped a bit. I take it that you like our efforts?"

Before she had time to answer, the bell on the door jingled.

"My gracious, who could be up and out this early on a winter morning? It's Monday, isn't it?"

She didn't have time to wonder as Nell, Vera, Howard, Joe, and Pete walked in.

"Merry Christmas!" they all yelled.

"Do you like them?" bubbled Vera. "Sandy did the whole thing." She crossed the room and put an arm around Sandy for a little squeeze.

"Well, not the whole thing. Who do you think made trip after trip here delivering stuff?" Pete added as he lightly pecked Vivian on the cheek.

Sandy laughed. "We all did it, but it was my idea. I got the idea from the windows at Fields so I asked Frank, my boss, to help me design something and he agreed. Besides, I think I can use this for extra credit for my D.E .class."

"Wow," is all Vivian could say as she walked back out to the front to see the windows again. They were even wonderful from inside the shop.

Each window was framed in colored Christmas lights and the walls had been transformed with wood slates and cardboard pieces to resemble a city street decorated for Christmas. Each window on the right and the left of the door held its own full-sized mannequin (thanks to Pete). On the left there was a man dressed in a natty suit and topcoat. He had a fedora on his head and he was posed as though he was in mid-stride. Behind him was the "city street" complete with artificial Christmas trees all decked out in lights and ornaments. *Was that Leon's little tree in with the rest?* she wondered.

In the right window there was a woman dressed in a red-and-white polka dot dress, short black boots, and an open winter coat as she faced the man looking too like she was in full stride. She had a green-and-white hatbox that she carried by the strings in one hand that read Band Box Cleaners & Laundry and in the other hand she had a leash on the end of which was a little stuffed animal that was a black Scotty dog wearing a red plaid coat. The lady wore a jaunty black winter hat and there was fake snow on her shoulders along with more snow on the ground beneath them; all the clothes compliments of Death Row.

The Christmas lights continued into the front part of the shop on both sides right above the wainscot paneling that Leon had only recently finished painting a darker green to compliment the soft sage that he used for the upper walls. The strands met and circled the doorway that led to the back workroom. At the very top of the door hung a large bunch of fresh mistletoe and several fresh Christmas wreaths with large red bows flanked each side wall above the strands of lights.

"Where did you ever find that hatbox?" she called back to Leon who was in the workroom with the others.

"It was in the storeroom. As soon as I found it, I knew that someday I wanted to do something special with it. That's why I didn't tell you about it."

"We used to use those when we cleaned hats," she said as she reentered the workroom. "Now we'll definitely have to have a Christmas party." Tears began to well up in her eyes. Knowing his woman well, Leon had a tissue handy and a cup of coffee for her to hide behind.

"Our biggest conflict," Sandy said, frowning, "was deciding which way the mannequins should face. Most of us wanted them to be both going the same way, like one was in front of the other walking to the train or something, but it was Leon who said they should be walking towards each other."

Everyone had crowed into the back room around the coffeepot and the donuts and they were all talking at once, making it hard to hear anybody clearly.

Leon, overwhelmed by the moment, turned to Vivian and said into her ear, "I think especially now that it's Christmas, people should walk towards each other." While he said that he took her hand and led her to the sofa and set her down. He then surprised everyone, including himself, when he dropped to one knee and as everyone grew silent, he pulled out a small, velvet box from his shirt pocket and said in a voice strong and clear voice, "Vivian Dumbrowski, would you marry me? Would you walk toward me from this day forward?"

After the words were out, he realized how truly stupid they sounded. In fact, he had had absolutely no intention of proposing in front of all these people. He wasn't sure how he would have done it, but ever since he and Vera bought the ring, he knew he wanted it to be a special time for just the two of them. What a putz! Now he had ruined everything!

She stared at the ring as everyone present held their collective breath.

"We have to talk," she said almost in a whisper.

"We can talk after you say yes," he said removing the ring and placing it on her finger, surprised by his own boldness.

Before she could say another word, Howard, who had slipped in unobserved, said, "Mazel tov!" Suddenly everyone joined in the celebration, slapping Leon on the back and pulling Vivian to her feet so they could hug her and get a better look at the ring. A party broke out spontaneously and they went through a lot of coffee before everyone finally left to go to their own jobs.

After everyone left, Vivian went back out in the front to gaze at the windows and at her beautiful ring and to be alone for a bit to catch her breath.

Leon came up behind her, holding a piece of paper. "Look what I found on the front counter. Evidently someone came in with their dry cleaning, saw our celebration, and left their stuff with their name and number. It even says Merry Christmas and congratulations!"

Her eyes were shining when she barely answered, "That's nice."

He turned her around and pulled her to him in a cherished hug. "I love you."

It was right. For the first time in his life, he was absolutely sure about something. "Do you like the ring?"

"I would be crazy not to," she answered holding it up for them both to admire. "It must be a full carat!"

"Yes sir, one whole carat. Vera picked it out."

"What?"

It was a good thing that business was doing it's pre-Christmas death crawl because it gave them the much-needed time to go from start to finish on the whole window decorating thing and the buying of the ring. Vivian was laughing by the time he finished telling the story of sneaking Vera downtown, and as he bent to kiss her he said, "It's so nice to kiss a woman who is laughing.... I plan to do it often."

The day flew by. Vera must have kept up a running conversation all day. By closing time she knew she had to finally say what she had been longing to say for so long. This ring had brought everything to a head.

After Vera had finally gone home and the front door was locked, Vivian stood admiring her incredible windows and tried to form her thoughts.

As she entered the back room Leon put down his paper and looked up from his chair. "Happy?"

"No."

"Did you say 'no'?"

She sighed deeply. "I have a few things that I have to tell you about me before this can go any further."

Leon's blood turned to ice. "Go on."

"I've been trying to tell you this almost from the very beginning when I first realized that I was beginning to care for you, but I just could never get it out and it's very hard to do now. I never should have waited so long."

"I can wait."

"You can, but I can't. I've deceived you from the very beginning. I know that I've told you about my husband. All that was true. In fact, everything that I've told you about myself is true. The part about the owner of this place living in Florida…that isn't true."

The phone rang and they both ignored it.

Leon's mind jumped ahead and linked Vivian with the owner in a clandestine way. Maybe they were secret lovers. No, that couldn't be right. She was at the shop all the time or else they were together. Maybe he was her rich father, or rich uncle. Before he could continue his thoughts, she spoke again.

"There is no owner in Florida. The owner of the cleaners lives here in the city." She struggled to continue, twisting her new engagement ring around and around her finger.

Now he was worried. Here in the city. Great—maybe he was infirmed and lived in a nursing home. Maybe he was some rich dude who lived in the new Marina Towers and was holding the shop over Vivian's head: "Marry me or lose the shop." Maybe they were already secretly married! He almost told her to stop. He was suddenly very

122

frightened. How bad could the information be that she had withheld it all this time? He almost wanted to ask for his ring back and then leave the shop never to return. He'd get into his car and never look back. But where would he go? This place and this woman had become his entire life.

So he braced himself and said, "Just spit it out," then added a desperate "please."

"All right, here goes. I'm the owner of the cleaners—both the building and the business."

The silence that now hung over them was thick and heavy.

Before he could respond she said slowly, while now twisting all her fingers together endlessly, "I told you that my husband left me well off with lots of oil stocks. Well, when the original owners—the ones who hired me—decided to sell, I thought, *Why not buy it?* I had the money and no plans for it and I liked working here. Besides, what else would I do? I like to travel, but not alone and I didn't have anyone that I would like to go with."

Deciding to make a clean break she added, "Then when the other two Ladies came on the market, I bought them too."

Now there was not only complete silence; it felt like time was standing still. He was totally dumbfounded. *She* was the absentee owner of the Three Painted Ladies? He didn't think he could even begin to absorb the news.

Before he had a moment to even catch his breath, she continued. "That's not all." She took a deep breath and talked to her hands. "I live across the street in the apartment over the hardware store."

"What?" he barely whispered.

"I've lived there for over twenty years. I told Howard that if he ever breathed a word that I'd kill him. Well, not actually kill him, but do him great bodily harm."

"You have to stop talking for just a minute. I need time to absorb all of this."

"Yes, I know, but now that I'm finally able to say these things, I have to say them all."

"There's more?"

"Not much more, but you need to know that I also own the

building the hardware store is in."

This was becoming too much for Leon to fathom, and he didn't want to hear anymore. He had stood to get a drink of water when she first said they needed to talk, but he put down his glass and sat back down heavily. After a few minutes of silence that seemed more like an hour, he asked, "So, if I understand you correctly, with you living upstairs across the street all this time, nothing has ever happened here that you didn't know about?"

"Yes, or is that no?"

He thought for a moment. "So you knew that when you first hired me that all I was doing was sleeping in the back and not doing the night watchman thing?"

"Yes."

He was quiet. Vivian dared not move.

"So for over a year you've watched my every move."

"In a way I did. I didn't purposely stare out the window when I was home, and you can't possibly know how hard it was for me to keep up the charade. I had to leave my apartment by the back way, walk behind the stores, cross the street, and look like I was coming up from the corner bus stop every day." She knew that she was trying to justify her actions, but she had to try to make him see her point of view.

"And that night that you ended up staying here, sleeping on the sofa?"

"Was the hardest night of my life," she continued his sentence. "Not only do I hate sleeping anywhere but in my own bed, but just knowing that it was right across the street and I couldn't get to it made it physically painful. I even thought about sneaking out several times, but then I didn't want to hurt your feelings, or worse, have you worry about me taking the bus home in the middle of the night. I didn't want you to try to find me or worse yet, call the police."

He rubbed his chin. "I can't even imagine any of this! An entire year you've seen everything here!" He paused as though collecting his widely scattered thoughts. "So, you saw us decorating the Christmas windows too?"

"Actually, no, I didn't have a clue. Remember I did have to go to church early to help with the coffee and because you met at the café first, I didn't see anyone. I was gone by the time you started in the shop."

"And now I understand that 'coffee helping at church thing' too— the reason I couldn't pick you up at your house. You got caught in a lie."

"Yes, I did, and I wondered why you didn't say anything when you took the call and caught me dead center."

Neither spoke for several minutes.

Vivian got up from the sofa and started to arrange some papers on her work desk. Finally she looked up from across the room to the still, quiet man she loved dearly and was desperately afraid of losing. "Leon, are you angry with me? Can you ever forgive me?"

"Right now I don't know how I feel. On one hand, I'm relieved. I've felt for a very long time that there has been something you wanted to say, but you never would come out with it."

"You're so right. I can't tell you all the times that I just wanted to say it...but couldn't. I had to make endless pretend calls to the 'office' when you were around; giving our work hours to the 'secretary' so she could write the checks. The longer I went not telling you, the harder it became. When I realized that I was in love with you, it got even harder."

"Why did that make a difference? I wasn't marrying you for your money because I didn't know you had any!"

"It wasn't that. You knew me as this old frump of a boss that had no life, few friends, and to your knowledge, very little in life."

"Pretty much, at least that's the role you played."

"And that's just it. It was only a role, and it got harder and harder to play as we did more and more things together. I had such a good time, but I often couldn't show you how much fun I was having because if you ended up liking me I would have to tell you everything and risk you hating me for deceiving you for so long."

"This explanation of yours is very interesting. In fact, now that I think back, your behavior since I met you has been very interesting."

"What do you mean interesting?" She was now twisting her hanky that she had retrieved from her pocket.

"It must have been very interesting keeping up the lie. Telling us you brought that breakfast casserole on the bus that day."

"You remember that far back? I never said I brought it by bus; you just thought I did. My gracious, that was over a year ago. How do you remember such things?"

"I'm sure as time goes by I'll remember lots of other things too."

"So, does this change things between us?" she asked at barely a whisper.

"Let me see." He paused for almost a minute while he paced the room.

Vivian was unable to move.

As he walked he raised a hand and started counting on his fingers as he continued, "One, the woman I love and proposed marriage to owns half the block in a now thriving section of Chicago. Two, she didn't tell me because she just couldn't." He looked directly at her. "Kind of like the things I had to work through before I could tell her about my life. Hmm." He put down his hand and sat down in his recliner. "I would have to say no, I'm not mad at all—overwhelmed, but certainly not mad." He picked up his paper and held it high so she couldn't see his face.

She moved quickly to him, removed his beloved *Tribune*, and dropped it to the floor. Seeing his smiling face, she sat on his lap and kissed him deeply. "I never thought this would ever happen to me," she whispered as she laid her head on his shoulder. "I thought I was too old to fall in love." She mussed his hair and smiled into his eyes.

"Well, little lady"—John Wayne was back—"ya better get used to it, 'cause now you're stuck with me."

He picked up her hand and kissed her ring, thinking briefly that she could have paid for it easier than he could with all her money.

"Let's set a wedding date right now," she breathed into his ear.

This thought took him completely by surprise; he hadn't thought about that part.

NINETEEN

Sandy asked to try the ring on when she saw it again. Vivian let her with mixed feelings. She hoped desperately now that Sandy was in her senior year and beginning her career in Art and Design that she wouldn't become infatuated with marriage and rings and do something foolish with Johnny.

"Wow, this must be somewhere around a full carat! It's beautiful!" She turned her own hand back and forth to admire the stone.

"Yes. I was quite surprised when I got it."

"You're kidding, right? Didn't you know that Leon has loved you for a long time? I think you loved him right from the start. Honestly, I don't know what took you two so long!"

Thinking this would be a good opportunity to talk about waiting before you jumped into anything, Vivian opened her mouth.

But Sandy rattled on. "I think it's really nice for you two. I would be absolutely floored if I got a ring like this, but there's no chance of that! Not only is there nobody I know who can afford a rock like this, at this age I don't even want to think about marriage."

Vivian sighed with relief.

"My mom had to get married at fifteen because I was on the way and she lived to regret it," Sandy continued as she handed back the ring and sat down at the table with a cup of hot chocolate. "She's been through a series of men since and never stuck to any one of them. She was married four times and the older guy who lives at our house now hasn't even mentioned marriage. It's really sad. This guy's wife is in a nursing home...some sort of a stroke or something...and he lives with us. Actually it's more like he lives with my mother; I just tolerate him. I think he uses his sick wife as an excuse not to marry my mom, but I think the whole thing stinks."

Dumbfounded at both Sandy's wisdom and confusion, Vivian continued sorting clothes that were heading for the washers as she tried to think of something wise to say. The bell on the front door jangled and Sandy said, "I'll go."

Later when Vera came in to work the afternoon shift and Sandy had gone, Vivian brought up her earlier conversation with Sandy and asked Vera her opinion.

"I think she's quite a remarkable person. I'm amazed at how she can see through it all instead of buying into it. Having a home life like that would make it easy to excuse your own behavior because no one would be able to say differently; or I suspect no one cares much about her in any way."

"I think you're right on that account," Vivian agreed. "I truly don't know how she manages to live right in the middle of all that mess and still come out unscathed."

"I agree, it's a mystery, but then you see it every once in a while."

"Every once-in-a-blue-moon, you mean."

They were laughing when Leon came in the back door, followed by the delivery guy with their dry cleaning solutions and laundry soaps.

Sam, the tall, slim driver for the cleaning supply company, always had on a neatly pressed blue shirt and clean pants when he came. His usual question was always, "So, is Sandy here today?" He usually asked the question while running his fingers through his hair nervously.

Vivian always had trouble with that question because she knew that Sandy did not find him the least bit interesting, and usually took the first opportunity she could to leave the workroom when he came. She wasn't sure if she should mention that Sandy was now "seeing" another guy or if she should leave well enough alone and just say, "No, she's not working today."

Sure enough, when Sam finished the delivery, he walked up to the front of the workroom and asked for Sandy. Still not sure how to reply, Vivian blurted out, "She's spending today with her boyfriend."

Sometimes Vivian wondered where it came from. She seemed to be able to be cruel at the drop of a hat.

"Oh, I didn't realize that she was going with someone." He didn't look crestfallen and he wasn't doing the usual hair thing with his fingers.

"Yes, she is seeing someone and she hardly even works here anymore. She's got a different job downtown." As soon as those words were out of her mouth Vivian wondered how she could be so stupid. *Now he'll ask where she's working downtown and Sandy will never get rid of him.*

"That's okay," he said, "I just wanted to ask her where she got that cute pink sweater she used to wear a lot."

"Huh?" said Vivian, her social graces and her command of the English language leaving her. "Why would you want to know that?" *Is he some kind of a weirdo stalker or something?*

"Because I want to get one like it for Debbie for Christmas."

"Debbie?"

"Yeah, you know, Debbie from next door? The beauty shop queen?"

"Debbie?" More intelligent conversation from Vivian.

"Yeah, we've been kind of going together since October, and I wanted to get her something really nice for Christmas. Her whole shop is pink inside, so I thought that must be one of her favorite colors."

"How did you meet Debbie?" asked Leon, who was coming out of the storage room after stacking the new supplies.

"Back last summer we met in the alley. I was making a delivery here and she had come out to get something out of her car. She noticed that she had a flat tire and I helped her fix it. We got to talking and then I asked her out. I guess you might say that we've been kind of going together ever since."

"Well, well," said Leon, "love is in the air!"

"Hey listen," Sam said as he turned to go, "if Sandy ever comes in, have her write down the place where she got the sweater, and I'll pick it up next week when I come back. Thanks!" He was out the door and gone.

"Okay, that's it. I am out of the relationship business as of right now," Vivian said. "I used to think that I could read people pretty well, but no more. I seem to be more wrong than I am right anymore." She slammed down the lid of the washer.

"Just so you're right about me," Leon said as he grabbed her hand and told Vera that they were going down to the Chinese place for lunch and to hold down the fort.

Vivian began spending more time away from the shop now that business had slowed down and Vera was always there to wait on the few customers who did come in. It was always interesting to see which people came in around the holiday and the kind of clothes they brought in. There were stories behind many of the items that were brought in—both Vivian and Vera were convinced about that—during Christmas or any other time of the year.

Dresses that had obviously seen many Christmas and New Year's parties were cleaned, once again, for several single ladies and they had done a bit of repair work on one in particular that had been torn several times. They spent hours speculating about this year's large tear because it looked more like a deliberate rip than a tear. The girl who brought in the dress seemed to be a frequent flier at various parties, and both Vera and Vivian agreed that her rips and tears were similar to ones that might have been torn by an irate date. They hoped she would soon realize what doorknobs they must be, whoever he was this year, and never see any of them again. There was something pathetic about her when she would come in, and they didn't doubt that she'd be back with similar repair work after the holidays.

Vivian thought about her customers as she rode the number twenty-two bus around downtown to the Loop as she finished her Christmas shopping. She also thought about this wonderful city and all it had to offer all year long. Along with Leon, she too loved Chicago. She loved the bus with its lighted Christmas soldiers attached to the sides during the holidays, and her heart was always touched by the decorating some of the drivers would do inside their buses just to make the season a little brighter for their riders—many of whom would skip Christmas for one reason or another. And many, despite themselves, couldn't help but smile a little when they left the bus and the driver would say a hearty "Merry Christmas" as they got off.... Okay, they didn't all smile.

She scoured the downtown shops looking for the perfect gift for Leon, her *fiancé*. It would take a long time to get used to that term. Longer still, she thought, to get used to the term *husband*.

On a whim she stopped at Fields, going in the doors under the famous square green clock on the corner of State and Washington. Vivian took the elevator to the eighth floor and got out purposely to look down on the Walnut Room tree on the seventh floor. Each year this magnificent forty-five-foot tree soared from the center of this historic dining room for a full two floors before it ended with the beautiful star on top. She gazed down through the open courtyard above and watched all the happy diners enjoying their meals. When she opened the Staff Only door of the design center, she was overwhelmed with all the Valentine pink and red hearts and gold cupids that were definitely out of place with Christmas.

She and Sandy had lunch downstairs in the basement, where the assorted small delis were located along with a large dining area in the middle. Vivian had eaten upstairs in the Walnut Room, under the tree, several times at different Christmases, but she knew from experience that it was by reservation only, and then you still had to wait an hour to be seated. The basement food was available for customers and employees. Vivian always found it fun to sit near the employees and listen to their conversations when she would eat there by herself. But today, she and Sandy kept up a running stream of conversation themselves, mainly about Christmas presents.

"So, are you thinking something to wear, or something he could use, like a radio or a stereo of something like that?" inquired Sandy as she bit into her sandwich. "We've got some great sales on men's fashions on the third floor, and I can get you my employee discount."

"That's the trouble. I can't think of a thing he needs."

"But is Christmas about needing or is it about wanting?"

"Ah, the age-old question. I don't know. Does a poor family spend its limited resources on socks and underwear or on toys?"

"But," Sandy said, "I don't think that Leon needs underwear or anything like that. I think he'd like a toy." She looked up and smiled.

"Great. I'll have to quit searching and start asking instead. Maybe I should talk to a few of his friends—Pete, Howard, Joe."

"It might not be a bad place to start."

TWENTY

There were only two weeks left before Christmas and Leon had put up another artificial tree from the Goodwill in the kitchen area of the workroom this time. He used the decorations he had saved from the previous year, the multicolored cleaning tags, the Italian Christmas lights and, of course, the star for the top. This little tree that had seen better days took on another Christmas miracle and actually looked really good once again. He was hoping that he and Vivian would have time to quietly sit on the sofa after the shop closed and be surrounded by the warmth of Christmas…enhanced by the lights on the tree and the soft seasonal music on the radio.

Vivian had taken Leon over to her apartment the following day after her confession and strangely saw it for the first time though his eyes. She saw how it was functional and clean, and totally impersonal. Everything was in its place and attractive, but it looked staged, like something out of a magazine—as if no one actually lived there. Okay, the small stash of tissues, nail files, clock, and reading glasses next to the sofa made it a little more personal, but it still felt cold. After that eye-opening visit, Vivian started to spend more and more time at the cleaners after hours.

"Where do you want to live after we're married?" she asked as she snuggled into his shoulder.

"I'd like to live right here."

Rising up and staring at him to see if he was serious, she said, "You're kidding, right?"

"Yeah, I guess I am, but you have to admit, this is awfully nice."

"I was just thinking the same thing, but honestly dear, we've got to start thinking seriously about where we're going to live."

"I thought we'd move across the street into your place. Keep an eye on things over here." He gave her a knowing nod and a soft elbow poke in her ribs.

She ignored his comment and said, "I'm ready to leave that place. I've been thinking about what you did to your house. When you first told me that you sold it lock, stock and barrel, I couldn't believe that anyone would do that. But now that it is, in essence, my turn to make the same decisions, I can see how easy it would be to just walk away. I too have lots of memories that I wouldn't mind finally walking away from."

"Let's not think of that now. How about if we sit here, admire the tree and cuddle."

Their Christmas party swelled to over forty people, and the place was full to overflowing. Vivian should have known that Leon couldn't resist getting everybody he knew together for any sort of a party.

Not only was the regular gang of Howard and Lois, Joe and Vera, Sandy and Johnny, Vivian and Leon there, but also Nell came from the café along with her sister Betsy, who would be helping out regularly after Christmas. Now that the street was much busier, the job had become too much for Nell alone, and since her husband was still "recuperating," she had asked her sister to move up from Indiana to help. Betsy was a recent widow and Nell thought she wouldn't come, but Betsy surprised them all. She sold her house to one of her kids and moved up. She was staying with Nell until she felt a little more comfortable in the city; then she would get a place of her own.

People from all up and down the block were there for the party, many stopping under the mistletoe that still hung above the door to see if there might be any takers.

The party was held on a Thursday night because the final weekend was too full of last-minute school and church concerts before Christmas on the following Wednesday.

It was finger-food potluck, and there was a wide range of foods, once again. Howard and Lois brought lox, cream cheese, bagels, and some macaroons. Leon thought it was odd until Sandy whispered that they were Jewish and it was great that they were even here.

Jewish, he thought. It certainly explained a lot. "That's probably why they don't decorate their windows for Christmas," he whispered back to Sandy.

"But if you remember they did go downtown with us to Moody for *The Messiah,*" she whispered back.

Everyone complimented Sandy on the windows. As Johnny held her protectively with one arm, she got quite a few queries about doing other windows up and down the block. The pink sweater Sandy had on reminded Vivian about her encounter with Sam. She barely had time to whisper the story to Sandy before Sam and Debbie walked in the front door, hand in hand...but no pink sweater, yet.

The new people from the flower shop had been invited, but chose not to come. Evidently they had had a death in the family, which made Vivian think that the place might be cursed with death. Leon told her not to be ridiculous and not to borrow trouble and let it go.

Not only did Pete come, he brought a date along. Sarah was a recently hired employee and there was nothing serious between them; it was all too new. But she turned out to be a lot of fun and a wiz at charades. Sandy and Vivian later talked about the fact that it looked like the relationship could turn into more.

Johnny had asked Leon earlier that week if he could invite his friend Steve and his friend Tony. Naturally Leon said yes.

The Christmas music was loud, the food plentiful as usual and everyone had a great time. Shop owners got to know each other's delivery people, because Leon had even invited them, and between the eating, a little business was done and new contacts were made. After the bulk of the people had gone home so they could get up early and open their own stores the next day, there were only Pete and Sarah, Steve and Tony, Sandy and Johnny, and Vivian and Leon left.

When the conversation was at a lull, Johnny said, "Hey, Tony, Steve has filled me in at work about how you two are doing, but I think it would be interesting for everybody else to hear. Last most of them knew, you and Steve were living at the factory."

"Whoa, that was months ago!" Tony said as he crossed his legs and broke into a smile, like he loved telling the story.

First he brought everyone up-to-date who didn't know about their living in a factory. Then he continued, "After Steve got a job at the hospital, I knew I needed something too. We were living on borrowed time at the factory because we had flirted our way into making a contact of one of the secretaries at City Hall who had something to do with the case. She said it looked like the city didn't have enough evidence for a case and that the whole thing might blow over soon. I still had the application for the Italian restaurant down the block so I applied right away. You ever hear of Annetties?" he asked the group.

Several people said yes or nodded.

"Well, wouldn't you know, the day I stopped in with my application, I got the job and they wanted me to start that night. It seems like the guy before me got arrested for something, so they weren't gonna hold his job. So I left a note at the factory on Steve's sleeping bag telling him where I was; then I went to work.

"I worked from four until midnight, and I liked the job right from the start. I was the second cook and all I did was what I was told to do. The main cook could tell that I didn't know anything about cooking, but he saw I was willing to do anything to learn. We get along great despite the fact that he speaks Italian better than English. The best part of all, in addition to learning to cook really great food, was that I got to wear a white chef's coat, so I didn't need any special clothes for the job. Remember, we kept our wardrobe down to the bare minimum and stored our stuff in a box in the factory itself just in case we had to get out in a hurry.

"So here I am, working almost every night because the place is always busy. I've got nothing else to do, so whenever the place is open, I'm there. I even go in early and help with the prep work when we have a party to do. It wasn't too tough to eat there either. We got one free meal—anything we wanted—and I tasted some really great and truly authentic Italian dishes.

"I started working in November and I didn't meet the owner for almost a month. It was real strange how we met, too. They were having a special party for the owner, because it was his birthday. The entire

136

family is Italian and speaks almost nothing but Italian. In fact, most of the customers speak a lot of Italian. Anyway, it took me awhile to realize that it's gonna be the boss's birthday party and everything had to be perfect. They closed the restaurant that night to everyone else and we set up one of the dining rooms for thirty people.

"The kitchen was busy for days getting stuff ready, and we were running out of room. I decided to clean off a couple of shelves in the back so we could use them for extra dishes and stuff. They were kind of dusty, so I pulled a couple of them out so I could clean underneath them. When I did, this old book falls out. Evidently it had gotten wedged behind one of the shelves years ago, because the head cook has been there lots of years and he had never seen it."

Leon got up to go to the bathroom and said, "Don't go on until I get back."

Everyone groaned.

As soon as he returned, Tony began again. "The main cook said to put the book on our break table there in the kitchen and we'd study it later. Well, he was so busy that I was the one to look at it later. It was a battered Italian cookbook that had to be ancient. The year it was printed was in Roman numerals, and neither of us could figure it out.

"When I had a chance to sit down to eat my supper, or sit and maybe peel carrots or something, I'd look through the book and attempt to read the recipes. One page was full of food stains, and the book kept falling open to that page. It was a recipe for some kind of a cake that really sounded interesting after the head cook interpreted the ingredients. Someone had underlined some of the ingredients and had written their personal changes to the recipe. There were even a few notes made in messy Italian underneath the recipe that neither one of us could figure out. We had all the ingredients, so I asked the main cook if he'd mind if I made it with his help, interpreting the Italian to English.

"He pointed out that we didn't have the special pan it called for, but I could try making it in a regular tube pan. So I whip up one of these cakes and it turned out pretty good. The cook says that it was a shame 'we' didn't try one earlier because he could have fit it into the birthday menu. I said, 'What do you mean *we*, white man?' and he had to laugh.

"We left the cake on the counter to eat as we worked during the meal. After it was all over, the big boss himself, Salvatore Annettie, walks into the kitchen to compliment us on the meal. You couldn't have gotten a better fit for a name like his if you went to central casting. He fit the name to a tee. He was a short guy that was kind of round and had a thick head of wavy silver hair. He was immaculately dressed in a dark blue three-piece suit and talked like a guy from the mobster movies; I almost thought it was an act.

"He introduces himself, says that he's heard great things about me from the head chef. Then he spies the cake. I thought we were in trouble for wasting money on something we weren't gonna serve. I'm thinking of excuses as he reaches for a bite. He stands there chewing awhile, then asks, 'Who made this?' Actually it sounded more like, 'who made-a dis?'

"I'm ready to head out the door because I can picture him pulling out a big gun with a silencer out of his waistband and shooting me full of holes. I'm not kidding. This guy is imposing! So when I realize that he isn't gonna shoot me for wasting flour and I could see that the main cook who had recently called it the cake 'we' made was pointing at me, I decided to come clean. I said I had made it and then boldly and stupidly asked if he liked it. Well, that's not enough for this guy; he wants to know where I got the recipe. I walked over to the table and got the book and gave it to him.

"'Where'd you get this book?' he wanted to know. Now I really am getting scared. I told him about cleaning the back shelves and finding the book. He walked toward me and said, 'You might be interested to know that this was my mama's cookbook, may she rest in peace. It's been lost for a long time. Then he says to me, 'After Mama died, God rest her soul, we hunted all over for it and never found it.'

"He took another bite of cake and asked, 'Did you say this recipe was in the book?'

"I gently took the book from him, and it fell open to the well-worn page; I pointed. 'I thought so. Mama's writing,' was all he said as he carried the book back to the dining room.

"After a short while this well-dressed and good-smelling woman comes in and hugs me, kisses me on the right cheek, then the left, and says something in half Italian, half English that sounds like, 'so perfect.' After she leaves I ask the cook what was going on. Naturally he didn't know, so we started to clean up the mess in the kitchen. Dinner was over, I didn't get killed, and we had more dishes than we could do in a couple of hours.

"Soon the door opens again, and it's some other Italian who speaks more clearly and says that I'm wanted in the main dining room. I'm to slice the cake thinly so everyone can have a taste and serve it. Okay, this is really spooky now. I look at the cook and all he says is that I'd better change my chef whites. (That's what we call the coats.) So I quickly do as he cuts and plates the cake. Then another guy comes to get me and says menacingly, 'Okay let's go.'

"We get to the dining room and he takes me right up to the head of the table to the boss. Mr. Annettie stands up and puts his arm around me while still holding his piece of cake; then he says in thick English, 'This is the genius that made-a my mama's cake-a. The very cake-a she made-a for me every year on my birthday. I knew it was Mama's recipe when I tasted it; she always made hers different from anyone else by putting in nutmeg instead of the cinnamonony. I'd know-a Mama's cake-a anywhere.'

"Everyone claps and he slaps me on the back and I'm more or less dismissed. I go back into the kitchen thinking that you couldn't write this kind of stuff and have anyone believe you. When the party is all but over, Mr. A comes back into the kitchen and says, 'By the way, what'sa your name, kid?'

"I tell him my name, and then he asks, 'Tony, is there anything I can do for you?' I'm thinking, *Like, what, rub somebody out?* Then he said, 'Anything you need?' Well, now we might have something there. I told him that I was between apartments and was looking for some place to stay if he knew of anything available. He puts his arm around me and says, 'Come with me.' We head for the back door.

"Okay, now he's gonna rub me out in the alley for stealing his mother's recipe book and using one of her sacred recipes. He walks me to the left when we get into the alley to a back door on the building. While I'm silently admiring his gorgeous car, he takes out a key, opens the door at the back of the restaurant, and we start up a long flight of stairs."

"All the time I'm thinking that I hope Steve gets worried and comes looking for me. Maybe there might still be enough left of me to identify! At the top of the stairs he opens the door with another key, reaches over to turn on the light, and says with a push of the door, 'So, what do you think of this place?' All I can see is a short hall from where I was standing, so he nudges me a little and we both go in. The hall turns to the left and I can hardly believe what's in front of me. This place could house a dozen people! There's a main hall that ends way down in a closed door that I presume is a bathroom. The first door on the left opens into a large kitchen, then farther down also on the left of the hall, a dining room that could hold a dozen people for dinner easily, and then the hall ends in a small room also on the left.

" 'The nursery,' he says as he peeks into the room. The next room is the one at the end of the hall and it does indeed turn out to be the bathroom. It has a well-worn black-and-white tile floor laid in a checkerboard pattern and all the fixtures are the old-fashioned ones...large and white. The other side of the hall has two bedrooms next to each other and the hall ends with a massive living room. We're at the end of the hall, back where we started, and he says 'So, what do you think?'

"I'm not sure if he means, do I think it's a great place, or do I want to live there? I take the middle road and say something like, 'Wow, great place.' He tells me this is where they lived, all six of them, when his mother and father ran the restaurant downstairs. It had been empty ever since his last sister (at forty-six) finally married a guy in real estate and moved to Florida. Then he says that I could rent it.

"Well, I know he's the guy that signs my checks and I know, that he knows, that there is no way that I could afford the rent, so I think that the question is really silly.

" 'For a guy like you that has such respect for the past and is such a dedicated employee, I think I could let you have it cheap,' Mr. A says. He told me the price, and we could indeed, putting our money together, afford the place. I didn't think he knew about Steve, so I told him and he said, 'any friend of yours must be okay' and 'when do you guys want to move in?'

"I think he was shocked when I said that tomorrow would be fine, but he took the keys off his key ring and gave them to me. 'We'll talk about utilities and other stuff after you're in and settled.' "

Steve jumped in before Tony could begin again. "Tony was so pumped when he got back to the factory that he woke me up out of a sound sleep at what must have been 2:00 AM to tell me the news. We moved first thing the next day, taking everything we owned with us, two boxes each!"

"Was there any furniture in your new place?" Sandy asked, stifling a yawn.

"Everything but beds! So there we were, still sleeping on the floor!"

"I know it's getting really late, but you've got to hear the rest of this. Believe me, its short." Tony sat forward.

"In for a dime, in for a dollar," said Vivian.

"Huh?"

"Never mind."

"Anyway, if you remember, the first snow we got a couple of weeks ago was just a dusting? Well, it was what we dreaded because we were going into the factory through the back window. To get to the window, we had to climb on some boxes. When there was no snow, nobody knew we went in. After the snow, you would be able to see our footprints easily. We would have been caught for sure. As it was, we made it out in the nick of time."

"Somebody should write this stuff down," said Johnny. "There are so many stories here in the room alone, you could write a book!"

"Somehow I don't think it would be a best-seller," said Sandy as she struggled up from the sofa and pulled Johnny up after she stood. "Time for a new sofa, guys. This one's had it!"

"We'll think about new furniture tomorrow," said Leon winking at Pete. "What we need is someone with an 'in' in the furniture business."

"I'll keep an eye out," Pete said over his shoulder as he helped Sarah on with her coat. While Sarah was still turned, Leon gave Pete the thumbs- up sign about her.

"I had such a good time that if it was up to me, Christmas could be over tonight," said Vivian as she surveyed the mess.

"Not me," said Leon as he looked at the same mess and moved away from it. "We haven't opened the gifts under the tree."

"But there aren't any gifts under the tree."

"My point exactly."

"I'm too tired to try to figure out what you're talking about. I'm going home."

"Me too," he said as he walked towards his room.

"I'll clean all this stuff up tomorrow. Don't worry about it. Vera opens, doesn't she?"

"Thank goodness, yes."

"Then I expect you to come in late. I don't want to see your face until at least 10:00 AM. Any later and you'd get spoiled."

She crossed the room and kissed him. "It was fun, wasn't it?"

"The best. Now go home. I'll wait and watch for your lights to make sure you're safe." He gave her a quick kiss.

She knew at this point that she could not kiss him good night again even though she desperately wanted to. There was never anyone in her entire life who cared about her so much. With the way she was feeling, it certainly would lead to something they were both determined was not going to happen until their wedding night. She touched his face lightly, turned, and said, "Night."

"Life doesn't get any easier with age," she grumbled to herself as she struggled with her key in the cold to unlock the door in the front of the building and walked up the stairs to bed, alone.

TWENTY-ONE

It was only five days until Christmas and Vivian began biting her nails. This was something she hadn't done since she was little and every time she caught herself doing it, she spread her hands on the table or the counter in front of her and said to herself, "Just stop it! Solve the problem."

Leon caught one of her demonstrations and she changed the subject. Vera witnessed the performances once and when Vivian realized that she had heard her mantra, she explained, "I still have no clue what to get Leon for Christmas and it's only five days away. That gives me only four days to shop!"

Instead of taking the usual tact for picking out gifts, Vera asked, "What's the nicest thing you ever got?"

Vivian was counting the till and only half heard Vera. When Vera stopped talking Vivian looked up and realized that Vera had asked a question.

"I'm sorry, what did you say?"

"I asked you what was the nicest thing you ever got?"

"For Christmas?"

"It doesn't matter!"

"Well, let's see, when I was sixteen I got a camera."

"Does Leon want a camera?"

"I doubt it."

"Well, pick again."

"Okay." Vivian took a deep breath and started again. "I got a watch one year, a really nice one."

"How about a watch for Leon?"

"You might have something there. I suppose I should see what kind he has now."

"So you're kind of thinking the way—who was it, Sandy? The one who asked what does a poor family give to their kids: toys or underwear?"

"I thought it was you that asked that question!"

"Whoever did, what's your answer?"

"I don't honestly know. I guess if I had been a poor mother, I would have given them some of each—a pair of socks and a little truck or doll tucked inside of them. But I would imagine that he doesn't need socks and he's too old for toys."

"Really?" Vera sat down at the desk and took out the file on deadbeat customers. "What do you think? Should we skip the letters for this month in the spirit of Christmas and give them another month's grace?"

"I say that we should have thought of this sooner and given them their cleaning for free if they could figure out what I could get my future husband for Christmas!"

"Well, we close at noon today so why don't you catch the bus and head into the Loop one more time?"

"You've got to be kidding. Do you have any idea what the stores downtown would be like today? It's just four days until Christmas—I don't think so!"

It was almost closing time and Vivian finally had a glimmer of an idea. She and Vera had spent almost the entire morning cleaning the workroom. Every once in a while they waited on a customer, but they were few and far between this close to Christmas.

"I think I'm going to walk down a few blocks to shop. I've got an idea."

"Thank goodness! Whatever it is, buy it!"

"I just might," Vivian answered as she flipped off the workroom lights and headed for the front door with Vera hard on her heels.

On Christmas morning there were several presents under the tree when Vivian arrived.

She and Leon decided to celebrate Christmas morning instead of Christmas Eve after much debate. "It's funny, isn't it? You wouldn't think it was such a big deal when we celebrate Jesus' birth?"

But when the subject came up originally, they each had definite reasons for celebrating when they did. Leon held out for Christmas morning and Vivian for Christmas Eve.

After a small discussion that almost ended in their first argument, Vivian remembered what Vera had said about using him to make you happy and she called the Villa Sweden for some information. Just as she thought she had remembered, the big Swedish restaurant was having their annual Christmas Eve smorgasbord and party and without asking Leon, she made reservations for both of them.

Explaining later that her being half Swedish and remembering the wonderful Christmas Eves she had spent with her own parents, wouldn't he like to go down to Andersonville for the smorgasbord on Christmas Eve? Her treat?

She was pretty sure that she'd get him with the food. She was right; for some reason, known only to him, this little Irish guy was very fond of potato sausage.

By the time Christmas morning rolled around, they were both happy.

"Bless that woman," Vivian said under her breath as she sat herself on the old sofa. "This is so nice," is what she said to Leon as she smiled and accepted a cup of coffee. He cut into the coffee cake that she had only a few minutes ago had taken out of her own oven and brought over.

It had snowed the night before, as though on cue, and there were still some lazy flakes coming down. It was going to be a late morning for the sun, so they had turned on all the lights in the front windows for the few passing cars to see.

Leon sat down close to her and put his arm around her and pulled her close. As they sat and drank their coffee, he said, while gazing at the tree and not her, "I don't think I can remember anytime in my life that I've been so happy. It's like my past life never happened and I'm just starting now." He then looked directly at her and added, "I'm not really good about talking about my feelings, but I had to tell you how happy and, I don't know, *whole,* that you make me feel."

She stretched and put their coffees on the table and took his hand in hers. "That's exactly how I feel. Looking around my apartment this morning I realized that nothing there has any hold on me. I want to be here, with you."

She made sure the kiss that he gave her was brief. This was no time and no place for more temptation. Getting up, she changed the subject. "So, when do you want to open your Christmas present?"

He got up and reached for a small box under the tree. "Well, now, of course!"

As she bent and retrieved a box for him, they decided that it was time for them to start making traditions that would be exclusively theirs. So, as the snow fell, the chicken baked slowly in the oven sending tantalizing smells of sage dressing into the room, and the radio played "Oh Come, All Ye Faithful" for the four hundredth time since Thanksgiving, they opened their gifts at the same time.

Both Leon and Vivian tore off the paper, opened the boxes, started incredulously at each other, and collapsed onto the sofa laughing as each one pulled out a watch: a Bulova for him and a Lady Bulova for her.

When Leon caught his breath he said, "Next year I'm thinking of getting you a car!"

When she got the joke, she laughed too.

Around one o'clock Sandy and Johnny stopped in on their way to his parents' house to wish them Merry Christmas and drop off gifts.

"We knew you'd be here," Sandy said and laughed as she gave

Vivian a small box and Leon another. "Open your gifts," she prompted.

Vivian said the appropriate "oh!" when she pulled out a pair of leather gloves from the traditional green Fields box. "Aren't they beautiful?" Sandy interjected. "They were on sale at work and with my employee discount; I figured I couldn't go wrong. Besides," she added as she squeezed Johnny's arm, "you and Leon are spending more time out of the shop than in it and I wanted you to be ready for long romantic walks along the lakefront!"

"Not in this weather," said Leon as he opened his gift. "Not with the wind whipping up the waves on Lake Michigan and sending the spray a block and a half! But I'm sure we could find someplace to go so she can show off the gloves." By now he had unwrapped his box of chocolates. They were the ones for which Marshall Fields were famous—the thick and creamy Frango Mints nestled in their signature green box. Before he could add his thanks, Sandy once again bounced in with conversation as she pulled Johnny to the front of the shop.

"We're going to Johnny's parents up in Winnetka—for dinner! I'm so excited!" With a quick "Merry Christmas" they were both out the door.

"Kids," Leon said with a smile.

"I agree. They're wonderful, aren't they?"

"Just like our own. You know, for two old people who never had their own children, we're turning out to be pretty good parents…if I do say so myself."

"Mr. Big Head," she said as she crossed the room to kiss him with all the Christmas love she felt absolutely oozing out of her.

Vera and Joe landed at O'Hare Airport at six on Christmas evening, and Vivian and Leon were there to pick them up. This weary couple had spent the holidays on a round robin of visits to all four of their children in three different states.

"We thought that we'd do something different this year, but I don't think we'll ever do that again! We are both exhausted!" said Vera as she sank into the backseat of Leon's car next to Vivian.

"What made you do it this year?"

"Well, like I was telling you before we left and you weren't listening because you were so worried about you-know-who's gift, we usually find a spot that's nearby all the kids and is centrally located, and then we find a neutral place, like in a hotel, so no one gets stuck doing all the work.

"We used to all go to our one daughter's—she lives in Iowa on a farm. Her house is huge, and because they milk cows every day they're home all the time. But this year she's expecting another baby, her fifth, and she's worn out. So we all decided that Joe and I would spend a little time with each of our kids and get in a good visit. Our usual family visits are a blur because between the kids, their spouses, and all the grandchildren, we leave feeling that we never did have time to really visit with anybody; it's more like a marathon than a visit."

"But it didn't work?"

"The visiting part worked fine, but we ended up having three Christmases with all the trimmings in three days. Three gift openings, three heavy meals...three Christmases."

"I can imagine that it could wear anybody out. Our Christmas was wonderfully quiet." She told them of Sandy's visit. "And see what Leon gave me," Vivian said as she pulled up her sleeve to show Vera the watch and tell her the story of their duplicate Christmas gifts. "I trumped him, though, because in the bottom of his watch box were tickets to three Cubs games that he never expected! Two tickets for each of three home games sprinkled throughout the season."

"So, Christmas wasn't lonely for you two?"

"It's been the best one ever!" she said as Leon turned slightly and smiled at her as Joe rattled on in the front seat.

More conversation, more laughter, and the ride and Christmas came to a close sooner than any of them wanted.

"Merry Christmas" rang through the air as they dropped off the weary travelers. "Merry Christmas," Vivian added as she too got out of the car and said, "I'll walk the four blocks home from here. It's a beautiful night and it's getting late. Got to be up and at 'em tomorrow morning; get ready for all the interesting people with their interesting laundry after the holidays."

"Do you think Miss Torn Sleeve will be in?" asked Vera as she grabbed a suitcase that Leon had unloaded onto the snowy sidewalk.

"I hope she is, and I hope there are no repairs to do. But remember we've still got New Year's Eve to go. She's got another chance to be foolish."

"Not exactly Christmas sentiment," said Leon as he waved good-bye to Vera and Joe.

"I know, I feel so sorry for her. I don't know what kind of guys she dates, but I don't think they have very honorable intentions."

"Honorable intentions! You are showing your age, Granny."

"Maybe so, but I also have very little to regret in the sex department."

"Sex! Now you do surprise me. I wasn't sure that word was in your vocabulary."

Vivian pulled him to her by his new Christmas scarf that had been a gift from Vera and Joe. "You'll just have to wait, big boy, to find out exactly what I know about sex."

With that she turned on her heel and headed in the opposite direction to her apartment.

A startled Leon stared after her, anxious to pursue the same conversation very soon. Maybe it would be a real good idea to set a wedding date, he thought as he got back into his warm car and pulled away from the curb on the oddly deserted Christmastime Clark Street.

Sandy was on Christmas break from school and not scheduled to work at Fields again until Monday, so she stopped in the following morning for a long visit.

"So, what are they like?"

"Who, Johnny's parents?"

"Who else."

"I really liked them, and I think they liked me."

"And?"

"And what?"

"And what are you not saying?"

Sandy realized that she could keep this inane two-word sentence conversation going on forever, but she really did need to talk to someone about yesterday. Now that Vivian was asking, she decided to talk.

"I lied."

"To whom?"

"To his parents. I sat there and told a whopper about my family."

"And Johnny?"

She completed Vivian's thought. "Didn't say a thing."

"Are you glad he didn't or disappointed?"

"I've thought of that all night and all morning, and I just don't know. I'm glad he didn't stop me halfway through and ask me what in the world I was talking about. But in a way I wish he would have, because once I got started making up this story of my fictitious family— you know, mom, dad, sweetness and light..."

"So you created your own reality."

"Pretty much. But they asked me these questions when I first got there and I realized by the time we left that I really like these people and if they would have asked me after I got to know them a little, I think that I would have answered differently."

"Answered honestly, or just differently?"

"Honestly."

"So, what now?"

"I don't know. That's the part that really puzzles me. I felt bad about it, but I didn't want to bring it up on the ride home because I didn't want Johnny to yell at me or, worse yet, give me that 'I'm so disappointed in you' speech. As it was, neither one of us brought it up, but by not saying anything, I think I made it worse."

"So what's the plan now?"

"I don't know. I've got the next four days off and he's got the weekend off. I usually talk to him several times a week on the phone and I don't know if I should wait for him to call or if I should call him and explain. Any suggestions?"

"Actually, I do. Call him. Call him tonight. Tell him everything and don't keep any secrets. Whether this goes farther than friends between the two of you or stays like it is, this kind of deceit will end up coming between you and making a barrier. If he thinks you can lie like that at the drop of a hat, he probably wonders if other things you've told him are lies too."

"I never thought of it that way."

"Well, think about it long and hard and call him tonight. Or better yet, make arrangements to go see him."

"But it will be much harder face-to-face."

"Yes it will, but it will count for more because it is harder. Somehow I think we get more credit somewhere when we make a clean break, face-to-face, and don't hide behind someone else, or a phone."

"I think that you're my guardian angel." Sandy gave Vivian's hand a squeeze. "Don't rope me into that position! I think I'm more like your Dutch uncle!"

"Angel or uncle, thanks for the advice," she called over her shoulder as she left and Vera passed her in the front part of the shop.

"I can't wait to hear what that conversation was about," Vera said as she removed her snow boots and shook the snow from her coat.

TWENTY-TWO

New Year's Eve came and went and no sign of Miss Torn Sleeve. Vivian and Vera weren't sure if this was a good or a bad thing.

Leon spent most of the month of January helping Pete over at the Goodwill store. Pete was making major renovations and turning the place upside down with new ideas, so he needed all the volunteer help he could get. Johnny helped some nights and so did Steve.

Since Christmas, Johnny was more pensive and not his usual flamboyant self that they had gotten to know.

"I think that going home for Christmas changed him some way," said Pete as he started to pull a large display case away from the wall.

"Hey cowboy, let me help you with that before you injure yourself and leave me to do all this alone."

"I've got a better idea. Let's take a five-minute break and both get back some energy. Besides," Pete said as he headed to the nearest chair, "I wanted to talk to you about Johnny."

"I'm beginning to excel in the parent business, so go ahead. Ask away."

He put his feet up with a groan. "Have you noticed a change in him lately?"

"I can't honestly say that I have, but then I've only seen him here. With school starting again and Sandy putting in every spare minute at Fields, we hardly see either one of them. Why, what's the trouble?"

"That's just it, I don't know. All I know is that he's not as happy as he used to be. You remember how downright goofy he could act. Well, not only is he much more serious, he doesn't seem to want to talk like we used to."

"Maybe it's something he has to work out for himself. You don't think it's something bad, do you?"

"That's just it, I don't know and I can't read him either way. So what do you think I should do?"

"I think the next time all four of us are together—you, me, Johnny, and Steve—we should take them out for pizza when we're finished for the day. We could go down to Pizza Uno. Are the guys going to work on Friday?"

"Yeah, I think they planned to. We were going to get a few things started, then finish up on Saturday. We're closing the store all day on Saturday to do some big stuff, so we'd have them for a day and a half."

"If we do this right, we can do it all Friday night," said Leon as he got up and slapped Pete's foot. "Come on, old man, the work is not going to do itself!"

"Slave driver."

"I've been called worse."

Leon arrived late and Vivian was still at the shop wrestling with the deadbeat letters that they hadn't sent out in December.

"You look all done in," she said as he came in the back door.

"I am. To be honest, I'm having a hard time keeping up with Pete. Not only is he probably twenty years younger, but he's a lot more used to hard physical labor; unloading all those trucks every week, well, he must get more exercise in one week than I do in a year."

"I know how you feel. We've been so busy that I'm either ready to add more help or retire. I can't decide which."

"Retire?" he asked as though the thought had never crossed his mind.

"Yes, I've worked hard all my life, and I'm ready for an easier life."

"Got anything in mind?"

"You mean besides finding an island in the Caribbean and doing absolutely nothing for a few weeks?"

"Well, after those few weeks in the sun, what would you have in mind?"

"I don't know. I would have to consult my husband and see what he'd like to do now that we're old."

"And rich," added Leon.

"And rich."

"So," she asked, "what would you do?"

"To be honest, I haven't even thought about it before now. But that Caribbean thing sounds nice. I've got an idea. How about a Caribbean honeymoon?"

"And just when would that be?"

"Soon." He kissed her before she was able to answer. "But right now, I've got to shovel more snow. I don't think we've had this much since that historic winter of 1875."

"And you remember that?" She smiled.

"I'm older than I look!"

"Evidently. Well, old man, you better get shoveling. Come on up to my place when you're finished and I'll have supper ready."

"Supper. That reminds me. I won't be back Friday night until late. Pete and I are taking the boys out for pizza."

"Good, they've been working hard from what you've told me."

"It's not only a reward; it's an opportunity for Pete and me to get deep in their psyches and try to find out what makes them tick."

"Good luck! If you find out, you won't have a retirement to consider. You'll be too busy writing a best-selling exposé on the brains of young men, 'Do They or Do They Not Exist?' Stay tuned; film at eleven."

"Very funny! Now get going, woman, and fix my supper." He gave her a peck on the cheek and grabbed the snow shovel.

Friday night came and went with no results in the questions about Johnny. Leon did notice, though, that Pete had been right. His spark was gone.

Work was going real well at the Goodwill, and Howard even stopped in to help one afternoon. Between all of them they figured that the store would be up and running in less than a week.

"It looks like it will be ready in time for the after-Christmas contributions," said Pete. "Evidently people either get new furniture for Christmas or else they go stir-crazy with the January snow and go out and buy new furniture. Whatever the reason, we always start to see furniture in January and February."

Pete was painting the back wall and sharing the pail with Howard who asked, "Hey, have you guys been down to the Museum of Science and Industry to see the international Christmas tree display? Lois and I went before Christmas and it was quite impressive. You guys should take your dates and go."

"Okay Howard, I might be getting myself in trouble here, but somebody told me you were Jewish."

"Yeah, so?"

"Well, you know, Christmas."

"Ah, well, whoever told you I was Jewish forgot to tell you that Lois isn't. She's Polish."

"Does that make it hard for you?" asked Leon as he stood stirring paint. "Hey, Pete, who picked out this color? It's really strange."

"I never look a gift horse in the mouth. A bunch of it came in the other day and I couldn't resist using it. It's free, you know."

"Free is one thing. Ugly is another!"

"You really think it's ugly?"

"Well, it wouldn't be my first choice."

"Mine either," added Howard. "But I think it will look better when it dries. Paint always looks different when it's wet."

"Man, you better hope so!"

Leon put his newspaper down and stared into space.

Vivian, who was stirring soup because it was her turn to cook for "The Lunch Bunch," as they were now calling themselves, noticed he was thinking about something and asked, "What are you thinking about?"

"What was the name of the guy who owned the Italian restaurant that Tony works at? Do you remember? Was it Salvatore Annettie?"

"I believe that's his name."

"According to the *Tribune*, that *was* his name. He's dead."

"What?" She turned the soup down and came over to sit on the arm of his chair and peer over his shoulder at the article he was reading.

Completely irritated when someone read over his shoulder, Leon handed her the paper and pointed to the large obituary.

"I can't believe it. He was only sixty-three years old. It says here that he died of a heart attack."

"I wonder what this means for Tony?"

"Hard to say. Next time you're at the Goodwill, why don't you talk to Steve or Pete and see if you can find out what will happen?"

"Yeah, I can do that. I'll see the guys tonight for what might be our last night of work. I'll ask tonight. You should see the store. It looks entirely different; looks good."

"You look good," she said as she kissed him softly.

"You've really got to stop that. I'm an old man too. You don't want to be reading my obituary in the paper next week do you?"

"Actually I was thinking that it would be nice to read our wedding announcement in the paper."

Leon surprised them both when he said, "Done! Now pick a date."

Now she was the one caught off guard. "I don't know. Would Valentine's Day be too soon?"

"Tomorrow wouldn't be too soon! I'll arrange to have the ad in next week's paper. By the way, what day is Valentine's Day?"

Vivian had wondered that too and was checking the large calendar that hung on the wall. "It's a Wednesday. Rats!"

"Wednesday's no good?"

"Well, it's not traditional."

"I wouldn't call our entire relationship traditional."

"True."

"So, Wednesday. February fourteenth?"

"Yes."

"Remember that word 'yes' or 'I do,' either one." He crossed the

156

room and flipped the calendar pages. "You have three weeks to decide which one it's going to be."

"Three weeks...oh my."

"No, 'I do.' And if I know you, you're going to want to talk to Vera about wedding plans, so I'll watch the shop if you want to see if she's home so you can start planning. Oops, I guess we'd better give our pastor a buzz too. Or do you want to get married downtown at the courthouse?"

"I'll call the pastor, then Vera. Thanks for watching the shop. I think I'll take a chance and walk down to their house. I need to work off some nervous energy."

"Not like me—nerves of steel!" He demonstrated by holding out his shaking hand.

The wrap-up night at the Goodwill store turned out to be more of a party than a genuine work night.

Because some of the day crew had come in and managed to get the majority of shelves and display units put in their new spots and got the bulk of them cleaned and polished, all there was to do was fill them and set up a few end displays.

Johnny, Pete, Steve, and Leon were the muscle, and Sarah said that she was the brains.

"You could use a few brains, Pete" was the only comment from Johnny.

The evening went fast and the pizzas were delivered around seven.

"Speaking of pizza," asked Leon, "anybody have more information on Tony?" He stared directly at Steve.

"Nope," he said as he dug into a thin-crust Chicago special. "Tony's still working because they're keeping the restaurant open until the reading of the will next week. Nobody knows anything, but there's plenty of speculation."

"Speculation?" asked Pete. "Speculation about what?"

"About everything!"

"Like?"

"Like what's gonna happen to the restaurant, what's gonna happen to us, and did he really die of a heart attack?"

Everyone put down their pizza and leaned in close as Leon asked, "Does someone think there was foul play involved?"

"No one knows for sure, at least that's what Tony said. It's all real hush-hush. No one's saying and no one's not saying, but there are innuendoes floating around that it might not have been a death by natural causes. Know what I mean?"

Sarah's eyes were as big as saucers as she whispered, "Is it possible he was murdered? Is that what you're saying?"

"There again, no one knows. But Tony thinks the guy might have had mob connections in some way because some of their private parties had some pretty shady looking guys there."

"What do you mean shady?"

"You know, flashy suits, big rings, big cars parked in the alley instead of out front, and lots of lowered conversations when any staff came into the dining room."

"It's pretty thin evidence," said Leon as he sat back and finally took a deep breath.

"All I know is what Tony says and the feeling I get when I stop downstairs for supper."

"You eat there?" asked a surprised Sarah. "Isn't it pretty expensive?"

"For regular customers it is, but I eat in the kitchen with the help."

"That must be tough for you; great Italian food and your own table for one reserved in the back!" Pete started cleaning up the pizza boxes and empty pop cans.

"I can't complain, but I am worried what will happen to us next. It was ideal living upstairs and now, we might lose it all. I can't see any of the family members running the place. It's no secret the head cook wants to go back to Italy; he talks about it all the time. If they sell the place, the new owners would kick us out right away, or triple the rent to get it up to normal."

"Hey Johnny," said Leon, "you're awfully quiet tonight."

"I've got a lot on my mind."

"Anything we can do?" Leon added his pop can to the garbage.

"Actually, maybe you can."

"Shoot," said a surprised Leon.

"Back at Christmas when I took Sandy to my parents they asked her questions about her family and she told some whoppers like she had this great family; mom, dad, sisters, brothers, nice house in the suburbs."

"Whoa," said Steve. "That must have been interesting."

"The interesting part was that my parents were so impressed with her that they encouraged me to keep seeing her. 'What a nice girl from a fine family,' they said. Believe me, it put me on the spot, and I'm still not sure how I feel about all of it."

"What do you mean 'all of it'—was there more?" Steve reached for his coat, as he got ready to leave.

"I think the rest of it was the stuff I added. Not verbally, but by not telling them the truth about Sandy I kind of got back into where I used to be when I still lived at home. I was the golden boy and was the one being trained to step into my dad's business and learn it from the ground up. I used to think that my family was a normal family. Then when I got to be a senior, someone pointed out to me that they were snobs. I had trouble with that at first, but the more I thought about it, the more I realized it was true. They only wanted me to date certain girls and be seen at certain places. They even wanted to pick out what I wore. I guess that's the reason I started dressing this way and combing my hair back like a hood; it was kind of like quiet rebellion."

Sarah stopped putting on her coat and asked, "Quiet rebellion? Can you do that?"

"I think everybody does it in one way or another," added Leon. "Especially those of us who don't have the guts to say what needs to be said, or needs to be done. I was like that for years, so I can relate, even at my age."

"So you know what I'm talking about!" Johnny smiled for the first time that night.

"Yeah, I do. And it's a tough thing to be saddled with, never feeling like you should say what you should say but knowing somewhere deep inside that you have to say it, but you don't."

"So what do you think I should do?"

"Well, I'm not an expert, but from my personal experiences, I think it would be best for everyone involved for you to go up and see your parents again, telling them everything, from Sandy's real home life, the reason you dress like you do and then tell them your dreams. They might not get it, but you'll feel better. Parents are funny. Sometimes they rebel themselves when their kids do this, but on the other hand, it shows that the kids have some spunk and parents often respect that."

Pete was walking to the door with Sarah to tell her good night and he added, "I think that's really good advice. I'd arrange to do it as soon as possible if I were you. Don't let this thing go. You've been a real dishrag around here and I'd like it if you got your *joie de vie* back!"

"My what?"

"Your zest for life!"

"Oh."

"I noticed that you haven't lost your zest for life," said Steve as he opened the door to leave just as Pete was giving Sarah a good night kiss.

TWENTY-THREE

"So, what did they say?" Leon decided not to beat around the bush, and Sandy might as well hear it here as well as anywhere else; if Johnny hadn't already told her that is.

The four of them were sitting around the table at the cleaners eating supper. Leon had Vivian purposely invite both Sandy and Johnny so he could find out what was happening and if they could help. Sandy was working overtime hours at Fields as they put in their Valentine windows, but arranged to make a late meal.

"If you brought us both here to figure out what to do about the Christmas dinner mess, Johnny and I have already had this conversation and I'm finally okay with it. I wasn't at first, but I am now."

"That wasn't an easy conversation either." Johnny reached over and took her hand. "But it worked out well."

"But your parents, Johnny?" asked Leon.

"My parents weren't nearly as understanding as Sandy was. I did what you said and told them everything. Like I thought, they didn't understand, but they did listen, which surprised me. I talked until I couldn't think of anything else to say and then, because they had no response, I went home. But I felt so much better. At least now they knew what I want and what I'm going to do to achieve it."

"And just what is it that you want?" asked an up-to-now quiet Vivian.

"I would like to pursue a career at the hospital. I like my job a lot, but I think that the whole department could be run differently."

"So, you gonna take over and do it right?" Leon asked, sarcastically.

"Actually, it's kind of like that. I asked around on the sly and found out that the guy who runs the department is some nephew or relative of some hotshot there and he really isn't qualified for the job. So I did some research and found out that they like people with business degrees so I'm going back to college while I still work. It will take longer, but that's not a problem. I'll get it eventually."

Vivian put her coffee down. "Back to college? You've been?"

"Yeah, I started out on a career path in business, then decided that since I didn't want to work with my father and eventually take over the business that I didn't need that kind of education. I dropped out at the end of my sophomore year."

"Amazing," said Vivian. She reached for his hand and squeezed it. "I think it's the best idea you've ever had to go back. I'm very proud of you."

Whether it was because he wasn't used to praise or because he felt uncomfortable holding hands with an older woman, he slid his hand out from under hers, turned a little pink and looked directly at Sandy. "It's not the only plans I've made."

Vivian groaned inwardly.

"Sandy and I have decided to go steady while we both finish college and then, who knows?"

"And that's okay with you?" Vivian asked Sandy.

"It's better than fine. I don't want to get serious now that I'm finally getting started in life, and I'm so relieved that Johnny doesn't want to either. No, I couldn't be happier."

"Neither could I!" Vivian's smile went from ear to ear.

Leon got off his chair and came around the table to put his arm around Vivian. "But when you two need some expert advice on both courtship and marriage, make sure you look us up."

"Speaking of marriage, O wise one, when are you going to set a date?" chided Sandy.

"We already did, young child. We're getting married in less than three weeks on Valentine's Day."

"Less then three weeks? You're kidding! You're planning a wedding for less than three weeks? It takes us longer to plan one counter display at work! What are you going to do—go to City Hall and get married?"

"We thought of that, believe me," added Vivian, "but I want our pastor to marry us and because it's a Wednesday night, he's available to go wherever needed."

"And where would that be?" asked Sandy.

"At this point, it's anyone's guess!"

"We don't even know where we're going to live," added Leon. "I want to stay here, but my future wife seems to frown on that idea."

Vivian smiled at him with indulgence. "Funny man."

"Why not across the street at your apartment?" asked Sandy.

"I suppose that's where we'll end up, but it isn't where I would like to stay."

"Crummy place?" whispered Johnny.

"Hardly!" responded Leon. "More like real swell." He moved his hand to silently indicate "ritzy."

"Yes, it is real swell, but I don't want to live there anymore. Actually, and I know this sounds really silly, but I would like to live in a house."

"In the city or out of the city?" Sandy was really getting into this while Leon and Johnny rolled their eyes.

"I'm not really sure. It's not like we'll always have to take public transportation, Leon and I both have cars."

"You have a car?" Leon stopped what he was doing and looked at her in surprise. "You didn't tell me you had a car! Where do you keep it?"

"In the back of the building in the garage."

"There's a garage back there?"

"Sure."

"Room for two cars? I could drive mine over and get it out of this terrible weather."

"No, there's barely room for one. But my car is small."

Now Johnny was getting interested. He took public transportation only because he had sold his car in order to pay the rent on his first apartment and to buy food before he ended up on the streets. Maybe Vivian would be interested in selling her car to him. "What kind of car is it?"

"It's one of those brand-new Fords. A Mustang convertible, if you must know. Hunter green with a tan top."

"Cool." Sandy's usual response.

"Way cool!" was Johnny's enthusiastic response. "Are you interested in selling it?"

"Number one, I doubt that you could afford it because it's brand-new, and second, I love it!"

Leon sat and stared at her. Finally he asked, "And just when were you going to tell me about your car?"

"I don't know. I figured that it would eventually come up in a conversation."

"I see."

"No you don't! I've been taking the bus for so long that I've pretty much forgotten that I had a car. I didn't dare think about it because then I might have let it slip that I had one. So there, Mr. Smarty Pants."

"But you said it was new. That means you recently bought it!"

Sandy and Johnny glanced at each other. Now might be a good idea to leave.

Good nights were said and even though the younger two left, Leon and Vivian continued their discussion for a while, never coming to an agreeable conclusion.

Vivian held that she had lived a double life for so long that it was second nature to not say anything to anybody. And Leon contended that once she had confessed all of her secrets, she really should have included this one too.

The discussion got heated, and then it got cold.

Vivian left without saying a word. Leon muttered to himself as he went around the shop turning off lights and then slammed his door, even though there was no one to hear it.

TWENTY-FOUR

The wedding was postponed by mutual consent and things were icy at the cleaners for several weeks.

Vera came to work but spent her lunch hours over at the barbershop, saying that Joe was getting busy and it was easier to stay there for lunch. Howard begged off, saying their store was getting so busy now that he had to stay over the lunch hours until they could hire more help; it was only half a lie.

Sandy came and did the windows at the cleaners in a Valentine motif like she'd promised, and Vivian was not one bit impressed that the male mannequin was now carrying a heart-shaped box of chocolates under his arm. After the windows were finished and Sandy had gone, she took the opportunity to turn the female mannequin around to face away from the male model; like they were both walking for the train, oblivious to each other.

Leon saw what she had done, and several nights later removed the fake box of candy and slid a *Tribune* through the male's arm instead.

They became the talk of the neighborhood, and their windows became their battleground. At the end of two weeks with constant "redecorating" going on every couple of days, the feud had lost its amusing qualities and was bordering on plain meanness.

Vivian arranged with Vera to work three days in a row for her; then Vivian just disappeared. She told Vera that she was going on a little trip. It was true, but everyone knew that it wasn't a pleasure trip.

Valentine's Day came and went, and Vivian finally came back after extending her trip for another two days.

It was a Saturday and Vera was ticked. As soon as Vivian came in, took off her heavy coat, and had a cup of coffee in her hand Vera asked, ever so nicely, "So, have a good trip?"

"No."

"So, why did you stay another two days, may I ask?"

"Because I didn't want to come back."

"Because?"

"Because after I was gone, I realized what an idiot I was. I don't know why I didn't tell Leon about the car. I didn't even tell him I was buying one or let him help me pick it out."

Vera sipped her coffee and thawed a bit herself. She carefully thought about her next question. "Do you think that it was your last act of independence, the slender thread that you were afraid would break and there would be nothing of you left?"

Tears were rolling down Vivian's face as she nodded yes. "I came to the same conclusion. After I spent the first couple of days just downright angry, I began to think about my feelings and ask myself why I was so angry. I came up with the very same reasons as you did. I think that I was scared about losing me. I've been alone for so many years. Even when I was married I was alone. I learned to be strong and independent because I had to, and it's hard to give up. I realized that was also the real reason I didn't tell Leon for so long about all my holdings. It isn't that the time was never right; I wanted to keep something just for myself. Oh, Vera, will I ever stop being so selfish?"

"Do you want to stop? No, before you answer that, think about the question. If you really don't want to change, you won't. You'll say that you have and you'll think that you have, but somewhere down the road you'll realize that you haven't really changed at all and things will be much worse. I think it's something you have to decide now, not later."

"I think you're right, and I think that I have decided. The five days I spent away from Leon were the loneliest days I've ever known. I realized that I love him so much; in fact, I love him more than I love myself."

Vera put her arms around her friend. "Then it's time to tell him."

"I know. That's the hard part."

"It shouldn't be too hard. He's been walking around here looking like he's lost his best friend." She paused only briefly. "He looks like he's got one foot in the grave; he acts like his dog just died; he—"

166

"Stop! I get it! You really are wise, and funny," Vivian said while finally smiling.

"Okay, I'll take the compliment, but only this time. I don't want to get a big head."

They were laughing when Leon came in the front door truly looking like all the things Vera said he did.

Before he could say a word, Vivian took his arm and steered him back to his room. "I have to talk to you."

They entered the room and Vivian quietly closed the door behind them.

Almost an hour later, two different people came out of his room; Vivian appeared sheepish and her eyes were very puffy; Leon seemed spent, as though he had fought the battle of his life. As they approached Vera, Leon slipped his arm around Vivian's waist.

Leon cleared his throat and began, "We have to apologize for our childish behavior. It was unbecoming, and we had no right to put you more or less in the middle."

"Forgive us?" added Vivian as she held out her hand to her friend.

"Only if you tell me that things are right between the two of you."

"Finally right," Vivian answered as she smiled at Leon, and stroked his arm.

Vera didn't let up. "So you're going to quit rearranging the front windows?"

They nodded.

"Good, because now it's my turn!" Vera headed to the front and picked up the female mannequin and moved it over to the male's window, reattaching the arm that fell off in the move, and placing them face-to-face as though they were about to kiss.

Leon reached back under the counter, retrieved the fake box of chocolates and put them back under the male's arm, removing the newspaper.

Vivian took the paper out of Leon's hand and placed it under the female's arm. "There," she said. "Much better!"

Now the windows were definitely lopsided. With both mannequins in the one window, the other was left half-empty with only a fake tree covered in pink and red hearts.

"Sandy's not going to like this!" Vera said. "I think you two should keep your hands out of the window displays and settle more important matters, like your wedding date."

"That's easy," said Leon. "Next Thursday."

"We'd do it today," added Vivian, "but we have to wait and go downtown to City Hall on Monday for the license and then wait three days for the blood test. That reminds me," she added over her shoulder as she walked to the phone, "I've got to see if someone is still at the clinic so we can get an appointment for the blood tests too on Monday."

"And, we'd like you and Joe to go downtown with us as our witnesses."

Now it was Vera's turn to be surprised but she recovered quickly "We'd be honored!" Her brain switched into fast-forward and added, "We've got so much to do to get ready! There's the flowers, our dresses, the rings…Leon, you haven't gotten them yet, have you? And you have to make honeymoon plans, call a travel agent…let's see what time is it? I wonder if they…"

Vivian was laughing as Vera rattled on. "I think it's time to cut off your coffee—or at least switch you to decaf."

"But there's so much to plan."

"Not as much as you think. We're wearing our regular clothes—okay, maybe our regular Sunday clothes—and we don't want you to dress fancy either, just something nice. We can order something simple from the new flower shop, maybe corsages and boutonnières, and we can always honeymoon over at my apartment."

"Gracious, you are ready! But I think that honeymoon thing needs work, though."

They were both sitting at the table now, doing what women do well: making plans.

Within a few minutes both women were heading next door to order the flowers. They both called back to Leon, who was planning on spending the rest of the day working on one of the washing machines. "Watch the store, will you?"

They didn't wait for an answer, nor did they even put on their coats as they left arm in arm.

Leon smiled and headed to the front counter. "Women," he said with amusement to himself. And then, as he watched them go arm in arm past the window, he added, "God bless them."

TWENTY-FIVE

Thursday, February twenty-second blew in at nineteen degrees with a frigid wind off the lake that would freeze any exposed skin within moments.

The sign on the door of the cleaners said, SORRY, CLOSED FOR THE DAY.

"I don't think that we're going to lose much business today," said Vera as she looked out the window down onto the snowy street from Vivian's apartment. There isn't a soul out there."

"Nobody in their right mind would be out today," Vivian said as she came out of her bedroom in an attractive light blue suit and beige heels.

"My gracious, that's beautiful! Is this what you think of as Sunday clothes?"

"Hardly. I had it in the back of the closet from the years that my husband and I had to look good for business dinners. I think it's silk."

"Well, if anyone should know, you should after all the years you've been in the cleaning business."

"I don't like leaving the shop closed today," she said as she clipped on an earring and peered down onto the street. "I think it's time to hire more help. It's getting too hard for the two of us to do it all. I know you have the energy of ten women, but it's time for both of us to take it easier. In fact," she sat on the sofa, "believe it or not, I think I'm going to get someone to do my job and maybe retire."

Vera sat down across from her and asked, "Anyone in mind?"

"For what?"

"For the job as manager?"

Vivian almost said no, but when she saw Vera's face, she changed instantly. "Well, I was thinking of offering it to my star employee. How about it? Are you interested?"

"Yes! I won't beat around the bush. I love the business and, with Joe new in the neighborhood and not a lot of clientele yet, I have to tell you, things have been a little tight."

"Vera, why didn't you say something before?"

"What could you have done? I was already working all the hours I could, and you just gave me a raise."

"True. So will you take the job, starting tomorrow, and be my shop manager?" Vera didn't even have a chance to say yes before Vivian continued. "It would mean that you'd have to hire at least two more people—one full-time and one part-time. I think we've pretty well lost Sandy; I'm happy for her, even though I really do miss her. It's kind of like my own little birdie leaving the nest."

"Now don't get maudlin on me! It's your wedding day." Vera got up and gathered their coats. "Come on, lady, we've got to get downtown. Joe and your groom will be waiting at City Hall for us to get there!"

"Don't forget the flowers! Wait, did you call a cab?"

Vera opened the door. "It's outside waiting. Didn't you hear him honk?"

"I'm so nervous, I wouldn't hear the last trump if it sounded."

"That one I don't think even you would miss!"

City Hall was a maze of long yellow hallways that joined every twenty feet or so. The brown office doors had various department names painted on each one. They found the office they were looking for and the secretary said that they could wait in the hall. Vera pinned Vivian's beautiful cymbidium orchid corsage on her and looked for the guys. Suddenly the bathroom door opened at the end of the hall and Joe poked out his head. "Pssst! Ready?"

"What's going on?" asked a perplexed Vivian.

"There has to be some tradition in this wedding, so the groom can't see you until they call your name to go in."

"They're going to wait in the bathroom until then?"

"You bet."

"Vera, you are absolutely crazy!"

"Thank you," she said as she straightened her own dress and saw the two boutonnières on the chair next to her. "Gracious! I'll be right back. They don't have their flowers!"

She grabbed the flowers and hurried to the end of the hall and knocked on the men's bathroom door. Someone other than Joe, who must have been coming out, answered the door with the strangest look on his face. "Yes, can I help you?"

Totally embarrassed, Vera started to stammer an unintelligible answer. She heard Joe laughing in the background as he came to the door. "Don't mind her, Judge. It's just my wife!"

"Judge?" she stammered, still holding the flowers that she had forgotten to give to Joe.

"Yes." He held out his hand. "Judge Jonathan Riordan. I'll be marrying your friends in a minute."

"Now I am embarrassed."

"Don't be. Believe me, I've seen much worse. In fact, you wouldn't believe some of the behavior we see every day. You're one of the milder cases!"

She turned and fled down the hall after throwing the flowers to Joe. She sat down next to Vivian with her head down, trying to keep from laughing.

Other people were filing in looking for the same office of the Justice of the Peace. Adults and children in pretty clothes, one couple dressed fit to kill in their wedding finery and their witnesses in down jackets, snow pants, and winter boots.

The Judge was right, Vera thought. *I'll bet he does see about everything every day.*

The secretary came out shortly after the judge went through his door and called their names. Vera knew she had to go back down to the bathroom to get the guys, and dreaded it. She told Vivian to go in and she'd be right back. Fortunately Joe opened the door and stepped out with Leon right behind him.

172

"The Judge told us that we were first and to come on in," said Joe as he pushed Leon forward and down the hall.

The ceremony was supposed to be short, but the judge had evidently taken a liking to Leon while they visited in the bathroom, so he added a few thoughts of his own to the ceremony.

Leon was handsomely dressed in a dark blue suit that he had bought at a regular store instead of his usual Death Row ensembles or something from the Goodwill. He wore a white on white shirt with a stunning dark blue shiny tie and black dress shoes.

"Like Tony's mobster," Vera said to Joe when she saw him, and giggled.

"You wouldn't laugh if you knew how much Carroll's Men Shop charged him for all of this." Joe whispered.

"But it's worth every penny! He looks marvelous. They both do." Vera's eyes were already tearing.

When the ceremony was over and Joe had snapped some pictures with his Christmas gift camera from Vera, they all took off their flowers and handed them to Vera so they wouldn't crush them when they put on their own heavy coats.

"Now the fun begins," said Leon as he smiled broadly at Vera and Joe while twisting his new wedding ring around his finger with excitement.

"Yes," added Vivian, "we have a few surprises for you too!"

"To start with," said Leon, "we're all going to lunch at the Palmer House!"

"Don't you need reservations?"

"You bet," said Leon. "They're all made."

"Whoa, this is shaping up to be some day!" Joe said as he grabbed his wife and herded them all to the elevator. "Maybe we should have made it the Drake and then I could have gone in like a real customer instead of a former employee."

"We want to talk to you about that too," said Leon as the elevator doors opened and he winked at his new bride.

By the time the elaborate and expensive lunch was over at the Palmer House, the four friends were sitting in the gorgeous second-floor lobby with its high-domed ceiling that resembled something Michelangelo could have painted. Vera and Joe were the new managers of the cleaners with an option to buy.

It had been something that both Leon and Vivian had seriously considered for a while, and it seemed the perfect time to offer them the position. Joe could finally leave the barber business and Vera could hire as many employees as she wanted, so she too could enjoy life a bit more. After all, neither Leon or Vivian needed the money. In fact, Vivian's taxman had advised her in January to start revising her income. He said that it wouldn't hurt to make a few losing investments to reduce her income. This idea couldn't have come at a better time.

Originally Vivian's idea was to be back at the cleaners in the early afternoon, take the Closed sign off the door and open for a few hours. But they had such a wonderful time downtown that they didn't get back until three, just ahead of the rush-hour traffic.

Besides, the emotions of the day had worn them all out and when the cab dropped Joe and Vera off at their place Leon had the driver take them back to Vivian's.

There were a few awkward moments between Leon and Vivian as they stood inside the door, until she started to laugh at how strange he looked standing there with his hat in his hand as though he would bolt at any minute.

"Now, really," she said, seductively, "whoever you are, stranger, stay awhile. It might get interesting." She glided her way across the floor, took his hat, and then his coat, laying them carefully on a chair. "Besides," she said, kicking off her heels, "I think there's something you need to see."

She led him into the bedroom, pulling him gently by his new tie."

"Hey now, lady, this is an expensive piece of clothing I'll have you know."

"Well then, maybe we should take it off." She undid his tie as she closed the door with her foot. "There's way too much light out there."

Leon looked around the dim room and realized that the bedroom curtains had been pulled shut and the covers on the bed had been pulled down. There were candles ready to light on the dresser, but later he didn't remember if they did or did not light them. At the time though, it made absolutely no difference at all.

When their flight left O'Hare Airport at 7:15 AM the next morning, they were ready for their weeklong Jamaican honeymoon, and Leon liked the idea of being married to Vivian—a lot!

Vera was beside herself with news and could hardly wait for the honeymooning couple to return.

Joe had already talked to his landlord about breaking his lease and found out that there was a notary public that wanted the space and that there would be no problem if Joe left. His landlord told him that he had been a very good renter the short time he had been there, and after all, he was only going across the street so if he needed him for anything, he knew where he would be.

By the time the taxi pulled up in front of the Band Box Cleaners & Laundry, the entire street was watching for them. Vera had mentioned the day of arrival just once at Nell's and it was up and down the entire block by the end of the day.

It was a strange sight for passers-by to see all the doors opened up and down the block waving to the Yellow Cab that pulled up. Vivian and Leon couldn't believe the reception and were glad that they couldn't make out the things people were yelling to them as the storeowners hooted and grinned.

Vivian was busy hugging Vera and Joe when Howard and Nell came through the front door at the same time.

"Welcome home, welcome home!" said Howard as he gave the bride a kiss, shook the groom's hand, and said that he came over to see if they had tans or not. "Just wondering how much time you actually spent out of your room!"

"Hush!" said Vivian as she eyed Sandy.

"Don't worry about me. I've got a clue."

"We probably saw more of Jamaica than most tourists," said Leon. "We ran into the daughter of one of Vivian's church friends who was there with the Peace Corps, so she showed us around the entire island and introduced us to lots of locals."

"It's a small world," said Nell. "I'm featuring coconut cream and banana cream pie all this week in honor of your honeymoon, so come on over later and get a slice on the house!"

"Thanks!" said Leon. He wondered briefly if Jamaica even grew coconuts.

"How's your sister working out?" Vivian asked Nell, pointedly more thoughtful than Leon.

"Pretty good. We've been so busy that we haven't had too much time to go sightseeing. But I promised her that as soon as this awful weather stops, we'd hire more people and spend some time touring the city. She wants to see it all, so I might have to hire a lot more employees." Nell sat on the sofa balancing some coffee and continued. "We're even thinking of doing like they do in other restaurants and turning our upstairs into a hall for parties. That Swedish restaurant in Andersonville seems to do real well with their upstairs room, so we've been talking about doing the same thing. Business is so good that we decided that if we're gonna do it, it better be soon. Neither of us is getting any younger."

No one asked her how her husband was because everyone's opinion was pretty much the same about him. She paused for breath and checked her watch. "That's not the time, is it? I've gotta go—congratulations!" Placing her cup on the counter, Nell added over her shoulder, "Don't forget to stop in for that pie." She headed for the door, holding it open for a man with a large basket of clothes.

"Wow, what a busy place," he said. "I used to drive by here all the time and I never noticed it until you painted all the buildings. Somehow you've become one of the most popular blocks in the entire north side. Glad I caught you here; I stopped by the other day and you were closed."

Vera said, "You're lucky we're open today. We have so much business now that we have to close periodically to get our work done. Pretty soon you'll have to make a reservation."

"Really? Wow." He left clutching his receipt in his hand.

"That was cruel." Vivian laughed.

"Well, it's partly true. We are almost busier than we can handle. We definitely are the most popular couple of blocks in the area. Oh Leon, I almost forgot, you have a phone message. Some guy called a couple of days after you left. He left his name and number and asked you to call. I left the paper in the till."

He crossed the room and pressed a key that made the drawer spring open and reached under the cash for his message. "Oh no, not him again," he said to no one in particular. "Not the guy from the *Tribune*!"

"I wonder if he's calling about Tony's guy."

"What guy?" asked Leon as he stuffed the paper into his pocket.

"You know that guy who used to be his boss that got killed by the mob?"

"Do they know that for sure? Have you talked to Tony lately?"

"Nobody's seen Tony for a couple of weeks and from what I understand, Steve's taken some time off of work, so Johnny hasn't talked to him for a while."

"Looks like we came home in the nick of time, Mrs. McKee."

"I think you're right, Mr. McKee. But until we can get the gang together to find out more, what do you say we go home and unpack? We've brought that delicious Jamaican Blue Mountain coffee for everyone," she told the crowd. "So, Sandy, why don't you arrange a night for a get together? Invite the regulars and we'll all get caught up on what's going on." She turned to Leon. "Did you ever tell Pete you were getting married?"

"I completely forgot."

"I thought so. Invite him too and, I suppose, Sarah?"

"I would imagine so, but I'll check and get back to you. Is there a better night?"

"Nope, now that this place belongs more or less to Vera and Joe, we have no time constraints."

By the look on Sandy's face Vivian could tell that she didn't know about the change in management. "See what you get when you work all the time. You really have to get out more and find out what's happening!"

"Evidently! I think there's a lot I don't know. But I'll find out what night is good for everybody and let you know. By the way, where do you want us to meet?"

Vera interrupted, "How about here again? This seems to be the ideal place."

"Only if you're sure you don't mind," said Vivian.

"Mind? We'd be honored to carry on the tradition!"

"Good. Then it's settled. Do your best, Sandy, and let us all know."

Everyone, except for the new shop managers, Vera and Joe, was gone within ten minutes. The shop grew quiet once again. There was only the gentle hum of the washers, the sweet smell of the fabric softener, and music from WMBI playing softly in the background. It was now Joe's turn to sit comfortably in the lounge chair and to sigh with contentment.

TWENTY-SIX

After the initial greetings were made, the wedding was discussed in depth, and Vera and Joe were announced as the new managers, the conversation turned to Tony. The story he told riveted his audience.

"It was unbelievable. The guy died in the beginning of February, and here it is almost a month later and we just had the reading of the will two days ago."

"Did they ever discover if he died of natural causes, or was he really bumped off?"

"You've got to stop reading crime novels, Sandy. He died of a heart attack."

"Oh." She sounded disappointed. "Really?"

"I don't know how that story got started, but none of it's true. He wasn't bumped off by anybody, much less the mob. Now, I didn't say that a lot of his customers didn't have mob connections, but they didn't kill him. It was a heart attack, plain and simple."

"Are they sure? Did they do tests?" Sandy continued hopefully.

"Give it up, girl! And yes, they did do an autopsy. His wife wanted one, so they did it and it was a heart attack."

"Fine," she grumbled.

"But here comes the interesting part, and the part that worried us the most. Ever since Steve and I got into the apartment upstairs we've kind of made a business out of it. We met a few people during our street days who still hadn't caught a break like we had, so we offered them lodging for free if they'd use the place to get back on their feet and start to find themselves again."

"We were up to about six guys when our landlord died," added

Steve.

"Yeah, we made sure they were very quiet and very good so we wouldn't get caught and kicked out, but when the boss died, we were sure we were going to be busted."

"Don't stop there," said Steve. "Wait till you hear this next part!"

"So anyway, here we are, the eight of us living upstairs, and the boss dies. We're all holding our breath. The restaurant opened again after the funeral and was busier than ever. Life just sort of went on as usual. When we wrote out our rent check I'd just take it down and put it in the till as usual. Well, last week I overheard some of the family—I think they were family, anyway—saying that the will was finally going to be read. I didn't give it any thought until one of them came in the kitchen with a piece of paper for me. It said that I was to be at the reading, and it would take place two days later at the restaurant."

"Cool, what happened?"

"This is where it really gets weird. I tried not to think if I was getting anything because I didn't want to get my hopes up. Mr. A already rented Steve and me the apartment upstairs for a song, and I figured that it was enough already. But I showed up because I got the letter. I figured that someone would realize their mistake and say 'thanks for coming' and maybe I'd get a cup of coffee, find out how much I owed for back rent, and that would be it. Then the lawyer started reading the will. I couldn't believe the amounts of money that were being given to the heirs!"

"What kind of money are we talking?" asked Pete.

"Big money—several million or two here, a million there. His wife got all their houses and most of the cars and enough cash to run them for the rest of her lifetime, even if she lives to be three hundred. His kids all got stuff and money, even the maids and chauffeurs got a half a million dollars each. Finally he read my name. I was instantly paralyzed with fear; I don't know why. When he read out in that irritating monotone of his that I got the restaurant and everything in it, I was dumbfounded. He went on to read a few more, but I didn't hear a thing after my name. What amazed me is that no one gasped when the lawyer said what I got. It was like they just took it for granted."

"So, you own a restaurant?" asked Howard.

"Yep, impossible to believe, isn't it?"

"So what now?" asked Leon.

"I have no idea. It didn't come with any money to operate it and we've managed to stay open because the head cook promised to stay until I found someone else. His name is Vincent something or another. I can't pronounce it, even though I've finally seen it in print."

"Are you gonna stay in business?" asked Johnny.

"I really like the business, but with my lack of experience I doubt that I could run it for long, especially if Vincent really does go back to the old county."

"So, what are your plans?" asked Vivian as she walked around the group pouring more coffee.

"Steve and I have been talking and we're thinking of selling."

"Selling? Why would you do that? I thought you liked owning a restaurant." Sandy said.

"No, I said I liked the job and everything it entailed, not the owning of it. Besides we've got what we think is a good idea."

"Well, don't keep us in suspense, tell us!" Pete was practically yelling. Sarah put her hand on his to calm him down.

"Wait a minute," Leon said. "What's that I see on your finger? Is that an engagement ring?"

Sarah gazed lovingly at Pete.

"You didn't think you were the only one who thought marriage was a good idea, did you?" said Pete, grinning.

"So when's the wedding?" Sandy asked before anyone else could.

"We haven't set a date, but we're thinking sometime this fall," answered Sarah softly.

"Once again, Mazel tov!" said Howard. "The only two left around here that are still unhitched seem to be Sandy and Johnny! Any plans?"

"Not us," Sandy said, taking Johnny's hand. "We're happy at this point to be just going together. We're both going to college...well, I'm going for the first time and Johnny's going to be going back to college here in the city to finish his degree in business. Either way, we've both got a few years to go before we can get serious."

"Good luck," said Howard. "Lois and I were going to wait too and ended up getting married when we were sophomores in college. Then she dropped out to have our first child and I think that she's resented it ever since." He looked furtively across the street. "I don't think she's ever said it outright, but it still bothers her."

"Why doesn't she go back now?" Vivian asked. "It's never too late to do what you want." She gave Leon a tender look.

"Here, here!" he said.

"I don't think she's ever considered going back, but that's a great idea. She has no excuse now; the store's doing real well and we've brought on new employees. I'll bring it up. If she doesn't go for the idea, I'll tell her it was your idea, Vivian, not mine!"

"Fine with me! Sometimes we have to be almost forced out of our self-made comfortable lives to get on with things...and that, children," she added in a schoolteacher voice, "is your life lesson for today. Now, please finish the story!"

"Right," Steve continued. "Johnny and I were just talking about how Tony and I were taking in a few guys to help them get a leg up on life and how most of them were doing really well right from the start. One guy didn't work out and we asked him to leave, but the majority of them really appreciate the help. We got to wonder if there weren't more that wouldn't turn down help if they could get it. Granted, there are a lot of loonies out there—lots on drugs and alcohol—and you've got to know that some are so far into their bottles or drugs that they'll never get out. But there are also guys like Johnny here, and Tony and I, who found ourselves on the streets because of poor life choices. Johnny dropped out because his parents were always pushing him to be something he didn't want to be; he kind of developed the 'I'll show them' mentality."

Johnny nodded.

"Tony's wife spent them into the street, then left him when they lost everything. And I got way ahead of myself as a trader. Not only did I lose my own money; I lost money for my clients. The court let me off relatively easy with community service and I had to pay back the money. As a result, I'm forever banned from trading anything. I'm still working on repaying the money."

There was complete stunned silence while Steve gave his narrative. Very few who were present knew any of this and it confirmed what

182

Leon had always thought: everybody had a story. There were things in everybody's life that they would rather keep quiet.

Tony took up the narrative. "So when all this happened at the restaurant, we were actually thinking of getting some corporate sponsors (Steve's still got lots of connections downtown) and turning the entire restaurant into a kind of hotel for the homeless. It would be a place with clean beds, individual rooms (small, but private), washers and dryers, and a kitchen for meals."

"It would give guys a place to start again, and another thing that most people take for granted—an address," added Steve.

"What do you mean, 'an address'?" asked Howard, fascinated.

"You can't get anywhere without an address. You can't apply for a job or welfare or a driver's license, nothing. Obviously you can't get mail either—no letters from home, no notice from anyone official...no junk mail," Steve added playfully.

"I never thought of that," Leon said.

"Me neither," added Vivian. "Who would ever think that something simple like an address could mean so much when you don't have one?"

"Go on," said Vera.

Tony began again. "Well, we tossed the idea around one evening with Johnny, who probably only got an hour of sleep that night before he had to get up for work. We talked far into the night discussing ideas. And one of the things that we were thinking of doing was to 'rent' out only the upstairs and keep the restaurant going downstairs to pay for everything and to feed the guys."

"That was just one of the things we discussed." Steve had jumped in. "We also thought about selling the restaurant and buying a building somewhere and using the money to run the place until we ran out of cash."

"That was not a good idea," said Johnny. "Evidently Steve didn't learn a thing from going broke in the market!" He punched Steve's arm good-naturedly.

"Hey, at least I didn't run away from rich parents just to show them what for."

"Okay guys, keep going. What did you finally decide?" said Leon, anxious to find out the outcome.

"Nothing," Tony said. "At least nothing yet. We all decided that we aren't the poster boys for good thinking, so we've decided to weigh each option and when we all agree, we'll act."

"All?" asked Howard and Leon at the same time.

"Yeah," said Steve. "The three of us decided to form a kind of corporation and see if there truly is strength in numbers. Maybe with three of us spending Tony's money, we'll do a better job than just letting him have all the fun!"

Vivian, who had been mostly sitting quietly and listening, then said "First of all, congratulations, Tony. I can't say I've ever known a restaurant owner personally."

"What about Nell?" asked Leon.

"Nell's is more of a coffee shop. Annetties is a bona fide full restaurant. Anyway, congratulations. Not only are your intentions wonderful, but banding together with these other two is a great idea. Just make sure it doesn't come between you and ruin this wonderful friendship that you've found. As you get older, you'll appreciate truly good friendships more than almost anything."

"Okay, lady." Leon put his arm across his wife's shoulders. "Enough advice. Not that it isn't good," he continued quickly, "it's just that it's getting late and tomorrow's another day."

"You sound like Scarlet O'Hara in *Gone With the Wind*!" laughed Vera as she pushed against her husband in order to get up from the sofa. "We've got to go home too. Thanks for everything! Good night! Oh, wait a minute—we're the managers here now. Everybody leave so we can lock up and go home!"

TWENTY-SEVEN

Everyone was so busy that it was the end of April before they all got together again. Vivian and Leon surprised everyone by going on another honeymoon. They called it a vacation, but everyone knew better.

The One Stop Coffee Shop did indeed hire more help. Nell found out that the local culinary school would let their students work for her for college credits because it was giving them valuable work skills and added to their learning experience, so she put an expensive ad in the Sunday papers with the information about their new hall for rent. The very next day she received several calls.

Nell's husband finally admitted that he had a drinking problem and signed himself into a clinic to get help. The program ran three months. He was already a month into it and doing better than Nell expected.

Nell's sister, Betsy, had a boyfriend. One of the neighborhood guys that came in every morning for breakfast began coming back in for lunch each day too, and it was he who was taking Betsy around showing her Chicago. They had made it through all the major museums already with just the smaller ones like the Doll Museum, the Chicago Historical Society, and Gelssner House to go. She told her sister that she had never been happier in her life.

Nell told her to see if she could get the guy's driver's license or social security number so she could have one of her cop friends run his history to see if he was who he said he was. Betsy believed that this made her sister the quintessential Chicagoan. Naturally she said no. She insisted she'd use her country common sense and Nell said she'd probably be sorry.

What Nell didn't know was that Betsy was so lonely she would almost prefer to have her heart broken by an exciting man to a dull life of endless cooking, cleaning, and sleeping.

Pete and Sarah were very much in love and found that spending time with Howard and Lois helped through some sticky situations for them. Where Howard was the Jewish one in that relationship, it was Sarah who was Jewish, and even in the sixties her family was making it very hard for her to continue seeing Pete. Suddenly they found that Lois had a tender side, even though it was tinged with some bitterness.

Tony, Steve, and Johnny were spending a lot of time together and Sandy was making graduation plans and also helping with the spring windows, using lots of pastels and larger-than-life flowers. She was still waiting to see if she'd been accepted into The Harrington College of Design on West Madison. It was only two blocks from the city's center of State and Madison. The school was highly touted by Frank, her boss, who went there himself. If she got a two-year undergraduate degree, he would put her on full-time and make her part of Fields' staff. He told her several times that she had talent.

Easter came in the middle of April, so Leon and Vivian decided that they would try to get everyone together either before the holiday or immediately after. After seemed to work better for everyone.

Most of the gang had never been to the apartment, and they were all surprised at how big it was and how beautifully furnished it was.

"My husband—oh gracious, excuse me, I mean my *first* husband— traveled for years for an oil company, so all of the unusual pieces that you see are the ones he brought back, like this leather vase." She picked up a large urn to show them how lightweight it was.

"What do you think they kept in there?" asked Sandy. "It doesn't seem like it would hold anything liquid."

"I have absolutely no idea and neither did my husband. He saw it and thought it was clever and bought it. I think that the Arabs probably make them by the hundreds for the tourists to buy."

"I still think it's cool!"

When everyone arrived, Vera helped Vivian serve the thick slices of key lime pie and the last of the Jamaican coffee.

"I hope it's okay," said Vivian, looking doubtful. "It's been a long time since I made a pie. In fact, it's been a long time since I've really cooked anything."

"I think you're a great cook!" interrupted her husband.

"Well, no one beats my take-out chicken from Nell's, that's for sure."

"How come you don't cook?" asked Sandy after biting into her piece.

Vera looked at Sandy and asked, amazed, "And just when would she have time to cook? If you remember, every minute the store was open, she was there."

"Oh... yeah, I just kind of thought that you would be the type of person that cooked. My mother never does, but then my mother is never home. Or when she is, she smokes a lot so she won't be hungry. She says she needs to watch her figure."

"Come on, sweetie, let it go. Those are her problems and not yours. Besides, you won't be there for long." Johnny winked at his steady.

Great, thought Vivian. *They* are *going to get married.* But to them she asked with a lightness she didn't feel, "So what exactly does that mean: 'you won't be there for long'?"

"Well, it's part of our news." When Johnny said that, he didn't look at Sandy, but faced Steve and Tony.

Steve started, "It's like this. We finally figured out what we are going to do. Well, actually, it wasn't just us. Johnny's father helped a lot."

"Did you say Johnny's father?" asked Leon before anyone else could. "I thought that was kind of a closed subject."

Vivian gave her husband a dirty glance for changing the subject from the possible marriage news.

Johnny took up the narrative. "I thought it was, too, after the talk I had with him. But my dad called the Goodwill one day and left a message for me to call him."

Vivian interrupted, "Leon, did you ever call that *Tribune* reporter back?"

"Nope."

"Are you going to?"

"Nope."

She was going to ask why not but decided that she would grill him later when they were alone. "So," she said to Johnny, "you were saying?"

"My father wanted to get together. We met at his office and he had lunch sent in so we ate there. I was surprised how different he seemed. At first I honestly thought that he might be dying and wanted to make things right with his only son."

"Was he?" asked Vera.

"Hardly! He was more alive than ever! It seems like he and my mom went on this church marriage retreat (needless to say, he went kicking and screaming, but he went). My mom told him that she was tired of being in the marriage by herself and it was lonely without him."

"Whoa, that must have been tough to hear."

"I guess it was. He told me during lunch that he knew that he was a selfish man and he used the excuse that he had to keep his job first in order to keep food on the table. The marriage seminar pointed out that this was an excuse to do and be what he wanted with no thought to his family, so he had to make some hard decisions."

"Did he?"

"Evidently he did, or at least he's trying to, because the day I saw him, he was almost the dad I used to have before he got so high-and-mighty. He even apologized to me for trying to squeeze me into his self-made mold. I couldn't believe it."

"So did you?" Vivian asked.

"No, I didn't believe him at first. Talk is cheap and I've seen my dad get interested in me only to use it against me later. I went really slow and figured that if he was serious about reconnecting, he'd call me again."

"Did he?" Vivian was truly interested.

"Yeah, he did. It surprised me and even made me a little suspicious. I thought that he might be doing some sort of penance and until I was his friend again, he wouldn't pass the class. I was so distrusting of his real motives that I called my mom and ended up talking to her for several hours. She said to give him another chance and yes, she thought that the change was genuine. Then she said that even if it was short-

188

lived, that now would be a good time to get his help on anything I needed—from college money to a 'real' place to stay."

"A 'real' place to stay!" sputtered Pete. "What a slap in the face!"

"I know. I didn't tell you that part because my mom, as nice as she is, is a bit of a snob herself. Anyway, he did call again, and this time he told me to pick the place for lunch. I purposely picked the lunch counter at Walgreen's to see if he was serious about going back to being a real guy. He didn't miss a beat when he said he'd be there right at the time we agreed on. I almost missed him because I started watching this guy demonstrate the Veg O'Matica and it was really interesting. He slices a tomato so thin that you could use it to feed a family of four for six months!" Seeing their amazed faces he added, "Not really."

"I thought you were serious," said Sandy, "Hey, Vivian, this pie is wonderful. See, you can cook!"

"Well, at least I can bake."

Leon gave them both a withering glance before he said to Johnny, "Go ahead. What happened then?"

"Wait a minute," interrupted Vivian again, "Does anyone want more coffee?"

"No, they don't," said Leon. "Sit down and shush!"

She sat.

"Go ahead," Leon said as he stared pointedly at Vivian.

She smiled.

"Well, when he asked me what I had been doing I filled him in on the fact that I had inherited a restaurant."

Vivian was about to speak, but Leon gave her the look and she kept quiet.

Vera picked up the ball, though. "You mean to say that you never told your father about the restaurant being yours?"

"I didn't think it was time. Besides, you remember that I didn't trust him the first time. I thought if he knew about Annetties that he would automatically step in and decide what I should do."

"Did you even tell your mother?" asked Vera as Joe gave her a withering look. "What?" She glared at Joe. "Don't you want to know if he told his mother?"

Before Joe could respond Johnny continued. "No, I didn't want to tell her something that could possibly come between them and hurt this new relationship they had going."

"Very wise," added Vivian.

Johnny smiled. "I'm not as dumb as I look. Neither of them knew a thing, and when I told my father there at the lunch counter I don't think he believed me at first. After I told him the entire story he said something that I never thought I'd hear him say."

"What was that?" Leon was caught up in the story.

"He *asked* me what my plans were. He didn't automatically tell me what to do; he asked me if I had any plans. I told him what the guys and I had come up with and he said that if that was the path I wanted to take that he would be happy to meet with all of us and work out a plan...but only if we wanted him to."

"Needless to say," said Steve, "we were all surprised and a little apprehensive. We knew about him from Johnny and we weren't too sure that we wanted him involved, but he's a very successful businessman and knows what he's doing. So we thought, *Why not? We don't have to take his advice, but it would be interesting to see what he'd say.*"

Steve paused long enough for almost everyone to ask almost simultaneously, "What did he say?"

"He said that our idea was basically sound, but it needed a bit of work. If we wanted him to contact 'his people' to lay out a plan, he would, and he would get back to us when it was done. I think Johnny was about to ask him what it would cost to do the plan, so his father hurried and said that it was free of charge. We could consider it his contribution, whether we used it or not."

Johnny took up the tale. "About a week later, his office paged me at the hospital and said that the plan was ready. Would I like to come pick it up, or should they send it? I said, 'Send it,' and it came by messenger an hour later. I thought she meant by the U.S. mail and it would take a few days. Needless to say, I was floored when it showed up shortly after lunch. That's when I began to realize how out of touch I was with real business. It did make quite an impression at the hospital, though. It had everybody talking."

"Johnny called Steve and me to tell us that he got the plans, but we had another party at the restaurant and we had to wait a day. I told him to open it and read it, but he said he'd wait until we could all see it at the same time. We arranged to get together the next day in the morning, seeing it was Saturday and I was the only one working, but not till later. We sat down and looked at what came. I must say, I was impressed."

"I think we were all impressed," added Steve. "Not only was it professionally done, but it made sense; even we could see that."

"So what did it say?" Pete asked. Sarah was getting tired and she had her head on his shoulder.

"Well, after all the verbiage and the legal clauses it mainly said that we should keep the restaurant to fund the other business we wanted to start. That way, if business number two failed, we'd still have business number one."

"So how do you feel about running the place now?" asked Pete.

"Better. Much better. Vincent decided that if he got a sizeable raise that he could manage to stay in the United States a bit longer and maybe send for his girlfriend. I didn't even know he had one back there, but once he decided to stay he told me about her and that he had heard that another guy was interested in her. With the extra money he decided to make the move, so he cabled her, whatever her name is, and asked her to marry him. He's going over to get married, so we're closing the restaurant that week for cleaning. By the time he gets back, we should be up and running."

"You must feel better about running the place," Vera said from the kitchen, where she was cutting the other pie.

"Most days I am, but special parties still terrify me. I'm trying to convince Steve to quit at the hospital and come to work for me."

"I tell him he's crazy! Why would I give up an eight-hour day job that runs only Monday through Friday? Besides, it's bad enough that I live with him, I don't have to work with him too."

"Thanks pal."

"Don't mention it."

"I won't."

It was good-natured banter, but the story wasn't finished.

Tony started the narrative again. "Not only was the plan

financially sound, but there was also a sheet from a realtor clipped onto the report. Evidently Johnny's father knew people in the real estate business and they had some property that had been on the market a long time. He must have thought we'd be interested in seeing it because there was a short handwritten note saying that this price was excellent and might work for us, but only if they had nowhere else in mind."

"Where was it?" asked Sandy

"Better yet, what was it?" asked Vera.

Tony looked around the room to make sure he had everybody's attention before he began again. "It's an old armory over on the northwest side. The three of us went over and checked out the location and it isn't bad. From the outside the building doesn't look too bad either. It's one of those buildings that have the curved roof...like a half circle from side to side.

"We poked around the place and thought that it might be doable. The bus even stops on the next block. So now we're going to call Johnny's father. All three of us will meet with him and see where we're going."

"Well, I wish you well," said Howard getting up to leave. "Stop in and see me when you guys have time. I'd like to talk to you too."

"You got it! Hey, Vivian, thanks for the pie! It was really great."

She hardly had time to dry her hands and come out of the kitchen before everyone was leaving and saying good night. When all the company was gone and as she was picking up the few remaining cups in the living room, she asked her husband, "What do you think of their idea? It's the oddest idea I've ever heard."

Leon came up behind her, took the cups from her hands, and placed them back on the coffee table and took her in his arms. "I have another idea that might interest you then."

"Oh, yes?"

She led him to the bedroom. This time they lit the candles.

TWENTY-EIGHT

Leon woke early the next day with one thing on his mind—the Memorial Day party. It was already the end of April and he only had five weeks to line up a band, get all the permits from City Hall, and make his annual trip from store to store with invitations.

The neighborhood had grown so much and he was so excited to get to know all the new people that he'd decided not to wait until Labor Day for their annual bash, but to move it up to Memorial Day. They had met the Andersons next door at the flower shop but the shop was so busy, they really hadn't had time to sit down and learn anything about them. All they did know was that they were a young couple in their thirties and they were both professional floral designers. Leon had teased them that they missed "their neighborhood" by about three or four blocks. When they didn't get it, he had to explain that Andersonville, the home of the original Swedish neighborhood with shops and residents in all, was only a few blocks down Clark Street and with them having the last name of Anderson. When he realized that they weren't getting it, he finally gave up trying to be clever and let it go. Evidently it would take these Iowans a while to understand Chicago humor, or at least Leon's humor.

He sat at the dining room table and made the blueprint for the invitation. Last year they had handwritten all the invitations, but this year they were giving out three times as many, so he was taking up Sandy's offer to have a friend downtown do the printing, but only as long as he could write the words himself and make it friendly and not formal. He thought that as long as they were going to have them professionally done maybe they could include a picture of the Three Painted Ladies on the front on the invitations. First he'd wait and see what the price was, though.

Vivian still thought that the number of people they were inviting was way too large and wanted it to be pretty much the same people who had attended the first party. "After all," she reasoned while they were discussing the guest list, "we are not going to have enough room in that one empty lot. It was crowed last time with a lot fewer people." She wondered what it would be if he indeed tripled the number of people.

She finally gave in because she saw that his mind was made up and he was doing all the legwork before and after the celebration. So as soon as he was finished with the wording, Vivian checked over the copy as he glanced down onto the street to the cleaners.

"I still find it a funny feeling being up here. You can see everything going on—in the street, at the cleaners. It's kind of like being a Peeping Tom."

"Uh-huh," she answered absentmindedly as she read through the invitations and was making a few corrections with her pen.

"I still can't believe that I never caught you up here looking out the window."

"Looking out the window at what?" she wanted to know.

"Well, at me, or at least at your store."

"You are a funny man. Believe me, you could sit there all day staring down on the street and see close to nothing. There's very little of interest down there. And you'll notice, Mr. Nosy Bones, you can see the front of the store, but not inside far enough to see where we stand to take in the wash."

"So you have looked!"

"In twenty years you might say that I have looked a time or two. But if you don't get going, you're not going to be at Fields in time to catch Sandy on her break so you can give her the invitation copy. Tell you what. Seeing that I am such a wonderful person who has agreed to all the extra people we're inviting, I'll even let you take my car...if you promise not to ding it up."

"I can't promise any dings, but it's a deal!" He grabbed the keys off the key holder by the door and was gone in a flash, which was good because Vivian had a phone call to make and she did not want him anywhere around to hear it.

She waited by the kitchen window peering down into the alley until she saw him back the Mustang out and start toward the street before she dialed.

The voice on the other end of the line answered, "*Chicago Tribune*, please hold."

As she waited, she struggled to open the piece of paper that she'd found in Leon's wallet. He had it in there so long that it was permanently creased. The voice came back on the line and asked, "Who are you waiting for?"

"Yes, thank you, I'd like to speak to—" and then she mentioned the name of the reporter that was written on the paper, hoping he still worked there.

"One moment please, I'll connect you."

Before Vivian had time to say thank you, she had been put on hold again and was waiting anxiously for someone to answer. She knew that this may not be the right thing to do, but this man had been calling for a long time, and if Leon wouldn't call back, she would. Whatever it was, she would handle it. She would handle anything that hurt him or worried him or made him sad. As she waited for someone—anyone—to pick up the phone she only half listened to the 'Muzak' playing to keep her content until someone finally answered.

"Hello," someone finally said from the other end of the line.

The resulting conversation was very interesting, to say the least, and Vivian arranged to go downtown two days later to meet with the reporter face-to-face.

Vera was busy interviewing a woman when Vivian slipped into the shop. Vivian almost never worked anymore unless the shop was very busy. They had already hired one woman named Helen, who was somewhere in her midthirties, and they didn't think that she'd stay. She had a lot of family problems with her children and a husband who came and went, so they decided it wouldn't be a bad idea to interview a few more. They certainly needed another employee, even if Helen did end up staying.

When the woman left, Vera came into the back and sat down briefly with Vivian and Joe.

"I was just telling Vivian what a welcome change this job is," said Joe. "I thought I'd live and die a barber.I never expected to end up like this."

"And you're an amazing cleaner employee yourself!" His wife smiled at him fondly. "He's even fixed that last dryer Leon started working on a month ago."

Vivian leaned forward. "I don't mean to change the subject, but I've got to talk to you two. I just got off the phone with that reporter from the *Tribune* who's been trying to get in touch with Leon for six months. You'll never guess what he wanted to know!"

The bell on the door jangled and all three let out a sigh of frustration.

"I'll go," said Vera.

No sooner had the customer left and the door opened again. Two more people came in. Vera called from the front for someone to come help. After a twenty-minute rush they were finally ready to sit back down when Leon walked in and asked whose turn it was to get lunch.

Vivian passed close by to Joe and whispered in his ear, "Don't say a thing about the phone call" as Leon walked over to the fridge and opened it.

Over a maddening lunch of sandwiches from the ingredients in the fridge, knowing there was no way to get rid of Leon, Vera tried to make light conversation. "Did you hear that Nell's husband's home?"

"No, I hadn't. How's he doing?" Vivian seemed to be the only one interested in the news.

"It's hard to tell. One thing good though. He's at the coffee shop every day now."

"I suppose he's getting under her feet."

"I don't think so. You know Betsy's gone, don't you?"

"Gone? What do you mean gone? Gone where? Back home to what was it—Iowa, Indiana? Wait a minute! When you said gone, you don't mean she died, do you?"

"Good night, no, she didn't die! She is gone because she got married and moved to her husband's hometown of Gary."

"Indiana?"

"Yes, Gary, Indiana."

"Did she marry that guy who was showing her the town or someone else? How did I miss all this?"

"It was the one that was showing her around town. If you two would stick around more, you might find out all the news in the neighborhood."

Vivian looked over at the men who were talking to each other. "Don't either of you want to know any of this?"

"Not particularly. It's more women's stuff than men's," said Leon as he checked out the fridge for something else to eat.

Before Vivian could ask exactly what men's stuff was, Vera continued. "I heard that Nell and Betsy had a bit of a falling out. Betsy said there was no way she could do all the extra work that was required to cater special events upstairs, and Nell said that now that she's put all the money into remaking the large room that 'inhaled' money, they had no choice but to open."

"What happened to the next-to-free help from the college kids?"

"I guess that didn't pan out because this time of year they're all looking for full-time jobs that pay."

"Great, so now what?"

"I have no idea. There's speculation that Nell's husband might have to kick in. Instead of sitting at the counter drinking coffee and talking to people, he might actually have to get up and go to work."

"Or start drinking again," Joe slipped in.

"Joe," Vivian said disapprovingly, "that wasn't very nice."

"Not nice, but true." He glanced at his wife. "But you know good and well there was a time when things got overwhelming and I slipped into the bottle."

Everyone sat in stunned silence as he haltingly continued.

"Most of our kids didn't give us any trouble," he explained to Vivian and Leon, who sat with astonished faces. "Well, hardly any trouble. But that last one would have driven anyone to drink."

"Trouble?" asked Leon, finally getting totally involved and

wondering if he had a right to ask that question.

Evidently Joe wasn't bothered because he continued. "Trouble wasn't the word for it. If there was something stupid that he could do, he did it, from little on. Every chance he got to shoot himself in the foot, he did. He's lucky he didn't end up going to prison."

"Now Joe, it wasn't that bad," interjected his wife.

"Pretty near."

"What finally happened?" Vivian quietly asked Joe while looking at Leon as if to say, *Should I have asked that?*

"What finally happened is that he got in way over his head with some punk kids and they all landed in jail for robbery. He says to this day that it was a stupid spur-of-the-minute thing. They had been drinking and ran out of beer and decided that the easiest way to get more was to take it from a grocery store. They got caught before they reached their car. Our son stole a six-pack of beer like he thought the plan was, but the other three guys had a bottle of the hard stuff under each of their jackets. For two of the the guys it was their second and third offense and they did more time than our son. He only got thirty days for a combination of the robbery and being legally drunk, plus restitution, but it cured him. Jail absolutely scared him silly."

"Good," said Vivian before she knew she said it. "No, I'm sorry, I didn't mean—"

"No, I not only understand your comment, but Vera and I thoroughly agree. We had finally realized that there was nothing more we could do. All the kind things we did, that the other kids appreciated, he took for granted. After the jail time he came out a different person. When he first went in, one of the cops took us aside and gave us some advice that he said we listen to or not. He said he'd seen this kind of kid lots of times before and the best thing for us to do is to not come for a while. Let him 'stew in his own juices' for a few weeks to think things through. He also said that we might want to attend this class for parents so we could get some help to hold our marriage together. This kind of thing can be very hard on a relationship, even a good one, because you find yourself quietly blaming the other person."

"It wasn't easy," Vera added, "but we realized that it was time to start listening to somebody else when it came to raising our own

198

children. Even with the classes, that's when Joe started drinking."

"My feelings swung back and forth between feeling like a failure as a father and not deserving this because I had been a good father. I didn't even feel like a very good husband because I thought Vera blamed me for the kid ending up that way. I beat myself up for a long time thinking it was somehow my fault. As you can see, even though I was going to the classes, I really didn't believe the stuff they were telling us. I was sure that it was my fault and believe me, it wasn't easy to accept that it was a decision that our son made, despite everything we tried to do for him: he, alone, was responsible for his own actions. The alcohol lessened the guilt, until the next day. Then I felt even worse because I had now proven that I was a lousy husband and father and that I was quickly becoming a drunk."

The room grew quiet and thankfully no one came into the shop with their cleaning. As they listened to the washers run and the dryers hum for a bit, Joe finally continued, "Vera should have been nominated for sainthood after that. It was bad enough that our son was being a jerk and breaking his mother's heart, but one night I realized that I was doing the same thing. I was no better and I was the adult in the situation. I quit then and there and never picked up a drink of any kind again. I apologized to my dear wife and we must have talked clear through the night. In an odd way, it was the best night we ever had."

Vera put her hand over her husband's. Both had tears in their eyes.

"So," said Joe, "there's always hope that Nell's husband will realize what he's got and make some better decisions because of it. Maybe I'll stop by someday soon and visit with him. I've never met him formally, but sometimes it's easier to talk to a stranger."

Sandy came by later in the day to say that not only had she been accepted to design school, but she was going to summer school too and it started three days after graduation. That way she would finish college even sooner. Vivian asked what her high school graduation party plans were and found out that she had none. It didn't surprise her any. Before

Sandy hurried out again, she left invitations for the commencement exercises on the table for everyone.

Joe pushed his invitation away with the comment, "I think I'll be sick that day. Have you ever been to one of these? They take hours! There must be four hundred kids in these graduating classes nowadays. When is it?"

"It's a Saturday," said Vera actually opening the invitation and reading it out loud. "Saturday afternoon, June 11, 1965, outside on the football field or in the field house if it rains at 2:00 PM."

"On the football field?" Leon was now thinking that the being sick ploy was pretty good. "Do you know how hot that's gonna be—a Saturday in the middle of June in an open field? I for one, hope it rains!"

"Now if you think you're going to get out of it, because it's going to be hot and long and boring, think again, mister!" said Vivian. "I think if you and I didn't show up, she would be greatly disappointed. Besides, maybe her mother will be there and we can finally meet her."

"I could care less if I ever met the woman," said Leon. "If I did, I'd probably end up having words with her. What she's done to that poor kid."

"So it sounds like you'll be going to see that poor kid graduate?" Vivian smiled at him. "Vera, why don't you and I plan a little party of our own for her? We'll find out what her plans are when she breezes though here again and we'll do something with just our gang."

"Sounds good to me," Vera said with a wink, "and while we're planning, we can discuss that *other* matter."

Vivian knew she meant the reporter and went along with the subterfuge by asking, "So what do you see of Debbie next door? Is she still going with Sam the deliveryman?"

Both men got up to leave—Joe to the front of the store and Leon to Death Row to get some stuff bagged up for Pete. He and Vivian had finally agreed that he could start getting rid of the oldest stuff and give it to Pete to sell. Leon had parked his old Caddie behind the store and would fill the trunk and backseat full to take over to the Goodwill before rush-hour traffic started...when the trip would be twice as long.

As soon as the guys were out of earshot, Vivian whispered the news to Vera. She didn't tell her everything in case she accidentally spilled the beans to anyone, but she gave her enough information to keep her in the loop. Vera was sitting there with a big smile of her face when Joe walked back into the room to say that the next interviewee was waiting in the front. He added, "What's up with you?"

She rose and ran a finger seductively across his shoulders as she passed. "Nothing."

TWENTY-NINE

The month of May was shaping up to be a scorcher. Even though it was only the second week, temperatures were already in the nineties and the Chicago beaches were full every day. Once school let out in June, every pool, beach, and park in the city would be packed and there would be fire hydrants all over the city turned on for neighborhood kids. Some turned on legally, some not.

The red geraniums that Vivian had planted in the urn she bought from the curb sale from Dennis's shop needed watering every day during the hot spell. They had placed the urn in front of the cleaners and it had stood there for almost two years now. Every time it caught her eye, she thought of him.

The dry cleaning business slowed down to a crawl, but the laundry business picked up.

"You could be coming out of a coma," said Vera as she folded a fresh-from-the-dryer batch of wash and was checking off each piece as she talked, "and know exactly what time of year it is just by looking at the type of wash people are bringing in. Look—" she held up a little jumper dress that maybe was the size to fit a two-year-old—"isn't this sweet?"

"Which reminds me," Joe added, peering down from on top of the ladder. He had been carefully greasing the track of the metal loop that the cleaning hung on as it made its way electronically to the front of the store and back to see if he could eliminate the maddening squeak. Vera said it sounded like they were squeezing cats in the back room. "Have you talked to Vivian about the kids?"

"Whose kids?" asked Vivian.

Joe stopped what he was doing and wiped his hands on a rag. "Our kids. We're getting kind of lonesome and thought that we might like to see a couple of them. Three of the kids and their families will be here in Chicago this summer for a visit, but our daughter, the one that lives on the farm, can't get away for a vacation, so we thought that we might like to drive out and see them."

"Any time in particular?"

"No, we thought we'd leave that up to you."

"Well, we're not very busy at all this time of year so I'd say that you could pick anytime between now and the end of July. Vera, do you think that Helen could be here alone?"

"I don't see why not. She's very capable and she's caught on quickly."

"Her family going to need her during the summer?"

"I don't think so. She was saying the other day that her kids love to go to Boy Scout camp each summer up in Wisconsin, so maybe we could coordinate our vacation with the camp schedule. She said that her husband has never taken her on a vacation, and from the sounds of it, he's not going to start this year."

"Well, that's a shame about her husband. Maybe you should tell her your mistress story."

"Come again?" said Joe with a puzzled look as he descended the ladder to pick up the rag he had dropped.

"It's nothing," Vera said, chuckling and waving her hand as if to dismiss the entire matter. "I'll let you know what we decide as soon as I know," she said to Vivian.

"I'll come in and help out when you're gone. It doesn't hurt for me to keep my hands in the business, and I wouldn't mind getting to know Helen better. Maybe I'll tell her about the mistress." Both women dissolved into laughter.

Joe simply shook his head and climbed back up onto the ladder.

"Great. I'll give Liz a call tonight," said Vera. "If we time it right, we can help bring some of the early garden stuff in and help her can it."

Joe groaned from his perch. "I forgot about that part."

"Has anybody gotten an update on the boys and their new venture?" Vivian placed another box on the table and continued folding.

"I don't think so," said Leon as he was heading out with his final load. "I'll ask Pete when I see him what he's heard."

"Don't be forever," Vivian called after him. "Remember the four of us are going out to the Flame for supper and if we don't get there early, we'll never get a seat. It amazes me that that place is still so busy even after raising their prices to $2.99!"

During supper Vera and Vivian talked graduation party and Joe and Leon talked baseball. Leon had already used one set of tickets for a Cubs home game and because Vivian had something going on at church, he took Joe. Joe had never really been a baseball fan, but he might be after the game.

"He might be sorry," said Leon one night as they took a walk around the neighborhood.

"Why's that?"

"Because 'once a Cubs fan, always a Cubs fan'. He's in for a lot of disappointment at least this year. The team is already doing lousy, but they'll be just where they need to be next year."

"But it's only a game," she said pointing to flowers in a window box on a very attractive house. "Isn't that attractive? What kind of flowers do you think those are?"

"What do you mean, only a game? I can tell that you know nothing about baseball, Why in 1947 the Cubs…."

Vivian knew it was going to be a long, one-sided conversation, so she mentally tried to remember to ask Vera if she knew about flowers and simply nodded and listened to him as he went on and on and on.

Because it was sports talk on one end of the restaurant table, Vera and Vivian knew they had the entire evening to talk to each other without interruption.

"Why don't we have a pre-graduation celebration at the Memorial Day party?" Vera asked. "We are going to have it on Sunday night this year and not Monday, right?"

"Definitely! But I don't think there are enough people there that know Sandy. She hasn't been around much for what, over six months or so."

"True. Are you thinking it should be just for the original group? Should we invite her mother?" Vera asked. "Should we make it a surprise or let her know?"

"I think we have to let her know because with her work schedule and school schedule, we will have to plan the party around her time available. And I don't think we should invite her mother, although it would be interesting to meet her."

"I hadn't thought of that. This might be harder than we thought to accomplish. No telling what the guys are doing and I would imagine that Tony still works nights."

"Say, have you heard anything about Pete and Sarah?" Vivian asked. "Have they set a date?"

"I haven't heard a word, but maybe Leon knows something. He spent awhile with Pete when he delivered the stuff from the back room."

"That's right, Leon," Vivian interrupted, "What did you find out this afternoon about the guys, and have Pete and Sarah set a wedding date yet?"

"Which question do you want answered first?" he teased.

"Either one, no, yes, oh, I don't care!"

"Well," he began maddeningly slow, "I didn't ask Pete about the wedding. I figured that he would tell us when it was time to tell us."

"Men!" said Vivian.

"Amen!" echoed Vera.

"Do you want to hear the rest of this or not?"

"Yes, Go on."

"Well, Pete didn't have a lot of time to talk, but he did say that the guys ended up deciding to do what Johnny's father suggested and keep the restaurant and buy the armory."

"Why would anybody sell an armory? Who even owns an armory?" asked Vivian.

"Isn't it the government?" queried Vera.

"Ladies…"

"Sorry," said Vera.

"Continue," added Vivian.

"Thank you very much. As I was saying, Johnny's father pitched in som cash as an investment. And get this—so did Steve's father and so did Howard!"

"Howard?"

"Howard. It seems like he and Lois have been doing well in the stock market and their business has really picked up, so they decided to invest in the new venture. They've become pretty good friends with Pete and Sarah and I guess they figured it was their contribution to the whole gang. It's becoming quite a little group too that's working on the project. Vivian and I have even put in a few coins."

"So when does all this happen?" asked Joe as he stabbed the last piece of steak on his plate.

"I guess it's already happened. They're getting some guy in to see what needs to be done to make rows of adjoining rooms in the main part of the building and then they have to expand the bathrooms and put in a laundry room and bumping up the kitchen a bit. I guess they've decided on using four-by-eight pieces of plywood for the individual room walls. That way they'll use two for the back and front of the room and three for each side, making it an eight-by-twelve room. I guess they're gonna cut a ranch-type window in the back of each unit for air circulation and of course, each unit will have a door in the front. The units will all be attached to each other like row houses, so they will share a common side wall and from what I understand, they are only going to have a main light in the middle of the room and no outlets."

"Why no outlets?" asked Vivian as she pushed her plate away.

"I guess the thought is, that way they eliminate anyone cooking in their rooms or having a loud radio or something, I don't know."

"I guess when you think of it, that makes sense; it's no telling what people would plug in and then forget to turn off. Maybe burn the place down," added Vera.

"The guys are hard at work and thoroughly focused and I think it's wonderful. Even if it should fail, which I hope it doesn't, this is an experience that they will never forget."

"I agree," said Joe. "Good for them, all of them." They raised their empty coffee cups and clinked them together.

206

"Now, how about pie?" said Leon, pulling Vivian's chair out for her. "I know just the place."

"No donuts?" asked Vera. "Amy Joy go out of business?"

"To be honest, if I never saw another donut in my life, it would be too soon."

"We'll see how long that lasts," said Vivian with a knowing wink.

"Probably as long as it takes for them to come out with another new flavor!" Laughed Vera as she followed the other three out the door.

THIRTY

Leon was disappointed that he couldn't get the mariachi band this year. When he stopped at the drugstore, Don and Maria were both there. As he sat in the back, visiting, he wondered why he didn't stop in more often. They told him that the band had broken up because two of the guys moved to California and the two guys who replaced them made the band so popular that they were booked solid most of the time. They did say that it was fine to use their empty lot again this year. Leon had never thought to ask and just assumed that it would be all right when he went to City Hall for the permits.

He remembered as he left that he needed to alert the police and wrote it down on the back of one of the invitations. They hadn't done that last year, and the cops showed up, but only to check. This year he would make sure they knew in advance.

He finally found someone who knew someone who played in a band, or his brother played in a band, or something. All he knew was he got a telephone number and once again, it was the only a suggestion that came with a telephone number.

This year they would need more tables and chairs because there were going to be lots more people. Howard said they'd need lots more Christmas lights too because last year it was kind of dark after the sun finally went down.

Leon remembered last year. Vivian had dragged him over to the laundry to tell him her secret of owning half the block. It had been Howard who had interrupted with that one hundred-cup coffeepot, asking if they could plug it in the front part of the store, so she kept her secret awhile longer. Things certainly had changed since then. In fact, as he walked the block, he thought a lot about the events of his new life. He never realized before that this was now the only life that he felt he had ever lived. It seemed like he had been here for a lifetime, a wonderful lifetime. How could he have made so many friends in such a short time? In the fifty years he had lived his other life, he hadn't made even a fraction of the friends he had now. He hadn't even known his own neighbors!

There wasn't a shop or an office in a three-block area each way that didn't get an invitation. He even slipped a few in the mailboxes attached to the houses near the end of the blocks, even though he thought that someone had told him it was illegal to use a mailbox for anything else but stamped U.S. mail.

He had never even stepped foot in the office of the new optometrist that was above the record store across the street and that had only been there four or five months. He was so impressed with the place, he promptly made appointments for both himself and Vivian. The neighborhood really had changed. All the buildings were full and business was good. Best of all, he thought, as he approached the Painted Ladies, they turned out well—very well. His very first effort in the neighborhood ended up being his best effort. He was pleased and he had to admit, proud. "Leon McKee," he said to no one in particular, "you are a very happy man."

The Memorial Day party started at four in the afternoon. The band showed up late, but they weren't bad. Come to find out, all *they* played was polka music and many people were frustrated because there was absolutely not an inch of room available for dancing! Someone suggested blocking off the street next year and making it a true Chicago block party.

Leon could just imagine the response from City Hall when he would ask to close off three blocks of Clark Street for an entire evening for a block party. First everyone down at City Hall would have a good laugh; then they would put him away on charges of insanity.

Howard had found plenty of tables and chairs, including

everything Nell had in her café. This year she was going to be closed during the party. Nell had decided to close early in the day to take some time out to have fun instead of always worrying about the next dollar that she could earn. She had started going to some of the church counseling sessions with her husband and had already learned more than she thought there was to know about his addiction, and in a way, her own addictions. There had been several large steps for her to take, but after losing her sister so quickly and realizing that she was angry at Betsy not so much for leaving her, but for leaving her to enjoy life, Nell realized that she had some changes to make before the restaurant became the only thing that mattered to her.

By six o'clock the lot was absolutely jam-packed with people looking for places to sit. Some from the year before wisely brought their own lawn chairs. As usual, the food tables groaned under their load of various cuisines. This year the Chinese restaurant begged off because of a special booking they had at the restaurant and it had to be all hands on deck and no one could come or send food. Needless to say, there was no moo goo gai pan, but there were plenty of other things. Neighbors who found invitations in their post boxes brought all kinds of favorite dishes—many large enough to serve twenty people by themselves.

Leon noticed that by changing the day to Sunday, different people were able to and not able to come. But when the next day dawned, the actual Memorial Day Monday, everyone could sleep in instead of trying to work a full day on only a few hours of sleep.

Sandy and Johnny got there late and said that Steve and Tony wouldn't make it, but that Tony had asked her if she would like a graduation party at the restaurant and she said yes. She would let them know when it would be.

"There's one thing off our list," said Vivian to Vera when Sandy was out of earshot.

Sandy also told them that her mother had left the county with some bozo from South America and left rent money for six months with the note saying she was leaving. Vivian thought that she would have been crushed, but Sandy seemed to take it very well, adding that she was using the money for schooling and moving into the place the boys were creating as soon as it was ready. She was also going to sublet the apartment and see if she could earn some money from it before her mother returned...that is, if she returned.

"So, is that what you're gonna call it, this new venture? The Place?" asked Leon as he passed around the punch.

"We don't know what we're going to call it," said Johnny. "We've tossed around hundreds of names and they all sound pretty lame. I mean, would you stay somewhere called A Leg Up, or The Shelter House?"

"I don't know," said Leon, "I kind of like Shelter House. How about A Shelter in the Time of Storm?"

"Isn't that a hymn?" asked Vivian, taking a drink of her punch.

Johnny ignored them both. "We're thinking of calling it The Five."

"Five what?" asked Leon and Vivian almost at the same time.

"The five things you *don't* have on the street: safety, privacy, an address, creature comforts, and a future."

"Now that you put it that way, it's not such a bad idea." Vivian was scanning the crowd.

"And it's in the fifty hundred block of west Armitage Street—get the connection? Fifty-five?"

"Not really, but I think that you'll come up with the right idea," said Vivian kindly.

"Leave it to my wife to think the best of everything," said Leon as he slipped an arm around her.

Funny, she thought. *I am getting kinder. It must be marriage to that man.* It was seldom anymore that she lashed out with a negative comment.

She and Leon danced a bit in a tight group of happy people packed together contentedly bumping off each other while she continued to watch the crowd as if looking for someone in particular.

About 8:00 PM the *Tribune* reporter showed up again with his camera. Leon groaned when he saw him and took Vivian by the arm to lead her away while muttering, "What's he doing here? I hope he's not looking for me again."

"I think it's still a free country and he can be here if he wants to. Did you ever find out what he wanted?"

"I never called him back, if that's what you mean. I thought that after six months he'd get the hint, or get the information about Dennis from someone else and leave me alone."

"Do you think he was looking for information about Dennis? Isn't that case pretty much closed and over?"

"I suppose it is. I just don't want to get involved in anything, especially with a reporter from the *Tribune*."

"This from the man who must have a lifetime of *Chicago Tribunes* piling up behind the cleaners? This from the man who cannot face the weekend without the Sunday edition? This from the man who believes everything he reads only if it's in—"

"Okay, okay, I get the point! Just make sure he doesn't see me."

"Oh no, bucko, you're on your own! I'm not going to spend the rest of this evening helping you avoid a reporter that you should have gone to see a long time ago."

"Thanks for nothing!" Leon called after her as she walked away arm in arm with Vera.

At eight-thirty the police showed up. Not one, but three cars. Well, actually the one in the front was a cop car and the one in the back was a cop car, but the one in the middle was a limousine; a big black Cadillac limousine. The three vehicles pulled up to the curb and double-parked. Cops, with blue-and-white checkerboard bands on their hats, making them appear more like cabbies than cops, got out from their cars, leaving their blue lights twirling on the squad roofs, and asked a few questions of the crowd. The music stopped and everyone looked around until someone spotted Leon and pointed in his direction. As the crowd parted, the cop closed in and asked, "Are you Leon McKee?"

Leon felt his legs buckle as he answered. "Yes, but we have a permit and your department was notified well ahead about this party."

"Come with me," said the cop as he put his big official hand under Leon's shaking elbow.

The reporter took a picture and the flash unnerved Leon.

There were a million thoughts that whirled through Leon's head as he took the short walk across the lot to where the band sat silently and the bright lights were shining. Was it about Dennis? Maybe it had something to do with that Annettie guy? Maybe someone saw him slipping invitations into the mailboxes and reported him. Maybe... his feet felt like he was already wearing cement overshoes.

"Leon McKee, there is someone here that has something for you." As the cop said those words, a guy in a shiny sharkskin suit and a thin tie opened the back door of the limo. Out stepped a short, pudgy man, also in a shiny suit. More pictures from the reporter. At first Leon thought it was a joke and then, on second look, he realized it was indeed Mayor Richard J. Daley standing there, rubbing his hands and smiling professionally at the crowd.

As the mayor walked to where Leon was standing rooted to the spot, he held out his big hand and, while shaking it, led him effortlessly to the spot directly in front of the band. Leon noticed that not only was it the best view for everyone attending, but it was also the best background for the many pictures the reporter was now taking. After extolling Leon's virtues and crediting him for single-handedly renewing life to this aging part of the city, the mayor went on and on.

Leon heard very little of it.

Finally the mayor said, in his peculiar way of speaking, "Mr. McKee, on behalf of the wonderful (which he pronounced 'wonnerful') people of Chicago, I would like to present you with this plaque commemorating your incredible efforts to make this section of Chicago, with true Chicago spirit, one of the most progressive communities in the city."

While everyone hooted, hollered, and applauded, Leon didn't even realize that the photographer whom he was trying so hard to avoid was now taking picture after picture of him with the mayor.

He finally saw Vivian in the crowd and motioned desperately for her to join him.

Both Vivian and Debbie from the beauty shop stepped up to where he was standing. Debbie then cleared her throat and, although she was visibly nervous, said, "I was asked to write a commemorative poem for this auspicious occasion and here it is." She cleared her throat again and began in a singsong way:

" 'Chicago Thanks Leon McKee,' an original poem by me, Debbie Herzog, owner of Madam's Boutique," she added quickly and then cleared her throat again:

"Your ability to attract new business here,
has opened the eyes of everyone all far and near.
Your selection of colors brought in so much light,
the Painted Ladies now, oh my, now what a sight.
Our dear precious ladies were all tattered and torn,
but now brightly they shine, with every new morn.
Even our neighborhood's bursting with business today
because you followed your heart come what may.
With appreciation, we thank you for all your good care,
because without you, we all might all be gone...
like the famous poet's old gray mare."

She briefly checked the last line as though she might have read it wrong because there seemed to be more words in it than she remembered. But she was overwhelmed when the end of the poem was greeted with loud applause—more for the effort rather than the poem. When everyone turned to the mayor, they realized that he had gotten back into his limo and the three cars were quietly slipping away into traffic.

Close to three in the morning, when it was all over and Vivian and Leon were lying in bed reviewing the unbelievable night, Leon found out that it had been Vivian who had finally called the reporter and learned that all he wanted was to get information about Leon, because he'd heard that he had "transformed" an entire neighborhood. When he found out that there was going to be another block party, he got in touch with his girlfriend, who knew someone that worked in the mayor's office. She confirmed his thought that the mayor ate things like this up and would love to make a big deal out of it and would even present a plaque as long as he could just present it and leave...after a few really good pictures for the next day's paper, that is.

Debbie had come over when she and Vera were discussing final plans and Debbie promised not to say a word. An hour later she slipped over with a piece of paper that she gave to Vivian saying that she had written a poem and did they think they could use it in some way? She had a gift of poetry and would often make them up on the spot at the shop for the customers to put in greeting cards. Everyone told her she should quit her day job and go to work for a card company.

"So you were in on this from the beginning," Leon said as he pulled Vivian close.

"Only because I knew it would get your name and picture in the beloved paper of yours. We'll probably have to frame it and hang it in the cleaners too. Fan mail will probably start pouring in as soon as it's printed and they probably *will* crown you king, well, King of Clark Street at least. Oh, that reminds me, did you see the letter on the desk in the living room?"

"No."

"It's addressed to you and it says to open it today."

"But today is Sunday. We didn't get mail today."

"No, it came yesterday, and with all the hoopla, I forgot to tell you. Don't you think you should open it?"

"I think something else would interest me more."

"Honestly!" she said as she threw back the covers and got out of bed. "It will only take a minute to read."

"I'll read it later," he called after her. "Don't leave!"

"You'll be asleep later," she said as she picked up the letter and returned to the bedroom.

He reluctantly took the letter from her and checked the front. "There's no return address," he said. "But the postmark is Chicago and on the back is what you read, 'open on Sunday.'"

"I know, I read it, remember? Now open it!"

Leon opened the letter and read it silently. His face paled as he paused and stared out into space. With a slightly shaking hand he handed the letter to Vivian.

It read:

Congratulations, Leon, on your four beautiful ladies.
I knew you could do it!

Dennis

About the Author

 **DIANE DRYDEN** is a feature writer for the *Washburn County Register* in Shell Lake, Wisconsin. She's also freelanced for numerous newspapers and magazines. She was born and raised in Chicago. "All the places I wrote about in *The Accidental King of Clark Street* existed when I was growing up," she says.

She's working on the sequel, so stay tuned for more about these wonderful, quirky characters.

For more information on Diane Dryden:
www.capstonefiction.com

Printed in the United States
87672LV00003B/79-87/A

9 781602 900578